HEATHER GRAHAM POZZESSERE

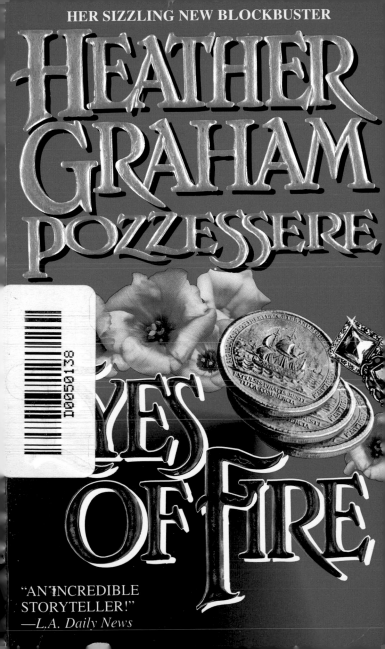

EYES OF FIRE

More great books by
bestselling author

Heather
Graham
Pozzessere

New York Times Bestselling Author
HEATHER GRAHAM POZZESSERE

They were bound by
danger and desire

A MATTER OF
CIRCUMSTANCE

New York Times Bestselling Author
HEATHER GRAHAM POZZESSERE

Over 10 million copies of her books in print

King of
the Castle

...an incredible storyteller; a weaver
of words." —L.A. Daily News

Bestselling Author of Slow Burn
HEATHER GRAHAM POZZESSERE

"An incredible storyteller!" —L.A. Daily News

Strangers
in Paradise

New York Times Bestselling Author
HEATHER GRAHAM POZZESSERE

SLOW BURN

"An incredible storyteller."
—L.A. Daily News

ISBN 1-55166-089-X

9 781551 660899

50599

MHGPIFC3

Sam heard a noise behind her and tensed.

She sat up straight and curled her fingers over the edge of the bathtub.

She listened. She'd imagined it, she told herself. She sat very still, barely breathing, listening once more. *Had* she imagined it?

No. A few seconds later, it came again. Something. Like a whisper through the air. Movement.

Sam grated her teeth furiously. Adam. He'd been like the sun in her life, all powerful, blazing, the center of her universe. And now he thought he could saunter in and out, and she'd be the same little obliging innocent she'd been before.

She heard the noise again, coming closer.

How had he gotten in? she wondered. She spoke at last, trying to control the contemptuous tone in her voice. "Adam, I don't know how the hell you got in here, but you can get yourself out of my private quarters right this second!"

He didn't reply. Not a word. Not a whisper of laughter, not a breath of mockery.

Furious, she twisted around. To her absolute amazement, it wasn't Adam. It was a man, or a figure, in black. Completely in black—down to a black ski mask. She was so stunned that she didn't even think to be frightened at first.

Then she realized that the figure was coming for her.

Also available from MIRA Books and
HEATHER GRAHAM POZZESSERE

SLOW BURN
A MATTER OF CIRCUMSTANCE
KING OF THE CASTLE
STRANGERS IN PARADISE

Coming soon

ANGEL OF MERCY
DARK STRANGER

HEATHER GRAHAM POZZESSERE

EYES OF FIRE

MIRA BOOKS

MIRA

ISBN 1-55166-089-X

EYES OF FIRE

MIRA and the star colophon are trademarks of MIRA Books.

To Don Stelzen, surely the world's nicest and best diving instructor, with thanks for always being so great and patient.

To my son, Shayne, for being my first "buddy" and learning with me.

To Sam Lawson, one of the world's greatest classmates, for his tolerance of so many scheduling changes.

And to Underwater Unlimited, one of the world's most wonderful dive shops; to Charlie Matthews, Chuck Beltran and all the folks there—thanks!

EYES OF FIRE

Prologue

Dead men tell no tales.

Or so he had heard.

Yet these dead men seemed somehow to cry out in silence, noiselessly shrieking out a story that had been kept secret for nearly four hundred years. Their skeletal remains lay about eerily, some held together by remnants of rusted armor, one with its head uncannily perched on a bookcase while the disjointed body sat on the desk beneath it. The sword that had probably brought about his death lay at his side. Perhaps it had once pierced through him, through flesh and sinew and organs; perhaps it had once been bathed in blood. Now the sword lay on the handsomely carved desk where the pieces of the dead man remained, side by side with the small bones of what had been a human hand, almost as if it was waiting to be used again. To be picked up and wielded in some form of ghostly revenge.

Dead men tell no tales....

But this one shouted silently of his own murder.

A tiny yellow fish, a tang, darted in and out of the cavernous eye sockets of the long-dead man. The diver moved closer, then pulled back, the sound of his own breathing loud in his ears as a moray eel suddenly shot its head out from one of the cubicles in the growth-encrusted shelving. Sea fans wafted over oak. Anemones rose against the rotted core of an inkwell.

Another skeleton startled him into a weightless jump. This skeleton lay by the side of the desk, shadowed in darkness. Though time and pressure had blown out the master's cabin window of the *Beldona*, the ship was down deep enough that the sun's rays offered little light inside. The diver flashed his light at the skeleton and nearly shot through the roof, ceasing to breathe.

Because the skeleton looked at him.

Looked at him...

Stared at him like a demon, a devil, dead hand drifting, fingers seeming to point...

Stared at him with blazing red eyes that seemed to blind him. He ceased to breathe, forgetting the first rule of scuba diving—breathe continuously. Experienced diver that he was, he forgot, but oh, God...

The skeleton was staring at him with eyes of fire. A dead man. A pile of bones. Nearly one hundred feet beneath the surface of the sea.

Get a grip, man! he warned himself.

Nitrogen narcosis, he thought. *A diver's disease that could cause absurd giddiness, a state of well-being, a state of panic. A state in which a diver might well see hallucinations. Described by Jacques-Yves Cousteau as rapture of the deep. A danger any diver knew existed beyond depths of one hundred feet, sometimes before, certainly after, no matter how immune a man claimed he might be.*

That was it—he was seeing things. He knew enough not to be doing what he was doing, especially at these depths! His rashness was taking its toll. He didn't dare stay much longer, but, oh, God! The lure had been too great.

He was seeing things.

No, he wasn't.

The dead men *were* there.

Even the dead man with the eyes of pure fire.

Sweet Jesus, but he hadn't been expecting such an eerie haunting from the past. So often, especially at these depths, time and pressure and the sea herself ate away the pathetic, mortal remnants of man, down to the bone itself.

She was a dangerous mistress, the sea. Days, weeks, years, centuries, played havoc beneath the waves. Salt, pressure, currents and sand all swept around the treasures, living and otherwise, captured by the wicked whimsy of the sea. Swept around dead men left behind.

And so often kept them from telling their tales.

His head was spinning, his thoughts careening into fantasy.

Breathe! he commanded himself, sucking air through his regulator at last. He went back to the basics he had learned, had taught. Breathe continuously. Regain control, respond, react.

It's just a skeleton. This poor fellow has been dead forever and ever. He's no danger to me....

The thought didn't help. He imagined that any second the skeleton would raise its hand higher, that the bony fingers would point straight at him, that the bones would begin to rattle and talk....

It was a dead man, for God's sake!

Just a dead man. With gems where his eyes should have been. He was a well-preserved dead man with remarkable ruby eyes, and that was that.

Regain control, respond, react. Fool! Didn't he teach those very words almost daily?

He didn't know what trick of pressure or temperature had kept these skeletons in such uncannily good shape, but they were miraculously here, inside what must have been the captain's cabin of the galleon. And though the windows had burst and the denizens of the sea had moved inside, perhaps the fact that the cabin walls had withstood the sea so well had helped preserve the dead who had perished within.

How they'd come to be here, he didn't know. But they had nearly done him in, nearly drawn a silent scream from him, and he had very nearly succumbed to a watery death himself. In fact, he was certain that his hair would be white from shock when he reached the surface again.

None of that meant anything to him at the moment. Nor did the fact that he should never have been diving alone, despite being an expert diver with several thousand hours of diving time under his belt. It was because of that that he should have known better. It wouldn't have mattered if he had come down a mere thirty feet instead of the nearly one hundred he was down now, he shouldn't have been diving alone. He taught the buddy system strenuously in his classes.

But he'd never imagined a morning like this one. The culmination of a dream. He had at last come across something in his research that had set off a light in his mind, and that light had burned so brightly that he hadn't been able to wait. He hadn't even been able to wait to tell Sam, to give her a clue, even knowing how much it would mean to her. She had been with Jem and some first timers and bubble watchers out on the *Sloop Bee*. With beginners, it would be some time.

And this . . . oh, God! With the right information, the answer had been so simple, and once he had realized it, he hadn't been able to wait.

Sam. Sam should have known. Sam should have been with him. Sam, with her ever-trusting, encouraging smile. Sam who never found fault, who believed, who laughed and teased and made life easy. She should have been here with him now. He couldn't repay her for not being here, not even with every single bit of treasure he found.

He simply hadn't been able to wait to test his theory.

His dreams had sent him flying across the waves. Intrigue and fascination had brought him here, near the Steps.

The Seafire Isle Steps.

The Steps, of course, were a mystery in themselves. They began a mere thirty feet below the surface in the water northwest of Seafire Isle; they deepened with the ocean floor for another twenty-five feet, then simply disappeared. Just like stone steps in other areas of the sea that were supposed by some to lead the way to Atlantis. Others thought them a doorway in the wicked mystery of the Bermuda Triangle. He was quite certain that there were logical answers for every mystery beneath the sea. Just as there was a logical answer to the mystery of the Spanish galleon *Beldona,* the prized ship of King Philip, which had sailed the golden corridor between the New World and the old so many years ago. Historians had thought for years that she had gone down in one of the vicious storms that raged across the seas, a hurricane of deadly proportions.

There was an answer to everything. An explanation.

Just as there had been an explanation for the fact that a skeleton had stared at him with burning eyes....

He could still see them blazing. Eyes of fire.

Nitrogen narcosis, he warned himself. He was seeing things. But the eyes did truly seem to burn. He bent low, studying them more closely....

There was something different about the skeleton. He should have been able to place his finger on it. He should know the truth about the ship.

His ship, as he thought of her.

The *Beldona*. He had found her! Sonar had missed her, radar had missed her. Shifting currents and restless sands had hidden her beneath a coral shelf.

Suddenly something about the skeleton caught his eye. He leaned closer, laughter bubbling in his chest.

Whoa, he thought. *Stay calm!* He warned himself.

But once again, far beneath the surface, he couldn't wait.

The magnitude of his discovery suddenly hit him. No, he couldn't wait. This was pure vindication.

He couldn't wait to tell *her*. Couldn't wait to share these secrets, deeper than any he had ever imagined. He'd discovered the past, and so much more. Many people had mocked him for being a dreamer. Very few had believed. And now...the laugh would be on them.

She would know that he'd been right to fight for the discovery. Maybe the time had come when he could divulge a few of his own secrets. Maybe this would make the time right.

He closed his eyes.

Or did he?

Because he was seeing things again.

The sea was playing tricks on him.

It was as if *she* was suddenly with him.

She couldn't be. But he could see her.

He could see her, hair waving like a banner, eyes as brilliant as those orbs of fire that had so shocked him. In his mind he could hear her throaty laughter, feel what they shared.

He blinked.

She remained.

She was there with him, her eyes glittering behind her scuba mask.

No...

He blinked again, this time closing his eyes tightly. He had known better—*much* better—than to dive alone, especially this deep. But it didn't matter now. He knew the truth. He had solved the mystery, and there was so much more to it than they had ever begun to imagine....

He had to regain control.

He opened his eyes again.

He was alone.

Bubbles surrounded him. His own, he assured himself. He was all alone.

Alone with a bunch of dead men.

Nitrogen narcosis...

He needed to go up. *Now.*

Because he needed help, of course. Needed Sammy and Jem, and probably others, too. But for now his ecstasy was like something ready to explode inside him. He wanted to share his sheer joy.

They would have to guard the secret until they were safe. There was so much more than just the treasure involved. If the wrong people knew what he had discovered...

He was going to need help. The truth was going to have to come out, and once that was done, they would be able to bring up the treasure.

By God, the treasure!

He turned, listening again to the sound of his own breathing, a continual hiss and heave against his ears in the confinement of the cabin. He tried to assess the magnitude of what he had found.

He was startled from his thoughts when something suddenly fell against him. He shifted his light around.

Another dead man. But this one...

Once again a scream rose in his throat.

It was swallowed by the depths.... And then he felt...something.

He turned. Saw.

Terror greeted him in the form of razor-honed steel. He wanted to scream and scream and scream....

Blood flowed, joined with the water. Miles beyond the ship, sharks sensed the blood and began to swim toward the *Beldona* with predatory interest.

Bubbles rose from his regulator. And then they ceased.

His unseeing eyes stared out at the shadowy phantoms inside the cabin of the long-dead ghost ship.

He had solved so many mysteries, had so much to say, but...

Dead men tell no tales....

1

There she stood.

Samantha Carlyle.

It had been a long time. Yes, a long, long time since he had seen her.

Hank had never actually described her, but from the moment he saw her, even from a distance across the water, he knew it had to be her.

Hank had described her with great enthusiasm without describing her at all. In his scholar's mental, metaphysical lust, if there was such a thing. It didn't matter. Adam had never mentioned in his correspondence that he could easily imagine Samantha Carlyle now because he doubted if she had changed a bit in the nearly five years since he had seen her.

She was one of those women who was simply riveting. Looking half-naked in a two-piece cobalt suit that was actually rather decent, considering how little women's bathing suits consisted of these days. It didn't matter. It was what was inside the suit that made it so compelling. She was tall, regal, legs wickedly long, slim, shapely. Honey-gold tanned. Rounded buttocks, flat stomach, skinny waist. Breasts...enough to create mysteriously shadowed cleavage against the constraints of the bikini bra. Good collarbone, nice long throat...

His eyes slipped down again.

Breasts. Very nice.

Body...very sensual. Long, slim, an athletic build that was still enhanced with...curves. Yeah, curves. Breasts...

Eyes up, old man, he told himself. Study her face. Her eyes. That's where the changes in a woman appear.

She wasn't wearing a hat or sunglasses, so she was easy to assess. She was standing on the bow, waiting to tie up at the dock. The boat came nearer, nearer; the engine cut. She was absolutely gorgeous, almost pagan, barefoot and perfectly balanced on those long, wickedly long legs. Her hands were on her hips as she waited. She defied nature, the wind, the water, like a goddess from the sea, Venus rising, red hair blazing in the wind, whipping behind her with the pride and majesty of a battle banner.

Her face...

Yes, her face.

Sophisticated. Beautifully boned, lightly tanned. Eyes large, bright, an extraordinary vibrant green that both clashed wildly against her hair like a winter's

storm and yet seemed to complement it, and the defined features of her face, majestically. Her nose was
perfectly proportioned and dead straight. Her face was
nearly oval, with just the hint of a heart shape to
soften perfection to beauty. Lips sculpted, arrestingly
defined. Brows arched, a slightly darker shade than
the blazing auburn that topped her head. Standing
against the wind, she compelled attention and admi-
ration. She was so dignified.

And yet somehow...

She reeked of sensuality, as well, he realized somewhat irritably, everything that was so perfect and se-
rene about her blending with the fire in her eyes and
the wicked length of her...

Yes, this was Samantha.

He hadn't expected to see her quite so soon, nor had
he expected her to be quite so vividly arresting. He'd
been younger himself, the last time he'd seen her. Too
young, maybe. Too impetuous, too quick to rise to
anger. Strange what the years, time and circumstance
could do to a person. But then, years ago she had been
way too proud herself. And she still had that cloak of
pride about her now, so it seemed. Ah, yes, she had a
look about her. Men probably still fell flat in her path,
and she probably still stepped right over them. Sometimes, maybe, she chewed them up, spat them out.

He knew. He'd been chewed up.

Spat out.

Something suddenly seemed to squeeze in his chest. The past hurt. No, seeing Sam hurt. Some part of her had stayed with him, no matter where he had gone, what he had done. Now Justin was gone. And Hank was gone.

And it hurt to wonder, not to know, to envision what might have been.

Well, he was back. And no matter what she wanted this time, she was going to have him on her like a leech.

No spitting him out.

Not this time, baby, he thought. This time, she was going to have to pay attention to him.

Because she had to have the answers he wanted. He knew it.

And she was going to give them to him.

He gritted his teeth, locking his jaw. He was determined that he wasn't going to give a damn how he got his answers.

Because she was in danger.

She didn't know it, and he didn't even know just how or when it was coming. He just knew it *was* coming.

Soon.

Very soon.

He came off the mail boat, arriving at four-fifteen on a Tuesday afternoon. Sam would never forget the time, because she had been returning with her small group of intermediate divers, standing at the bow, ready to hop ashore to tie up.

Instead she plummeted into the water, missing the dock at the sight of him.

He was back.

Amazingly, she didn't recognize him at first.

She just saw the mail boat pulling into the Seafire Isle dock at the same time as the *Sloop Bee.* Then she saw the man, standing in the aft section of the boat.

It wasn't that she wasn't fairly secure in herself, nor was it that Seafire Isle didn't draw its share of men, many of them single, and many of those handsome, adventurous, good-looking—even nice.

She'd just never seen anyone quite like him arrive at all, ever—or so she thought at first.

He was dressed casually, a tailored jacket worn loosely over a knit shirt against the wind, soft, worn jeans, sneakers. He carried a duffel bag, no more. It lay at his feet while he stood in the aft of the approaching mail boat, arms crossed over his chest. He had the easy stance of a man accustomed to boats, to the sea; his feet were set apart, and he stood balanced against the waves and rocking of the sea.

He was a good six-foot-three—Sam could easily judge his height, since she was almost five-ten herself. Half the heartbreak of her school years had been in trying to find a boy who wasn't eye level with her breasts at the dances.

He carried himself extremely well. His shoulders were attractively broad; his chest appeared well-muscled, his waist very trim, his legs long and powerful. She found herself imagining what he would look like undressed. Not *that* undressed, of course, but in swim trunks.

"Hey, Sam! The line!" Jem called to her.

"Got it!" she called back, leaping out right before she fell in. Luckily for her, she'd spent the majority of her life on the island, with much of her time on boats and in the water. She could recover quickly—even as she wondered if she had actually been gaping and if the new arrival was laughing behind his Ray-Bans at the way she had so nearly fallen for him.

Because he *was* watching her, she thought. She couldn't see his eyes because of the dark glasses, but the tilt of his head was toward her. He wasn't exactly smiling, but there did seem to be the slightest curve to his mouth. A generous mouth, very sensual, well-defined and beautifully shaped. His cheekbones were high and broad, somehow both cleanly hewn and rugged in appearance. His jaw was square, firm. His hair was dark, almost ebony, touched at the ends by a natural reddish tinge given by the sea and salt air to hair, no matter how dark it might be, when the body to which it was attached spent too much time in the sun and water. His face was almost bronze from the sun as well.

Men could, perhaps, be more conventionally handsome, but she'd never seen anyone so completely electrifying and compelling in all her admittedly somewhat sheltered life.

Never seen . . . except for once.

Oh, God! It couldn't be. . . .

Beneath the Ray-Bans, his eyes were blue-gray, a color that could be like mist, like metal; it could warm, cut, pierce, demand, burn with silver flames. . . .

No, it couldn't be him. But it was.

Dear God, it was.

Her entire body seemed to twist into knots, to freeze.

And it was then, at precisely that moment, that the *Sloop Bee* banged softly against the dock and she was unbalanced and tossed cleanly into the water.

''Sam?'' Jem Fisher, the tall, ebony-dark Bahamian who had been her best friend the majority of her life as well as her partner in most things, called from the deck of the *Sloop Bee*.

Sputtering, furious with herself, Samantha surfaced, caught hold of the end of the wooden dock and pulled herself up.

The water had been good. It had washed away the shock.

And the startling pain, she assured herself.

She didn't glance toward the mail boat as she slicked back her newly soaked hair, waving a hand toward Jem. "It was just so hot!" she called. "Too much sun. I thought I'd cool down a little."

Jem arched dark brows over his deep brown eyes, his handsome black face set in a mask of puzzlement.

It was obvious that she'd fallen in. She was lying, and he knew it. The rest of the passengers stared at her politely, trying to pretend that the wind on the way in hadn't been cool enough to combat the heat of the sun.

It didn't matter. She lowered her eyes quickly, tying the bow rope to bring the *Sloop Bee* to rest at the dock, then scampering to tie the stern rope and wait while her guests stepped from the boat with whatever personal equipment they had brought aboard. The mail boat docked behind the *Sloop Bee*. Zeb Pike, the mailman, offered her a casual wave, tossing the mail packet on the dock. He looked tired and seemed to be in a hurry today. Apparently Zeb wasn't coming ashore.

But *he* was.

Definitely.

The back of her spine seemed to stiffen, and she determined to absolutely ignore him. Actually, at the moment, she had little choice. Her dive party was disembarking from the *Sloop Bee*, her Seafire Isle guests demanding her attention.

"It was great, it was beautiful!" a very attractive young brunette told her with glowing eyes. The woman was accompanied by a young man with glossy blond hair and equally bright eyes. He smiled and nodded at her words. The Emersons, Joey and Sue, on their honeymoon. They hadn't looked at a thing beneath the sea except for each other.

Sam smiled. "I'm so glad you enjoyed the outing."

"Oh, we did!" Joey Emerson assured her.

"We'll see you for cocktails," Sue said.

Sam nodded. I'll bet, she thought. They were headed off for one of the cottages that flanked the main house of the Seafire Inn. Despite her own suddenly slamming heart and rising temper, she smiled, watching them go.

She didn't imagine anyone would see them until the next day, and late the next day, at that.

"We could have stayed down a little longer the second time."

Sam started and turned. She was being addressed by a guest in his mid to late forties, a tall, taut, well-muscled fellow with iron-gray hair, nearly black eyes and a stern, sun-leathered face. He probably did know diving—but if so, he should have known that she was going by all the proper rules and regulations.

"Mr. Hinnerman, we're a commercial enterprise, out to entertain you. We go by the dive tables, and that's that. I'm so sorry if we disappointed you."

"I didn't say I was disappointed," Hinnerman said, inhaling heavily. "I just said we could have stayed down longer."

"Perhaps we could have, sir, but we shouldn't have, I'm afraid. Do you need some help with anything?"

"Help?" He arched a brow. The look told her that he found the idea of needing help with anything ludicrous. And he probably *didn't* need help with anything—unless it was his personality. Strange man. Tough as nails. Yet his girlfriend—still sleeping up at the main house when the dive boat had left that morning—was just the opposite. Though Sam couldn't quite determine her age, she decided that Jerry North couldn't be very young, perhaps near forty, or even older. It didn't matter. Jerry North was extremely attractive and would probably be so to her dying day. She was pure froth. Slim, small—just adorable. A blue-eyed blonde who didn't do anything that might mar her manicure. She loved Seafire Isle anyway, or so she said. She liked to lie around the pool and walk on the beach. She liked cocktail hour, and the fact that they built fires in the parlor of the main house at night against the slight chill of the air after sunset.

She seemed to be a very nice woman, but, like Hinnerman, she sometimes made Sam uncomfortable.

She always seemed to be watching Sam.

"Mr. Hinnerman—"

"Liam," the man corrected.

"Liam," she agreed, and forced a smile, "I do hope you enjoyed what you were able to see."

One of those flashes of unease Hinnerman could evoke in her swept through Sam as his gaze moved over her. Almost like a touch.

Just innuendo, never anything more. Still, she felt little shivers upon occasion, wondering what the truth about her guests might be. Perhaps they were just moderately kinky voyeurs. The looks Hinnerman gave her were definitely sexual.

But Jerry North's weren't. They were strangely sad, if they were anything at all.

So she was sad *and* kinky, Sam thought.

"I enjoyed it, all right," Liam Hinnerman said, smiling at her broadly. "I always enjoy being with you. You are an excellent dive mistress."

"Sam!" To her relief, Brad Walker, a lanky, green-eyed, freckle-faced thirteen-year-old with stylishly half-long-half-shaved reddish hair, the youngest diver aboard, came rushing up. "Sam, that was neat!"

"Neat," Hinnerman muttered, and moved on.

"I loved it!" Brad continued to enthuse. "Especially that World War Two ship. So sad, huh? Do you think there are bodies in it?"

She shook her head, smiling. "No bodies, Brad." To Brad, World War Two was as much past history as the American Revolution, yet she still had divers who came to see the navy wreck because they remembered comrades who had perished aboard it.

"Sorry, Brad. Luckily, most of the men escaped when she sank. The navy went after the few who didn't. But they left the ship there, and it's a memorial to all of them now."

"It was cool. So cool," Brad said.

"He's just immature." Brad's slightly older sister, Darlene, a very pretty strawberry blonde with a nicely budding figure and who was fifteen going on thirty, sauntered lazily up beside him. She shook her head at Sam, as if they shared a knowledge regarding the total immaturity of men at any age. Sam had to grin— agreeing with Darlene's secret assurance to some extent. "It wasn't cool, Sam, it was an enormously gratifying experience."

"It was *cool,*" Brad insisted.

"Just so long as you both enjoyed it," Sam said.

"It would have been more fun if I'd had a real dive buddy," Darlene said.

"I'm the one without the real buddy. Thunder thighs here kept tugging at me the whole trip, squealing every time there was a barracuda within a mile," Brad said contemptuously.

Darlene shook her head in disgust. "There've got to be real men somewhere, don't you think, Samantha?"

"I'm sure there are a number of them," Sam murmured. *Where was he now?* She jiggled Brad's baseball cap. "There are lots more wrecks out there. We'll do some different ones tomorrow, huh?"

"Coo—el!" Brad agreed, running happily off, dragging his heavy dive bag along with him. The Walkers had been on Seafire Isle four days, but inclement weather had made this the first time they had been able to dive.

Darlene shook her head again. "It can be so trying, you know. These family vacations..." she murmured.

Her folks came up behind her. Judy and Lew Walker. They were very young for having half-grown kids. Judy had confided in Sam one night that she'd been just a junior in high school when she'd found out that she was going to have a baby. She and Lew had split up, gotten back together, discussed abortion— then run away and had the baby, Darlene. They'd spent the next few years struggling, but they'd been lucky. Both sets of parents had stepped in to help, and they'd both made it through college by working part-time. "The most miraculous thing, really," Judy had told her, "is that we made it as a couple and that we didn't totally destroy one another." Then she had gone on to say, "This vacation means so much to all of us. We struggled for so many years that it's extra-special now to have the beach, the moon, the sand, the fishing, the swimming. It's heaven!''

"Sam, a great trip,'' Lew told her. He was lean, sandy-haired, still a big kid himself. A big responsible kid, Sam thought. She had liked both him and his wife—and their family—right away.

"Super!'' Judy told her. Judy was very tiny and thin to the point of skinny. She had freckles, sandy-red hair and dimples. She was in constant motion, pretty in her vividness, sweet as could be.

"Super!'' Sam agreed. She tried to keep smiling, but it was difficult when she didn't know where *he* was. "Is that like coo—el?''

"I think. No, I'm certain,'' Lew said. He slipped an arm around his wife's shoulder. Their dive bags were on wheels. They only needed one hand each to drag them behind them, leaving the other hand free for each other.

Sam doubted she would be seeing the elder Walkers for cocktails, either. "Thanks,'' she said.

"Super, cool—*and* I had the best dive partner,'' came a husky male voice.

Jim Santino. Darlene called him "Romeo'' and giggled all the time when he was around. He was good-looking, with a charming smile and blond hair that was long enough to fling out of his face frequently, something like a mating ritual. She'd partnered up with him today because Liam Hinnerman had gone with Sukee Pontre, who was right behind Jim now. Sukee was in her early twenties, with short dark hair and eyes and flawless ivory skin. Her father had been French, her mother Vietnamese, and Sukee had benefited from both. She wasn't just attractive, she was exotic. She had told Sam that she had come to Seafire Isle because she had heard that not just guys but *rich* guys came here for vacations. She was the kind of woman who would probably have made other women hate her except that she was so blunt and funny and forthright.

"Really, handsome?" Sukee drawled to Jim. "And here I had thought you might consider me to be the perfect partner."

"Um, er..." Jim stuttered.

"It's difficult when there's so damned much perfection around, isn't it?" another voice cut in.

Sam's eyes were drawn upward, over Jim's shoulder.

It was him. The man from the mail boat.

Adam O'Connor.

Smiling below his Ray-Bans, his voice husky, deep, resonant. Somehow mocking.

He lowered his glasses and locked eyes briefly with Sam—an antagonistic look, yet one that somehow warned her that he didn't intend to acknowledge the fact that he knew her.

Nor did he want her to recognize him.

Jim turned, looking up at the newcomer. He seemed to acknowledge some kind of competition—he had to, the way Sukee was staring at the man—but he was quick to redon his charming manner. "The perfect guest, the perfect hostess." He smiled at Sam, then at Sukee, then stared at the new addition to their number once again. "You're right. So much...perfection." He offered a hand to the man. "Jim Santino," he said. "Welcome to—"

"Perfection Isle?" Adam drawled. He smiled, accepting the handshake in a friendly manner.

He's a snake, Jim, Sam longed to say in warning. Yet, somehow, she managed to keep from doing so, despite the fact that each time Adam spoke, she could hear a slight, *slight* underlying tinge of mockery in his voice.

The others laughed. Sam wasn't sure Adam had meant to be amusing, even though he kept smiling. A killer smile. He had a dimple. Just one, in his left cheek.

Adam looked at her then, smiling innocently. "You must be the perfect hostess, I imagine?" He stretched his hand out to her.

If only she could bite the damned thing.

"Welcome to Seafire Isle," Sam said smoothly, offering her own hand. She took note of his when he gripped hers. Large, powerful. The nails were bluntly cut, clean. She had very long fingers. His engulfed hers.

She drew her hand back quickly.

"Thanks," he told her.

"Have you come to stay, or are you with the dinner party coming in tonight from Freeport?"

He shook his head. "No, I'm staying."

"Really?" She forced herself to sound interested. "Do you have a reservation?"

Why was she playing this game? she asked herself.

"No, but your agent back at Freeport—Miss Jensen, is that right?—said that it's slow season and you'd surely have one room left, at the least."

"Did Miss Jensen say that?" Sam murmured. She could imagine how happy Miss Irma Jensen would have been to say it. Sam had only recently hired her to book newcomers, dinner parties and day trips to Seafire Isle. She was a sixty-year-old spinster who was certain that Sam needed to marry soon—or become a hopeless old maid herself. Irma was always delighted to book single men onto the island. She was convinced she was eventually going to make a match.

Not this time, Irma, Sam thought.

"Are you a diver, Mister, er..." Lew Walker began.

The newcomer nodded his dark head. "O'Connor. Adam O'Connor. And yes, I dive."

"You'll love the trips. The reefs are magnificent. And the wrecks are fascinating."

"Wrecks are always fascinating."

"Yes, but these are special. Sam entertains us with the history of each wreck before we reach it," Judy said.

"Sam is always entertaining—I imagine," Adam said politely.

"Best dive vacation I've ever taken," Sukee offered. She smiled. "Mr. O'Connor. The best," she ended sibilantly. It had a nice sexy sound to it. She'd come to flirt with all the free males—and maybe a few who were not so free. She'd concentrated on Jim so far, but now it was evident that she'd discovered a new quarry to pursue. "I just know you'll enjoy Sam."

Adam stared at Sam, those damned Ray-Bans back in place. "I'll do my best," he said politely.

She wanted to slug him.

God, she'd last seen him so long ago....

And the way she felt hadn't changed a whit. Yes, yes, it had, she assured herself. She still wanted to kill him, still wanted to...

That was it. She simply wanted to throttle him. She was no longer crushed. She wasn't a young woman barely turned twenty-one who was still madly, hopelessly in love with a slightly older man. A man with whom other women had been in love with as well. She wasn't broken, desperate, longing for his touch, wanting to be held in his arms....

She felt her cheeks reddening. She remembered the first moment she had seen him today, not knowing then who he was, wondering almost academically what he would look like minus most of his clothing. Well, she knew, and...

She was over the bastard, she assured herself. Had been for a very long time now. A dozen things had happened in the years since that had made her forget him. Okay, not forget him, exactly, but relegate him to the past. Where he belonged.

Still...

If she'd never seen him before, she would have thought he was the type of man a woman might turn to in times of trouble—even if she was a woman confident in her own abilities. He had a touch of machismo about him. In fact, as she knew all too well, he could be damned irritating.

But that didn't alleviate a woman's urge to get close to him. To touch him. Feel his warmth, his energy.

Like a moth to a flame, she ridiculed herself. And her wings had been badly scorched.

Just be cool, she warned herself now. Be mature.

Darlene would certainly recommend maturity.

"Well, Mr. O'Connor, I'm sure Yancy will see to all your needs at the reception desk." She turned to the others. "I think I'll shower for dinner if you'll all pardon me."

Adam was the only one looking at her; the only one who seemed to notice that she was excusing herself. Jim, Sukee and the Walkers continued to watch Adam with interest.

Jem, who had pulled out the hose to wash down their equipment, was staring at her curiously over Adam's shoulder. In fact, he was grinning, damn his hide. The hell with them both. No, the hell with men in general. She'd only ever met one who was simply honest and sweet, and he . . . he was gone.

Hank.

Hank, with his open blue eyes, his continual search for knowledge. His determination, his enthusiasm, his honesty, his naiveté, his nose always on a map, in a book.

What the hell happened, Hank? she wondered, the question a silent scream within her mind. *Why did you let it happen? Why didn't you let us help you? What happened, what happened . . . ?*

What the hell had happened?

And where the hell had Adam O'Connor been when Hank had disappeared? Not to mention when her father had disappeared?

Was that part of what hurt so badly now? He'd gone, yes, and left her. But when she'd been desperate, she'd sent for him. She'd thought that enough feeling, enough history, had remained between them that he would come to help.

But he hadn't. Her pleas had gone unanswered.

She bit her lower lip and turned swiftly, anxious to put some distance between herself and Adam as quickly as possible. Damn him. This wasn't fair. It was the surprise of seeing him that was throwing her so badly now. Definitely not fair. But then again, when had he ever played fair? He surely had the advantage today. Coming here, he'd known that he would see her.

Sweet Jesus, she could have used some warning. It would have been nice if Irma Jensen had given her a call.

Why? she taunted herself. What did it matter? Come on, come on, she was an adult, a big girl, and he was history, *ancient* history.

She started walking quickly, heading toward her private beach house off the south side of the main lodge.

First her father . . .

Then Hank.

And all over a cache of pirate gold.

Or had it been? Had they disappeared . . . had they *died* for another reason?

Adam O'Connor chased live men. Present-day pirates. And Adam was on the island.

Why the hell was he here?

Sam suddenly stopped in her tracks, staring at the smooth concrete path that began where the wooden decking ended. She had come about halfway up from the docks and stood between the docks and the main lodge. And she was looking down at a trail of drops on the smooth concrete.

A trail of crimson drops, bloodred drops....

Oh, God.

Adam was back in her life, on her island.

And there were drops on the walkway.

Red drops.

Blood?

2

Sam quickly bent down to study the crimson drops. She reached out a finger, touching one.

"Sammy!"

She jumped, coming to her feet. Ahead of her, in the doorway of the lodge, stood Jerry North, Liam Hinnerman's exquisite little doll. Her blond hair was a riot of soft waving curls around her gamine face. She was dressed in slinky white, a chiffon halter-dress creation that bared her shoulders and formidable cleavage and a fair length of her slim tanned legs. Her feet were encased in stiletto heels despite the sometimes tricky terrain of the island.

"Sammy, how was the dive?"

"Nice, you should try coming one day!" Sam called. She bent down, reached out, touched a red drop.

Studied it.

Was it blood?

"You should try one of my drinks! I make a mean Bloody Mary!" Jerry called to her cheerfully, lifting her right hand. She was holding a glass. A big, tall glass. A celery stick was rising above the rim of a glass that was practically overflowing—with something red.

A Bloody Mary.

Sam almost groaned aloud, wiping her finger on the grass by the path. She stood, smiling at Jerry, feeling like a fool.

Tomato juice had become drops of blood in her own slowly decaying mind.

It was because that damned man was back.

"Oh, did I spill? I'm so sorry!" Jerry called contritely.

"Just a drop, no problem. It's nothing."

"Still, I'm sorry. Everything is so immaculate here."

"Nearly perfect," Sam muttered.

"What was that?"

"Nothing, nothing. It will rain soon, a few little drops of tomato juice are no problem," Sam said.

"Thanks. Still...I can get something and clean them up."

"Jerry! We're outside! Trust me—the birds never apologize for what they do to the walks."

Jerry smiled and laughed softly. "You really grew into a beautiful young woman."

"What?"

"You're just a sweetheart," Jerry said. "The island is great, and you do a wonderful job here."

"Thanks."

"Must have been a good dive. The others are right behind you. They look tired."

"It was," Sam agreed. She wanted to escape. She needed time alone, and Jerry, as usual, wanted to draw her into conversation. Most of the time she liked Jerry. Just not now.

"Those little cuties are all scattering to their own cottages. A few of them will be coming our way soon, I imagine. Come join me before they get their hands on you. I'll make you a Bloody Mary."

"Thanks, but I really want to bathe and change first. You go on in. I'll join you soon."

Still feeling like a fool, Sam waved Jerry inside and started walking quickly away once again.

In a pleasant room inside the lodge, a phone rang.

He quickly picked up the receiver. "Yes?"

"You've got company."

"O'Connor?"

"Yes."

"I know. He's already arrived."

'You've seen him?"

"He came in on the afternoon mail boat right when the dive party was returning."

"Hmm. Did he say why he was on the island?"

"A dive vacation."

"Right. What else?" There was a moment's silence. "What was Miss Carlyle's reaction to his appearance?"

"No reaction."

"She was polite?"

"She pretended not to know him."

"O'Connor is never anywhere unless something is going on. The stakes have just doubled. You'll have to keep your eyes wide open. What did he bring with him?"

"Not much. A duffel bag."

"No electronic equipment?"

"Not so far as I could see."

"Check it out."

"Sure. I like grabbing a tiger by the tail."

"Don't tell me you're afraid?"

"Let's say I have a healthy respect for the man."

"Healthy respect or—"

"Don't worry. I'm on it."

"He's one man. He can't be everywhere at once." Again there was a brief silence. "Remember that. He's just one man. Human. Things happen. And when they don't, people make them happen. Do you know what I mean?"

"You're suggesting something could happen to O'Connor?" There was a note of derision in the question. "He's one of the best divers in the world."

"Justin Carlyle was one of the finest divers in the world, too. The sea ate him up. It can happen to anyone. Bear that in mind."

"Justin Carlyle was a marine biologist who loved the sea. O'Connor has been both a Navy and a police diver. He's here with his guard up, you mark my word."

"*You* mark *my* word. No man is invulnerable. Especially when you go through a woman to reach his Achilles' heel. You stay awake there, you hear?"

"Yeah. Who is O'Connor working for?"

"It's the damnedest thing—I don't know. Not yet, anyway."

"Great."

"Give me time. I'll find out."

The receiver went dead.

He replaced it slowly, then stood and walked into the bathroom, dropping his clothing as he went. He paused before the mirror, pleased with what he saw. Naked, he shoved aside the toiletries in his overnight bag until he revealed a dark velvet bag that might have carried men's cologne or talc. But it didn't. He ran his hand carefully over the outline of his specialty custom-made thirty-two-caliber pistol, a small weapon, easily concealed, but one that packed a deadly punch nevertheless.

Assured, he locked the door to the bath, his overnight bag on the commode, within arm's reach of the shower. He started the water and swore vociferously as it shot out at him, steaming. He adjusted the temperature, still swearing.

Well, hell, that was just it, wasn't it? They were all getting into hot water now.

But didn't they always tempt the devil?

For big payoffs, you had to take big risks.

He began to lay his plans as he quickly showered.

Don't think about him, Sam warned herself. Humph. Might as well tell herself to quit breathing. Not that it meant anything. She was hardened. Older. Mature.

Burned.

But she still wanted to know....

What the hell was Adam doing here? Go with the obvious, she advised herself. He was after someone or something—he was not on a pleasure trip, that was certain. He'd been with the Metropolitan Dade County Police the first time he'd come here, searching for a drug runner out of Coconut Grove reported to have gone down about two miles off the island. He'd found the sunken speedboat—and arrested the two men who were pretending to be sports fishermen while visiting the island in their attempt to recover their lost treasure. In the meantime, he'd made a conquest on the island—her.

Sam didn't head straight for her refuge. She walked quickly along the concrete path, skirting the front of the lodge, still feeling like a fool. Anything could have been on that damned path. Anything. It led from the docks, first skirting the white sand of the beach area on the northward slope of the island, then winding through the manicured lawns toward the lodge itself.

Hibiscus grew along the path in flowering beauty, while palms lent shade, and crotons and wild orchids added deep slashes of color along the way.

With Jerry having disappeared into the lodge, Sam paused in the center of an orchid-covered gazebo near the far corner of the lodge, catching her breath and looking at the inn.

The main lodge itself was Victorian. It had been built by Sam's great-grandfather in 1880. Cosmetic touches and several major additions had been built on over the intervening years, but every member of the family since her great-grandfather's day had remained true to the integrity of the Victorian era. The lodge house was painted a soft coral with white balconies, porches and gingerbreading. It was encircled by a magnificent broad porch and sat atop a small knoll. She loved the house, and she loved the island, just as she loved the water and the breezes, the boating, the diving. It was a fantasy life—hard work, but a fantasy. She enjoyed living it and working it. This had been her home as long as she could remember, except for the three years she had spent at St. Anne's Fine Arts College for Women.

Too bad it had been an all-girls school, she reflected sourly. A little more exposure to men and she might have been better prepared for Adam when he had arrived on the island. At the very least she might have had a more accurate perception of her own weaknesses and inexperience.

Well, it was all in the past now, and though Justin Carlyle had disappeared over four years ago, she still had Jem Walker with her, and Jem was great. He was as close as a brother could be, her best friend, her partner in all things.

Her life and the island were damn near perfect.

Except that now Adam was back.

She stared at the house, inwardly swearing and breathing deeply to calm herself. She heard voices, guests returning to their rooms. She closed her eyes, hoping she was concealed by the healthy tangle of orchids. The voices faded.

Only two or three. Had Adam's been among them?

She slipped out of the gazebo, looking toward the dock.

The entire group was now gone. Amazing what his damned appearance had done to her. She'd rushed away, imagined she'd seen blood on her walk, then walked around like an idiot while everyone who'd left the docks after her was probably already relaxing in a hot tub.

Even Jem had finished up with the business of rinsing down the equipment and was no doubt comfortably submerged in heat and bubbles in his cottage.

Everyone had disappeared.

Disappeared. God, how she hated that word!

Don't start thinking about disappearances now! she warned herself.

This was customarily a quiet time on the island, after the daily dive trip and any of the other activities and lessons, and before the traditional cocktail hour—unless you were Jerry and liked to start cocktail hour early. Though the island was a casual vacation destination, people always had a tendency to dress up for cocktail hour and dinner, at least a little bit. Her guests napped, bathed and indulged themselves—and one another—during this quiet time, as she thought of it after talking with one guest, a kindergarten teacher.

Quiet time. She needed a little quiet time of her own, with an early start on the cocktail hour thrown in.

She turned away from the empty dock and hurried along the path, anxious to reach the calm refuge of her own abode. Once her house had been a kitchen for the lodge, but with the installation of smoke detectors and a sprinkler system, the one-time kitchen had been adapted into a charming cottage. There was a central living area, a sunken office off to one side, a small kitchenette, and then her bedroom and bath, the latter huge, with a separate shower stall that offered a dozen jets and a huge Jacuzzi set high atop elegant, tiled steps. It was surrounded by glass, with privacy shutters built along the outside wall. From the bath, she looked out onto a garden area with purple bougainvillea twining over the shutters and a small fountain with a graceful Venus pouring water onto concrete flowers.

Sam carefully locked her door. She didn't want to assume that Adam's being on the island meant he intended to come anywhere near her, but then, she knew the man, and if he wanted something, he would come after it.

She checked the lock, then leaned against the door, studying her living room walls.

They were laden with paintings and prints. A few were period pieces and very valuable. Galleons, warships, privateers, all lined her walls, along with some beautiful charts and maps.

There was a map of Seafire Isle with its surrounding coral reefs and shelves. Once upon a time, the small island had been a dangerous place, teeming with pirates. It had been passed between the Spanish and the British a dozen times. Because of the coral reefs surrounding it, the island was accessible only by smaller ships, and in days gone by, many a poor vessel had been wrecked on her reefs. This map had been sketched in pen and ink during her great-grandfather's day. It showed the more modern pleasures of the island, the lodge, the scattering of cottages, the docks, the beach, the tennis courts and the golf course. It was quite charmingly drawn, and little had really changed since it had been done.

But Sam's eyes were drawn from the Seafire Isle map, and she moved across the room, looking at her father's favorite. It was a treasure map, drawn in the early eighteen hundreds, encompassing Florida with all its islands, the Gulf Coast and the Caribbean. There were stars and notes attached to every possible "treasure" trove—or sunken ship—location in fine, minuscule handwriting. "Here lyeth the *Santa Margarita*, the *Ghost Galleon*, sunk in the Year of Our Lord 1622, in the Eyes of a Storm, may she rest in peace." The treasure recovered from the *Santa Margarita* had an estimated worth of about twenty million. She had sunk at nearly the same time as the more recently discovered *Atocha*, a ship that had yielded its own trove of treasure, both fiscal and historical.

Closer to Seafire Isle, west of the south Florida mainland, was the mark for the *Beldona*, her father's love, his great passion—the mistress of his life.

The *Beldona* had, in the end, claimed him, or so it seemed. And without giving up a single one of her secrets. She'd gone down in 1722, also in "the Eyes of a Storm," and she'd carried her crew, her prisoners and her treasure to a watery grave from which there had been no reprieve. She'd been something of a mystery ship from the very beginning, a British ship carrying secret documents as well as a doomed crew of Spanish privateers. No one had ever been able to tell a pirate tale like Justin Carlyle. No one. No one had ever been able to weave such a spell of magic, adventure and chills. And no one, perhaps, had ever been so caught up in the spell of his own lore.

Justin had also been an excellent diver, strict regarding the rules of safety.

But Justin had followed the *Beldona*. And he had never returned.

Strange, for all his hard, contemporary tactics and cool determination, Adam had been as seduced by her father's tales as any other man. He had sat up hour after hour with Justin, while they had drunk cheap whiskey together, laughing, imagining, weaving tales of what had happened the night of the storm. And they had speculated as to where the ship might have gone down. Yes, Adam and her father had been great together.

She inhaled raggedly again, backing away from the map. Great. Just great. She had gone from wondering about Adam to agonizing over her father, and now she couldn't stop remembering them both.

No, she would never waste time on such a rotten bastard again, and that was that. She turned toward the kitchen, walking slowly at first. Then more quickly.

Her walk became a run. She reached into the refrigerator and, more desperately than she wanted to, dragged out a bottle of zinfandel. She poured herself a glass, her hands shaking. She gulped down the wine.

She shuddered, her entire face puckering. Wine was not meant to be guzzled. She poured herself a second glass, determined not to think about Adam. She decided, as she made her way into the bathroom to start hot water running into the massive Jacuzzi, that he had one hell of a lot of nerve, thinking that he could just walk in here and expect her not to betray him.

Maybe she'd misread him and he really didn't care if she betrayed him or not. Maybe he was really on vacation.

No. Never.

By the time the Jacuzzi had been filled, she had her third glass of wine at her side. She crawled into the tub and leaned back, determined to relax, to unwind. Impossible. She laid her head back, feeling the water pulse against her back, her neck.

Damn him. What was he doing here now? Where had he been when things had gone badly for her, when her father had disappeared, when Hank had followed the exact same way? She'd been desperate enough then to write to him, to beg him for help, and he hadn't shown up. Where the hell had he been, and what possible right did he have to come now?

She sipped her wine, feeling its effects at last, soothing her body if not her soul. Great. She was guzzling zinfandel. Trying to get sloshed on wine. She hadn't done anything so stupid since she and Jem and Yancy had been sixteen and downed a bottle of cheap burgundy they had gotten hold of in Freeport. Think how sick she'd been. . . .

No, she wasn't going to make that mistake again.

Right, she taunted herself. Her wine wasn't cheap anymore.

She shook her head, warning herself to slow down. She had a business to run. She didn't want to get sloshed at all—couldn't afford to—but his presence on the island was really getting to her. And she was usually so moderate. She hadn't overimbibed in wine or anything else since she had gotten so carried away that night when they had first . . .

She heard a noise behind her and tensed, sitting up straight, her fingers curling over the rim of the tub, listening.

She had imagined it, she told herself. She sat very still, barely breathing, listening once more.

Nothing. . . .

Had she imagined it?

No, no. . . a few seconds later, it came again. Like a whisper through the air. Movement.

She gritted her teeth furiously.

Adam.

He'd been like the sun coming into her life, all powerful, blazing, the center of her universe.

She'd been like a stick of gum to him. Easily spat out and forgotten, exchanged for another.

And now he thought he could saunter in again, and she would be the same obliging innocent she had been before.

The noise was coming closer.

How had he gotten in? she wondered. The bastard. She spoke at last, controlling her contemptuous tone to the very best of her ability. "You son of a bitch, I don't know how the hell you got in here, but you can get out of my private quarters right this second!" she snapped.

He didn't reply. Not a word. Not a whisper of laughter, not a breath of mockery.

"Damn you!"

Furious, she twisted around. To her absolute amazement, it wasn't Adam.

At least, she didn't think it was Adam.

It was a figure in black. Completely in black—down to a black ski mask.

Sam was so stunned that she didn't even think to be frightened at first, just curious.

A ski mask? Nights on the island could be cool, but never cold enough for...

Oh, God. She was an idiot.

"What on earth..." she began to murmur. Then she realized that the figure was coming toward her, carrying some kind of a black cloth in its black gloved hand.

She stood up, drawing in breath she could expel in a shriek as she tried to leap from the tub and escape. But she was cut off from the doorway by the figure, left standing there naked, dripping.

She made an attempt to sidestep the figure and leap for the door. No luck. She stared at it hard. Male, she thought instinctively. Tall—no chest. But that was it. There was nothing else she could tell about her silent attacker.

For seconds they just stood, staring at one another.

Then she realized her situation. She was naked, unarmed, and an intruder was in her bathroom, completely camouflaged and staring at her.

"Help!" she screamed. Her cottage wasn't that far from the main house. And there were other cottages near hers. Someone might be walking on the beach. Someone...

This was ludicrous. A black-clad figure in a ski mask on a Caribbean island—attempting to attack her!

"Help!" she shrieked again.

The figure lunged for her.

"No!" she cried, beating her fists against his chest, kicking him. He grunted as one well-aimed kick connected, then seemed to find his own spurt of fury. He grasped one of her arms, and she was drawn, still kicking and screaming, against his body. He struggled to force the cloth over her face. She kept struggling to keep it away. She tried not to breathe. She could already smell the sickly sweet scent of the drug that soaked the cloth.

"Help!" she shrieked again, still kicking. The cry cost her what little breath she had left. She had to breathe. Had to inhale....

The scent was awful. Filling her nose, her lungs, seeping into her blood, deadening her limbs. She couldn't keep fighting, couldn't force her arms to move the way she wanted them to. She tried to claw, to scratch his eyes with her fingers.

Oh, God, she was losing her strength. She was being attacked . . . assaulted. . . .

Murdered?

She still couldn't believe that an intruder had come here for her. This was her damned island!

Blackness . . . stars . . . weakness . . .

That awful, sickly sweet smell, closing in around her, filling her . . .

She was starting to go limp in the fierce hold of her attacker.

Suddenly the arms that held her were wrenched away. She was dimly aware of a thudding, crunching sound as a blow was thrown and connected with flesh and bone. She heard a groan, footsteps taking flight....

All in a matter of seconds.

"Sit!" someone snapped at her. "I'll be back."

She reached out blindly. "Ca—can't!"

She lacked the strength to stand, yet she couldn't manage to tell her limbs to set her into a sitting position. She was going to fall against the unforgiving tile.

"Damn it!" she heard someone say. "He's going to get away."

She didn't fall, she was swept up. She blinked furiously against the effects of the drug, trying to fight again.

"Damn it, Sam, I'm trying to keep you from killing yourself!"

Her vision started clearing. It was Adam. Right in front of her. No, holding her. She was still so dizzy. The room was spinning. No, he was walking. Carrying her. Laying her down on her bed.

He left her for a minute and the darkness began to recede. She drank in the fresh, salt-tinged night air that whispered over the island. She tried her fingers. They moved. Her toes. They wiggled.

There was a sensation of weight as he sat down at her side. Cold, as he pressed a washcloth rinsed in cool water over her face.

She inhaled through the cloth and felt her temper reviving the rest of her.

Adam was in her room—and she was stark naked.

He lifted the cloth from her face. His eyes were burning and sharp, his features tense, yet his lips seemed to curve in a mocking smile.

She struck out wildly, her palm swinging toward his cheek.

"Stop it, Sam! It's me. Adam!"

The Ray-Bans were gone. She could see his face clearly, if she could only focus. She blinked, making the attempt. She saw the silver glitter of his eyes against the striking, angled lines of his profile and tried to strike out again. He caught her hands, leaning over her, his weight bearing her down, preventing her from attacking him.

"Sam, damn it, it's me!"

"I know perfectly well who it is!" she cried out. Still struggling furiously, she managed to free a hand and tried again to strike him.

Once again, before her blow could land, her wrist was captured.

And she realized that she was lying naked and completely vulnerable... with Adam O'Connor not just back on her island, but lying on top of her in her bed.

3

"Fine! Next time a stranger is trying to drug you, kidnap you, maybe even kill you, I'll remember to keep my distance," Adam said evenly. His tone was husky. Angry.

His eyes were directly on hers, gleaming. A knife-like silver. Not giving away an iota of emotion.

Only his voice hinted of his feelings.

She stared at him. Not moving, not breathing. Not daring to, because the slightest motion would bring her bare flesh into closer contact with him.

He'd aged nicely over the years. He was even more attractive in his mid-thirties than he'd been in his late twenties. His voice had deepened; his chest had broadened. Even the lines in his face gave it the character that men seemed to achieve so easily, while women battled the ravages of age with expensive creams and potions. His dark hair was longish, collar length. It was tousled now from the fight he'd put up. One dark wavy strand had fallen over his forehead, where it looked too damned good. Sexy, sensual. Very masculine. It was great hair. Very thick. She knew, because once-upon-a-very-long-time-ago, she had run her fingers through it. She was tempted to touch it right now.

She would like to touch it and yank it right out of his head.

He'd changed clothes for dinner, making her current, uncomfortable situation seem all the more ludicrous. He was dressed in casual evening attire, black pants, jacket, bone and crimson vest over a dress shirt. He was in absurdly good condition. He wasn't breathing hard—only his hair had been mussed. Even his tie had remained straight, helping to maintain his look of casual elegance.

She was going to die, she realized, if she didn't breathe soon.

She might have died! She'd never been afraid on the island, never even thought to be afraid. What might have happened if...?

She inhaled, trying not to gasp too deeply for air. She couldn't gush out a thank-you-for-my-life. She just couldn't do it.

"He—he shouldn't be a stranger anymore," Sam gasped, rallying. "You should have caught him. You should be after him right now rather than humiliating me."

"You're humiliated?" he demanded, silver eyes cool.

"Adam—"

"Humiliation has never been your strong suit."

"What would you know about my strong suit? You don't know me at all. You passed through my life years ago. Hundreds of people have passed through it since."

"Hundreds with whom you've had affairs? In this day and age? Shame on you, Samantha. Really."

She stared at him with all the careful restraint she could manage, eyes narrowed. "Get off me and get out of my bedroom. Now."

"Yeah. You're welcome. But please, don't deluge me with any more gratitude. I can't deal with it. It would just go straight to my head."

"God forbid. If anything else went to your head, it might explode."

"Oh, really?"

"Damn right!"

"In contrast to the Queen of the Seven Seas here, eh?"

"O'Connor!"

He rose—carefully, ready for her to start swinging again.

She wouldn't have minded doing so. Except that it wouldn't have gotten her anywhere. Because he would have been right back on top of her. And that would *not* have been good. Because it was amazing just how vividly memory could serve—even when half a decade had passed.

He stood above the bed, looking toward the door to her room. The room was shadowy; dusk was falling. She was grateful for the darkness, since she didn't seem to be able to move and get any clothes.

It just seemed so absurd for him to be here. She should have forgotten him; he should have forgotten her. They were hardly friends now. They hadn't exactly parted on good terms. The words that passed between them now had quickly become sarcastic, scathing, when they should have been casual. But something remained after all that time.

Bitterness. Anger. And more. Things left unresolved. Being near him was like entering an energy field where slashes of lightning cut furiously through the air.

He was still in her room. Too close. Far too close.

Some things changed. Chemistry stayed the same. And she was still . . . frightened. She could strike out at Adam, or cling to him.

No. Oh, no.

"You should be going after him!" she said.

He looked at her again. She was sorry she had spoken. She felt as if her entire body was blushing, as if her skin was burning right down to her feet.

"What if it was a her?" he demanded.

"What?"

"It could have been a woman."

"It was a man. The height—"

"They're making taller woman these days. Whoever it was, they weren't much taller than you."

"It was a man."

"Because the chest was flat?"

"How amazing! I hadn't thought you were aware that female chests could come in flat."

He leaned over her again, a half smile curving his mouth. "You'd be amazed at the amount of wonderfully sensual, sexy women who come in size small."

"Your tastes have broadened."

"Ah, let's see, I just passed through your life and know nothing about you, but you can judge my tastes?"

She smiled, determined not to cringe or allow him to realize in any way that her nudity in front of him made her feel as vulnerable as a day-old kitten.

"I know that when you left here, the woman you left for was incredibly well-endowed. Not particularly tall, but—well-endowed."

"You're mistaken. But then, you so often are."

"How could you possibly know that?"

"How could you possibly know my taste in breasts?"

"I'm only familiar with my own observations, of course."

"Very mature ones," he commented. "But then, you were just past being a child back then, weren't you?"

There was something disturbing about the way he asked the question.

Just past being a child.... She had been in her early twenties at the time. He'd just been accustomed to a faster crowd. Women who knew what they were doing.

Well, he had seen to her education.

"I do apologize," she said coolly. In perfect control. "We're certainly both adults now, and this has to be one of the most ridiculous conversations I've ever had. Whether that was a man or a woman, you should have gone after them."

"Oh, really? I get beaten up for saving you, and then I'm supposed to go after the intruder anyway?"

"You don't look beaten up."

"Trust me, I am."

"You—"

"Not only was I struck by the intruder, but then I got you throwing punches, as well."

"Aftershock," she said evenly.

"Um."

"That doesn't matter now."

"It doesn't matter to you because you weren't on the receiving end."

"You are *not* hurt! You should be chasing—"

"Chasing who—and where?" he demanded curtly. "Your cottage is surrounded by others, and by the main house. All that intruder had to do was shuck the ski mask and black pullover and slip on a shirt or a jacket and you'd never recognize him or her in a thousand years."

"It couldn't possibly be a guest!"

"No, a large stork delivered him to the island!"

"Well, you should have caught him!"

"Silly me. I should have let you crack your head on the tile so I could chase the intruder. Fine. Next time I'll let you crack your damned head!"

"What kind of a cop are you? You could at least look for clues."

"I'm not a cop anymore."

"No? Then what are you doing on the island?"

"Vacationing. Boating. Diving."

"Lying."

"Do you subject all your guests to the third degree?"

"Only you."

"I'm here to dive."

"The hell you are."

"I love to dive. This is a great location."

"So is Aruba."

"I like the diving off Seafire Isle—and the dive mistress here has quite a reputation. I hear she's perfect—and perfectly entertaining."

"Do you think you could possibly remove yourself from my room?"

"Do you think you can quit questioning me long enough for me to get out?"

Her eyes suddenly narrowed on him. "How did you get in here to begin with?"

"The same way your attacker did, I imagine."

"I was careful today. I locked the door."

"Not good enough, Sam." He pointed to where one of her bedroom window curtains was floating inward on the breeze. "The window, Sam. Easy access."

He turned to leave the room, and she started to shiver.

She rolled quickly under her bed covers, hoping he wouldn't realize how much he had unnerved her. But he was leaving the room without glancing her way. She wondered if he had actually taken a look at her to begin with.

If he'd even noticed that she was naked, or, if he had, if he'd cared in the least.

Wonderful. She'd been attacked, nearly... what? Kidnapped? Murdered? Yet here she was, worrying about Adam. What in God's name was the matter with her?

She leaped up when he was gone, hurrying to dress. She threw on panties, a bra, black pumps and a long-sleeved black knit dress. When she was dressed, she drew a brush through her not-really-washed-and-half-damp-hair, wincing as she hit the tangles. She told herself to toughen up, dragging the brush through her hair until it had a semblance of neatness to it, then hurried out of her bedroom—anxious to see if he had really left her cottage.

She didn't think he had.

And he hadn't.

He was seated in her living room, comfortably leaning back in the deep Victorian brocade sofa. Despite his evening attire, he'd managed a pose of casual ease, his feet propped up on the cherrywood coffee table. There was a bottle of beer in his hand, and he sipped it slowly, reflectively, as he stared at the treasure map on the wall. He lifted the bottle, indicating the map. "I'm surprised you keep that."

"Why?"

He shrugged. "Your father."

"I'd have to discard the entire island if I couldn't bear memories of my father."

"I didn't mean the memory," he murmured. "I meant—he disappeared searching for the *Beldona,* right?"

"Yes," she said.

His eyes suddenly seemed more veiled than her own. "He loved that ship."

"He didn't love the ship—he *couldn't* love the ship—he never found her. He just loved the sea, the adventure. And he loved the island. Look, forget my father for now, what about tonight? Should I call the mainland police? Make out a report?''

''You could.''

''Could? What does that mean?''

''Well, the police will come out, question you and question all your guests. You won't find out who attacked you, and you might well empty the island.''

She hadn't thought of that. ''But—but what about the danger to my guests?''

''I'd bet my life that the attacker is very specifically after you.''

''Great. Then I'm in danger.''

''Yes. You'll have to be extremely careful.''

''And how am I supposed to do that?''

''Stay close to me.''

She folded her arms over her chest. ''That could be difficult when you're running around with your well-endowed—and not-so-well-endowed—women.''

''Did I arrive here with a woman?''

''No, but they always seem to appear around you.''

''But I'll be watching *you.*''

''But—''

''Look, if the police come, they won't be able to do a damned thing but file a report. Your innocent guests will leave the island. And you'll still be in danger.''

''That's your opinion.''

"You're right. That's my opinion. Hank Jennings disappeared searching for the *Beldona,* as well, didn't he?"

She frowned, thrown by his abrupt change of subject—or determination to return to the original one. "Did you know Hank Jennings?" she asked, trying to keep her voice level.

"I heard about his disappearance," he said, his eyes on the map once again.

"Naturally you heard about it. I wrote to you, asking for help. You didn't come. But then, you didn't show up after my father disappeared, either, and you'd become bosom buddies with him."

He didn't offer her a sarcastic reply, which she might have expected. He didn't even remind her that she had asked him to leave Seafire Isle.

He just shook his head, taking a long swallow of beer. "I didn't get your letter for nearly a year after your dad disappeared," he told her. His voice seemed a little husky.

The beer, she thought.

"I was down in the Everglades on a sting operation when it came."

"Well, that would have been years ago now. Are you always so quick with your correspondence?"

"A neighbor was picking up my mail. The letter wound up on her counter, then fell behind her stove, and she finally found it over a year later, and by then . . ." He shrugged.

It sounded like one of the worst stories Sam had heard in her life but, oddly enough, she believed him. Not because the story was believable, but because of the way he told it.

"*She* was picking up your mail, huh?" Sam murmured.

"*She* was sixty-six. I don't think there was any ulterior motive behind the accident. If you'd really wanted me, you could have called."

"It's difficult to call someone who has ignored your rather desperate appeal for help."

"You know damned well I would have done anything I could to help your father."

"Well, at least I don't have to feel like such a fool for attempting to reach you last year when Hank disappeared. But what happened then? Was your neighbor collecting your mail again?"

His glare assured her that he didn't find her amusing. He shook his head, lifting the beer, taking another long swallow. Then he looked at her, his eyes silver and very sharp. "I was out of the country last year, working for private concerns. My mail was all held at the South Miami post office—feel free to check on that."

"Oh."

He exhaled in exasperation. "I was in Africa, river diving for industrial diamonds."

"I didn't ask you for a detailed explanation."

"You don't seem willing to believe one, either."

She shrugged. "So what are you doing here now?"

Once again he lifted his shoulders, and she knew she was going to receive an evasive reply. But he suddenly stared directly at her. "Unusual things have been happening in this area with some frequency."

"My father disappeared, Hank disappeared. Other than that, not a damned thing besides your run-in with the drug dealers years ago has happened here."

He arched a brow. "Nothing *unusual* has happened? What about just now? Or was that your usual evening? Were you just indulging in some kind of kinky sex in there tonight? Should I have kept out of it?"

Sam refused to dignify that with an answer. She walked across the room to the treasure map, studying it as she spoke. "I haven't had the first unusual thing happen here—until your arrival."

"Your father's disappearance wasn't unusual?"

She spun on him, fighting a wild tug-of-war to keep her emotions under control. She had loved her father. She'd never even known her mother; Justin had been all she'd had. And he had made her the center of his universe. When he had first disappeared, she had refused to believe it, yet as the days went by and no sign of him was found, she had known that he was dead. He would never have stayed away from her if there had been a breath of life left in him.

"My father is dead," she said softly.

He didn't deny it. He merely asked quietly, "And don't you want to know why?"

She shook her head stubbornly. "I do know why! The sea is a vengeful mistress."

"What about Hank?" Adam demanded. "Didn't he disappear just the same damned way—without a trace?"

She threw up her hands. "They both went out alone in small boats. Adam, the sea doesn't always give up her dead."

"Yeah, well, if I understand things correctly, she didn't give up so much as a jagged piece of lumber after the disappearance of either man."

"Adam, you know that massive ships have disappeared completely. The ocean is huge."

"Sam, you're being blind. And things are getting worse. There's more to this picture than you realize. People have been dropping like flies all around you."

She swung around, staring at him. "What are you talking about?"

He leaned forward. "Three different sets of divers—ostensibly sports divers—out from Key Largo, Coconut Grove and Fort Lauderdale—have disappeared entirely in the past year."

"But we're not in South Florida—"

"Oh, right. We're on an island not far from it. In all three cases, they were headed for the waters right around Seafire Isle."

"You just said you weren't a cop anymore."

"I'm not."

"Then . . ."

"I'm working for private concerns," he told her.

She lifted a hand in exasperation. "Okay, so your divers were heading for these waters. They could have disappeared anywhere. We're within the boundaries of the so-called Devil's Triangle out here. Pay attention to me. Ships have disappeared. Whole fleets of airplanes. I'm sorry about the divers, but I don't understand why that should suddenly make you show up on Seafire Isle. Especially on the night I just happen to be attacked in my bathroom. Then again, it's incredibly good luck that you just happened to be at hand, ready to come through my window after the intruder."

He smiled then, lifting the beer, swallowing. "I heard your scream. I couldn't get in the front door— it was locked. I came around the house. Found the window. No great mystery."

"Okay, then. The great mystery is why someone would suddenly want to attack *me* because *you've* come to the island."

"I'm sure I had nothing to do with someone attacking you."

"I've never been attacked before."

"There's a first time for everything, isn't there?"

"I'm still convinced that this first time has something to do with you."

He shook his head, finishing the beer. "Nice attitude. God knows what might have happened to you if I hadn't been here, and I still haven't heard a 'Thank you, Adam, for saving my life.'"

"But what if I was attacked because of you being on the island? Am I supposed to thank you for having put my life in danger?"

He leaned forward suddenly, with startling speed and agility that reminded her how dangerous he could be when he chose, that any time he gave the impression of casual relaxation it was just that—an impression.

"Samantha, use some damned sense, will you? Your father disappeared because he got close to something. And then Hank disappeared."

She swallowed hard. "My father knew that no matter how good you were, it was never safe to dive alone. A dozen things might have happened. He could have had a heart attack. He might have gotten excited about a discovery and tried to come up too quickly. I've had to accept the fact that he probably drowned."

"Where's the body? Where's the damned body?"

"You're not listening. You're refusing to see the obvious! The sea doesn't always give back her dead, you know that!"

"Oh, Sam, come on! You're trying to say that your father and Hank both disappeared because of some Devil's Triangle bullshit."

"It doesn't have to be anything strange or mystical! People have disappeared—"

"Yes, and there were sea monsters before men discovered the truth about giant squids and whales. There's an explanation for everything. You know it, and I know it."

"Right. Like there might be a real explanation for the fact that you're here."

"You *are* persistent."

"I'm in danger, or so you say." Sam waited for him to say something reassuring. He didn't.

"I just told you that three groups of divers—"

"Disappeared during the last year. Hank disappeared just over a year ago. So that's four disappearances. I have an older gentleman here right now who can quote you statistics regarding all the disappearances here. Even some scientific experts believe that there might be magnetic poles or something like that in the waters around here. Why should your missing divers have anything to do with my island?"

His silver eyes were sharp, and he groaned in exasperation. "Pay attention, Sam. They were all heading for waters just north of Seafire Isle."

"I head for waters just north of Seafire Isle almost every day."

"Yes, I know."

"I haven't seen or heard a single thing that was the least bit strange."

"I'd say your father did."

"My father has been gone for years."

"A long time, yes. But we've just agreed that Hank and the other divers all disappeared within the past year."

"So what the hell do you know about Hank?"

"He *was* looking for the *Beldona,* wasn't he?" Adam demanded.

"He—he . . ."

"Well?"

"I don't know exactly what he was doing. I had already gone the day he disappeared. He took one of the little motorboats and his diving equipment, and he never came back. Neither did the boat."

"Are you trying to tell me that Hank Jennings just decided to motor away?"

She stared at him, folding her arms over her chest. "No, I don't believe that he just motored away."

"Was he looking for the *Beldona?*"

"I just told you—"

"What was he doing on the island?"

"He—he was a researcher. He studied the Steps and everything beneath the sea."

"The wrecks?"

"Of course."

"The *Beldona?*"

Samantha let out a frustrated cry. "Yes, yes! He was as fascinated by the stories of that stupid ghost ship as my father was! She's sunk beneath the sea, hidden, exactly where she belongs, and I wish to hell that people—especially people around me—would leave her alone where she lies!"

"You probably know more about that ship than anyone else on earth. You know that, don't you?"

"I'm not a researcher or a marine biologist. I run a resort, and I *don't* know everything there is to know about that ship, and I don't want to know anything more than I do about her."

"No one knows everything. But I imagine a lot of people consider you to be the current expert on her. You *are* your father's daughter, after all."

Sam sighed in complete exasperation. "When did this conversation start being about me? I want to know what you're doing here, and you're switching everything around so that *you're* questioning *me!* It's not going to happen. If you'd just tell me—"

He stood up suddenly, impatiently. Almost violently. She took a step back, but he didn't even seem to notice. His empty beer bottle clinked on the top of the coffee table as he set it down. He dragged his fingers through his dark hair, staring at her. For a moment, just for a moment, she saw a flash of passion within him, yet she couldn't begin to pinpoint exactly what that passion was for.

"All right, Sam. Someone on the island has been corresponding with SeaLink for several days now."

"SeaLink?" Sam murmured, confused. She knew the name, but she couldn't place it right away. "The marine supply company?"

"Marine supply company!" Adam muttered.

"They are a marine supply company, aren't they? A big one. They sell boats, scuba equipment, maps, electronics."

"Yes, yes. It was founded in 1970 by James Jay Astin. He's also a treasure hunter. He and his employees have managed to dig up a fair amount of salvage from at least a dozen of the ships that have gone down off the coast of Florida."

"I read an article about him in one of the diving magazines. He turns his finds over to the government, endows all sorts of museums—"

"And he keeps what he wants in his private collection, or sells it on the black market around the world."

She wasn't going to argue with him when she didn't really know anything about Astin—except that he appeared to be a model citizen.

"Astin was friends with your father."

"How do you know?"

"They went diving together once when I was here. I didn't know who Astin was myself at the time, but I've had the opportunity to meet him since."

Sam shook her head stubbornly. "I never met him. My father had his own life, and when he was alive, I didn't necessarily meet and greet all the guests. So this Astin knew my father. Lots of people did. And it's not illegal for Astin or his people to be visiting the island."

"I didn't say it was illegal. Just curious."

"Besides, you're not a cop anymore."

"No."

"So what is it to you?" she asked coolly.

"I told you, I'm working for private concerns."

"And what do I know about your 'private concerns'? I still think you're at the center of all the trouble."

"He was trying to drug you, not me."

"I give up. You're trouble, and you're impossible."

"Want to try throwing me off the island?" he asked pleasantly.

"Cause enough trouble, and I will."

"This is a public vacation spot. I could sue the pants off you."

"I could have you arrested for breaking and entering."

"That's what I get for trying to save your ass!" he exclaimed, hands on his hips. "Tell me, Sam, *are* you going to throw me off again?"

"I never threw you off the island."

"You asked me to leave."

"Your interests were elsewhere."

"So, are you?"

"Like you just said, Seafire Isle is a public vacation spot."

"I'm glad you see it that way. Because I don't give a damn what you think, or what you want—I won't be leaving until a few mysteries are cleared up."

"Is that so?" she inquired politely.

"And you should be glad."

"Really."

"Yes—damned grateful, in fact."

"Then thank God for your presence," Sam muttered.

"Sam, my love, you can be one stubborn bitch," he said wryly. He took the few steps needed to come close to her, lifting her chin. She managed to keep herself from wrenching it away.

"You bet!" she promised him softly. "The worst bitch you've ever come across if you're trying to put something over on me."

He smiled suddenly. "Aren't we getting just a little bit carried away here? I didn't come to pick up the pieces of an old argument right where we left off. And I probably did save your life."

"Okay. Thank you for saving my life. Now, will you please get the hell out of my house? Maybe I can't throw you off the island, but I know damned well I have the right to throw you out of here!"

"Miss Carlyle, you need me."

"I do?"

He shrugged. "Well, if you do decide to try to throw me off the island, you'll have to hope someone else is around the next time you're in trouble."

"I thanked you, didn't I? Of course, it would have been helpful to know just who was attacking me, but then, you're not a cop anymore. You couldn't possibly have been expected to nab the attacker as well as save my life."

"Okay, the next time you're about to fracture your skull, I'll consider you expendable in the pursuit of justice."

"Will you please get the hell out?"

"Nice. I should just leave you to the next ski-masked attacker who crawls into your bathroom."

"Look at it my way. I haven't seen you in years. The next thing I know, my bathroom is filled with strange men."

"Strange *men?*"

"I consider you very strange."

"Maybe you'd better consider me dangerous, instead," he warned her suddenly, softly, a thoughtful look in his eyes as he studied her.

"Maybe I should," she murmured, agreeing. "Damn it! I just want to know exactly what you're doing here."

"All right. Fine. Tell me, do you know exactly who all your guests are?"

"You know how the island is run. My father is gone, so yes, of course, I meet all my guests."

"I didn't ask you that. I asked if you knew who they were."

"I'm not a cop. People don't have to fill out their life histories on arrival. I don't have dossiers on everyone who sets foot on Seafire Isle."

"I didn't think so."

He sounded so damned self-satisfied.

"You do, of course? Have dossiers on my guests?"

"Yes."

"You're kidding."

"Well, I don't exactly have dossiers. But I imagine I know a great deal more about them than you do."

"All right, who's on my island?"

"You really have no idea?"

"I really have no idea."

He stared at her, then smiled suddenly, cocking his head. He turned away from her, heading toward the door.

"Where are you going?"

"Out."

"Out?"

He paused, looking back. "You wanted me out, right?"

"Damn it! That was before—"

"I'll see you at cocktail hour, Sam."

"Damn you, you didn't answer my question!"

"I didn't, did I? But then you haven't been particularly cooperative either, have you?"

"Cooperative! Are you insane?"

"See you later, Sam. Maybe we can exchange some information then. Go in and close that window in your bedroom. Unless you want to take the chance of having a few more strange men enter."

"Damn you, Adam!"

"Sam, pay attention. Make sure you close and lock that window. And when you leave your cottage from now on, make damned sure that you lock it carefully. You need an alarm system, actually."

"This is an island! We've never needed any kind of alarm system!"

"Maybe you never did before."

"Adam, this is ridiculous! What we've had has always been sufficient. Normal hotels don't have alarm systems in every room."

He arched a brow. "Yeah, well, a lot of your big guys have some kind of video surveillance. That's beside the point now. You should think about moving into the main house for a while, maybe. For your own protection. Yancy lives in the main house, right? And Jacques?"

"I don't want to move into the main house. I'm quite comfortable where I am—"

"With strange men in your bathroom?"

"Damn you, Adam, you have no right to do this! Talk to me, tell me—"

"Sam—"

"You know, Adam, that's the basic problem with you. You always want something for nothing. You don't seem to have the concept of *give* and take down yet."

"Sam, so far, you haven't given me a damn thing."

"Son of a bitch! I always gave you everything."

"Wrong, Sam. You never gave me a chance to give you anything before—"

"What?"

"You never gave me a chance to give you anything—"

"Like what?"

"Like explanations! So this time, you're just going to have to ask and ask damned politely when you want something. I didn't give, is that it? I went through one hell of a wringer."

"Adam—"

"You took a hell of a lot more than you ever seemed to know, Miss Carlyle," he interrupted.

"Damn you, Adam!"

But he walked away and the door closed firmly behind him.

4

The bar in the main house where the guests gathered before dinner was old-fashioned, very Victorian and very comfortable. There was a huge double-sided fireplace running the length of the far wall; it connected with the dining room. The hardwood floor was covered with numerous thick Persian carpets in shades of burgundy and mauve; the bar itself was carved oak; and high-backed, brocade-upholstered chairs and love seats were set about at intimate angles. Beyond the velvet over linen drapes, wicker chairs with similar upholstery lined the porch.

When Sam came into the bar via the porch, Yancy was just setting out crystal bowls filled with nuts. Sam didn't speak to her at first; she went behind the mahogany bar to uncork a bottle of her favorite Chablis. She poured herself a glass and stared at Yancy, who was watching her with condemning eyes in return.

"Go easy on that. You're not a good drinker, Sam Carlyle. Especially not with wine."

"Excuse me, are you my keeper?"

"No, I'm not," Yancy assured her. Like Jem, though, Yancy had grown up with Sam. They were best friends. They had laughed together, matured together, weathered all their losses together, survived together. Sam and Yancy were almost exactly the same age; they'd been born a month apart. Sam had always considered Yancy to be one of the most beautiful women she had ever seen. She was Sam's height, with black hair she kept cropped almost to her skull, olive eyes, and skin the color of pure honey. Her father had been a Creole sailor, her mother, Katie, had been from Trinidad, and she had been the first chef Sam's father had hired when old Jimmy had passed away. Jimmy had been in his nineties, still ruling the kitchen, when he had suddenly expired while making gumbo. They had all mourned him deeply—they had by that time rather come to believe that he would live forever. But then Katie had arrived with Yancy, and Sam, three at the time, had quickly come to understand that Jimmy had lived a long, fruitful and happy life, and that it was okay to love Katie, as well. In addition, Sam had found herself thrilled to have another little girl to play with, so Yancy had become the sister she'd never had, and Katie, who was patient and gentle, had certainly done well in the mother department. Years later, when Katie had died of heart failure, they had both felt as if they had lost a mother. In the same way, Yancy had shared every bit of pain, anger, frustration and loss when Sam's father had disappeared without a trace.

"I simply love a sip of good wine," Sam told Yancy defensively.

"Careful. It might love you back a bit too much. And I think that you've had more than a sip already."

"Yancy!"

"Oh, don't worry. No one else will be able to tell. I simply know you."

"Yancy, damn it—"

"Don't you go yelling at me. I didn't tell him to walk back into your life."

Sam poured the wine, set the cork in the bottle and walked around the bar. She headed to the set of chairs directly before the fire, leaving her glass on the counter. Yancy came over and sat down beside her. Sam stretched her hand out. Yancy took her fingers and squeezed them.

Sam had to smile. "I'm sorry I yelled at you. He just took me by surprise. But, Yancy, that's not the worst of it! You wouldn't believe . . ." She hesitated, wondering how much she should say. Then she remembered that she was talking to Yancy. "Yancy, someone just attacked me in my bathroom."

"What?" Yancy nearly shrieked.

"Sh, sh!" Sam said. "You'll have everyone checking out."

"Well, girl, they should be checking out if that's what's going on. Who attacked you? Not—oh, I don't believe it!"

"No, no, Adam didn't attack me. He stopped the man who did."

"Out of the past and straight to the rescue," Yancy murmured. "But who . . . ?"

"I don't know."

"How can you not know?"

"He was wearing a ski mask."

"A ski mask!"

"Sh!"

"No one is here. You were attacked by a man wearing a ski mask—on a Caribbean island?"

Sam nodded, turning around to make sure that Yancy was right and that they hadn't been joined as yet. "I was in the tub when this guy appeared, dressed all in black, trying to drug me, I think."

"You think," Yancy murmured skeptically.

"Yancy, he had some kind of a cloth in his hands."

"Black?"

"Right. Damn it, Yancy, this is serious."

"I'm sorry. So tell me—"

"He was definitely trying to drug me. I can still recall the awful scent of the cloth. I was nearly knocked out, but then the guy in the ski mask was pulled away—"

"Adam?"

"Yes."

Yancy was quiet for a minute. Then she shrugged. "Well, he is useful," she said.

"Yancy..."

"Okay, so did you try to breathe wine because of the attack, or because of Adam?"

"Yancy!"

"Ah, because of Adam," Yancy said.

"Yancy...."

"He did save you, right?"

"Yes, he did."

"And you said thank you."

"More or less."

"Sam!"

"Yancy, you're missing the point."

"I'm not missing the point. There's a dangerous whacko running around the island. We don't want everyone to check out of the hotel, but neither do we want anyone else attacked by the whacko."

"It's strange, but I don't think this particular whacko is a danger to the general public."

"Now you're losing me."

"I don't think our guests are in danger."

"Why not?"

"The whacko *is* one of our guests," she said, evading a direct answer to the question. She didn't want to admit that she was relying on Adam's judgment.

"My, my, my. What is the world coming to? Imagine. We're letting the riffraff onto Seafire Isle."

"Yancy, it isn't funny."

"Of course it's not funny. You could have been . . . hurt. Or worse. Maybe we should call the mainland police."

"I—I decided not to."

Yancy arched a brow. "Did Adam suggest that you not do so?"

"Not exactly. He pointed out that it might not do me much good, and that I might wind up in greater danger."

Yancy lifted her hands and let them fall back on the armrests of the chair. "Why?"

Sam didn't answer her. She frowned suddenly. "Yancy, where's the baby?"

Yancy smiled. "Upstairs. Lillie Wie is staying overnight because of the dinner party. She and Brian are napping right alongside each other."

"Oh!" Sam said, leaning back into the chair with relief. Brian was six months old—and the love of all their lives. He had his father's blue eyes and toffee brown hair, and the most winning smile known to man. Lillie was one of the day maids. There were four of them altogether; they came in the morning from Freeport and usually left with the mail boat in the afternoon, along with the two grounds keepers. Sam hadn't been quite twenty-two when her father had disappeared, but between herself, Jem Fisher and Yancy, they had divided the duties on the island in a manner that had worked well right from the very beginning. Jem supervised maintenance, tennis, golf, lawn care, pool and beach care, and any repairs that became necessary. There were only two tennis courts, and the golf course was only nine holes. There was also only one pool, so Jem didn't find his responsibilities overwhelming. Jem's younger cousin, Matt, had taken a job with them during the last year, as well, acting as lifeguard, scuba instructor and jack-of-all-trades, but he only came over on weekends, when his college schedule allowed.

Yancy managed the main house, the reservations, the kitchen and the household staff. Sam was dive mistress, scuba instructor, social director and official hostess. It all fell together well. Yancy had always loved the house, which worked out well, because now she usually had the baby at her side, no matter what task she was up to.

"Were you afraid somebody might be after the baby?" Yancy asked her.

"I guess not. I'm just...unnerved," Sam told her. "Is dinner all set up?"

"All set and ready to go," Yancy said. "Jacques has everything in control."

Jacques Roustand was the only other live-in employee on the island. He'd been their chef since Yan-

cy's mother had passed away eight years ago. He'd
found himself in a sad position at first, of course, but
he'd been so different and so entirely unique that
Yancy herself had been the first to fully accept him.
He was in his mid-thirties now, and appeared almost
a caricature of the typical French chef, down to a slim,
twirling mustache he had worn continuously ever since
his arrival. He wasn't exactly French, for though he
had attended school in Paris, he had been born and
bred a Louisiana Creole. Sam was convinced that it
was more his mother's influence than the French
school that had made him a great chef. He never ran
out of different ways to prepare crawfish, shrimp,
Florida lobster or any creature they pulled from the
sea. His dishes were colorful, exotic and could always
be prepared for each individual guest in either a spicy
or mild manner. She, Jem and Yancy all considered
him invaluable—and any one of them was customarily willing to drop anything he or she was about to do
when Jacques called. If he wanted garlic chopped,
they chopped. Glasses filled, they filled them. Silver
polished, they polished. Sam had once told Jem that
she might own the island, but Jacques indisputably
ruled it.

"Good evening, ladies!"

They both jumped up, turning to greet their first
arrival for the evening.

It was Avery Smith, an elderly gentleman visiting the island on his own. He was tall and very slim, with a full head of iron-gray hair and iron-gray eyes to match. He was intelligent and charming. And wealthy, Sam assumed, judging by his impeccable clothing. He was very fond of Versace, elegant gold cuff links and silver-handled canes. He never appeared for dinner in less than a complete tux.

"Mr. Smith," Yancy said. "Good evening to you. Would you like your customary brandy, sir?"

"I would indeed, my dear young woman."

As Yancy went to get his drink, he smiled at Sam. "I wish I were just a few years younger. I would love to join one of your dive parties. I could hear the children laughing—so excited!—when they returned this afternoon."

"I hope they didn't disturb you," Yancy said, giving him a snifter of brandy. "I tried to make sure I gave you and the Walkers cottages far enough apart."

He sipped his brandy, waving a hand her way. "I like the sound of laughter." He smiled again at Sam. "They say you are very, very good, like a fish *in* the water and charming with your tales *atop* it."

"Thank you. I enjoy the water very much."

"Every day?"

"Every day."

Brad and Darlene Walker chose that moment to come scampering in, both asking Yancy politely for soda.

"Play you in backgammon, Sam?" Brad queried hopefully.

"Later, okay? Play your sister for now."

Darlene groaned. "He cheats."

"I do not!"

"Where are the parents of these little hellions?" demanded Liam Hinnerman, entering the room in a handsome tweed suit, Jerry North, small, fragile and lovely at his side.

"Liam!" Jerry murmured.

"Where are your charming parents?" Liam said.

"Oh, they're coming along!" Brad said cheerfully, sliding into one of the big chairs that encircled an antique gaming table. "I'm red," he told his sister.

"Yancy, I'd just love a Bloody Mary," Jerry said, smiling graciously.

"And I'd kill for Scotch on the rocks," Liam muttered, still eyeing the children balefully.

A deep, masculine voice suddenly spoke out. "Let's get the man a Scotch before he decides to kill!"

Sam swung around. Adam had come into the room. He smiled at Hinnerman, walking around behind the bar himself, something the guests were more than welcome to do if they chose. He set a tall glass and a short one on the antique bar.

"Um—hello," Jerry said, blue eyes wide as she stared at Adam.

Liam Hinnerman stared blankly at him.

"Hi," Adam replied pleasantly to the two of them.

"You haven't all met as yet," Sam heard herself say smoothly. "Jerry North, Adam O'Connor. Adam, Jerry. Liam Hinnerman, Adam. Adam, Liam."

The three exchanged greetings, both Liam and Jerry staring at Adam.

"Sam," Adam murmured, "this must be your wine here, huh?"

"Thanks ever so much," she murmured, coming for it. Their fingers brushed as she took the glass, and he smiled mockingly. She drew away quickly, retreating across the room, seeing Avery Smith by the fireplace. He was watching Adam, as well.

"Oh, Adam, this is Mr. Avery Smith. Avery—"

"Yes, yes. Mr. Adam O'Connor," Smith said, stepping forward with graceful dexterity to shake Adam's hand. "How do you do, sir? A pleasure."

"Thank you, but the pleasure is mine."

"Come join us," Smith said, indicating the chairs surrounding the fireplace.

As they chose seats, Sukee and Jim Santino arrived. More pleasantries were exchanged, and Sam was somewhat annoyed to realize that all her guests seemed fascinated by Adam.

And which one of her guests had entered her room, attempting to drug her, at the very least ... and for what reason?

"I really can't tell you how much you're going to enjoy the dive trips," Sukee said, drawing a chair close to Adam's. He smiled, seeming to enjoy her company.

"Sam is an excellent dive master," Hinnerman noted.

"She sure is," Avery Smith said, eyes sparkling, "but then, taking nothing away from our hostess, you must think about the waters she travels."

"The Bermuda Triangle—the *Devil's* Triangle!" Brad—who had apparently been engrossed in his game—provided for them.

"Precisely!" Smith said with pleasure.

"You don't really believe in all that crap, do you?" Hinnerman asked him.

"Liam," Jerry murmured.

He looked somewhat abashed. "I mean—it's all just stories."

Sam glanced at Adam. He wasn't saying anything. Arms crossed idly over his chest, he sat comfortably in the plush chair, awaiting Avery's answer with interest.

"True stories."

"Mr. Smith knows!" Brad told them, turning around, his eyes wide.

"Ghost stories," Yancy murmured.

"I love a good ghost story," Sukee drawled. "Please, Mr. Smith, the fire is crackling, the lights are low. Tell us about the Devil's Triangle."

"We could all become afraid to dive!" Jerry warned.

"You don't dive anyway," Brad reminded her dryly.

"Please, let's hear the stories," Darlene said.

Avery Smith offered them a rueful grin. "I imagine that Mr. O'Connor there, Sam and Yancy, maybe even you others, have heard a few of the tales about the Devil's Triangle. And, yes, we are in it. The triangle stretches from Miami to Bermuda to Puerto Rico. It's been responsible for the losses of ships, planes and human lives since man first began to traverse it. All the way back into the 1600s, Lloyds of London came to realize that they were paying dearly for ships that went down in the particular area known as the Devil's—or Bermuda—Triangle. Before that, Christopher Columbus reported disturbances with his ship's compass when he was in the area of the triangle. He made note, as well, of something that the astronauts have seen from space—strange, eerie streaks of white water appearing within the typical azures and deep blues of the sea."

"Perhaps," Sukee whispered mischievously, "the long-lost continent of Atlantis sits beneath the triangle, and ancient electronic equipment pops on and off to suck in a ship now and then."

"Or," Jim suggested, "Atlantis is now populated by alien beings, and they reach out giant tentacles to slurp up human men and women to bring back to their dying world."

"I think, Mr. Santino, that you watched too many B movies as a boy," Avery Smith said, still smiling, unoffended by the sarcasm his story was drawing. He wagged a finger toward the gathered company. "Whatever the cause, I promise you, history tells a stranger tale than ever a man could weave! There are over three hundred Spanish wrecks in the waters of the Bermuda Triangle, and that's just the beginning. Coming far closer to contemporary times, of course, is one of the strangest disasters, that of the planes that disappeared in 1944."

Brad had forgotten his backgammon game and turned his chair toward the adults, one of his game pieces curled in his fingers. Even Darlene seemed awed.

"You're referring to the navy planes?" Adam said.

"I am."

"Well?" Liam demanded.

Adam shrugged, looking at Avery Smith as he spoke. "Five torpedo bombers left the Fort Lauderdale Naval Air Station at two in the afternoon on December 5, 1944. A routine patrol that was to have lasted about two hours. They were in radio contact with the base at all times, as well as with one another. An hour and forty-five minutes into the flight, when they should have been heading back, the patrol leader radioed in to say that they were off course, that they couldn't see land. They couldn't figure out which way was west, but they should have found west very easily, just following the sun.'' Adam paused to breathe.

''What happened?'' Brad demanded anxiously.

Adam shrugged.

''They all died, kid,'' Liam said.

''Liam,'' Jerry remonstrated softy.

''Well, they did, didn't they, O'Connor?''

''They kept in contact with the base for another half hour or so. They said that the ocean didn't even look the way the ocean should look. A different pilot took over talking to the base. He said something about it looking like they were entering into 'white water,' that they were completely lost. Then there was no more contact with the pilots. None at all.''

''Whoa,'' Darlene murmured, wide-eyed.

''And that wasn't the worst of it, was it, Mr. O'Connor?'' Avery Smith asked, still smiling, a little gleam in his eyes.

Adam grinned at him—a knowledgeable skeptic. ''No, it wasn't.''

''Do tell us what happened next!'' Sukee demanded.

"A rescue plane was sent," Adam said.

Avery picked up the story. "A huge plane called a Martin Mariner flying boat was sent out just as soon as it was established that all contact was really lost. The plane had all kinds of equipment aboard, everything that might help in the rescue of the pilots if they could be found. Only they weren't found. And..."

"And?" Brad asked.

"And the rescue plane was lost, as well," Adam said. "She vanished. Disappeared without a trace. The Coast Guard was called in, and nearly three hundred thousand square miles were searched. The beach was combed from the tip of Florida to St. Augustine. The largest rescue effort ever put together was in force, and nothing was found. Nothing. Not a body, not a fragment of a single plane, nothing, absolutely nothing at all."

"That's right," Avery said, still seeming both pleased and amused. "Several times in recent years, people have thought they located the planes on the ocean floor. But it was never them. They're still just as missing as they ever were. But those planes are just a part of the mystery. There have been hundreds of incidents. Thousands of them, perhaps. Another one of the more major incidents occurred when the coal ship *Cyclops* disappeared in 1919. She was five hundred feet long, nineteen thousand tons. She vanished with three hundred and nine men aboard, and, once again, not a man, a bone, a fragment of the ship was ever discovered.''

"Then there is, of course, the story of the *Carroll A. Deering*," Adam said, still watching Avery Smith. He smiled at Brad. "You'll like this one—it's definitely a ghost story. The *Carroll A. Deering* was discovered wedged in the sands off Cape Hatteras, North Carolina, in 1921 within the angle of the triangle. There had been absolutely no storms the night before, and the ship was discovered in very eerie shape—the tables were all set, and half-eaten meals remained on the plates. Food still waiting to be served was in pots on the stove. The lights were on, bunks were made, books were lying about. Everything about the ship spoke of life—except that there was no life to be found aboard her. Not a sign of a survivor existed anywhere. Nor was anyone ever found who had been aboard her. Yet, as she remained trapped in the sand, people from the nearby shore swore they could hear screams and creaks and groans by night, coming from the haunted ship."

"Wow," Brad said, his eyes round.

"And we're in this Devil's Triangle?" Darlene asked on a squeaky breath.

"Dead center," Sukee told her.

"Well, I've yet to hear of an entire island disappearing," Yancy said matter-of-factly.

Smith cleared his throat as if to contradict her.

"An *island* has disappeared?" Sukee asked skeptically.

"Not really," Smith said reassuringly. "But there is Bouvet Island, in the South Atlantic. I'm sure Mr. O'Connor can tell you about it, as well."

Adam grinned, looking at Smith. "Named for Jean Bouvet, the French explorer who discovered it in . . . 1750 or thereabouts?" He looked questioningly at Smith.

"Thereabouts—1739," the older man said.

Adam turned to Sukee. "It's appeared and disappeared several times since it was discovered. Naturally it sinks, but exactly why it rises and falls isn't really known as yet."

"And there are no disappearing islands anywhere near us, dear girl," Smith assured Darlene.

"I know, but when we dive—" Darlene began.

"Maybe you shouldn't be diving, then," Liam suggested dryly. He grinned, lifting his nearly empty glass toward the children. "The triangle is one thing—bet you don't know where the word cannibal comes from."

Brad shook his head, eyes bright. "Where?"

"Roast loin of people, boy, roast loin of people. Columbus found these fellows with piles of bones and skulls in their homes in the Lesser Antilles. The folks called themselves Canibales, though they were really Caribes—just had a different dialect than some of the others. Columbus went on home, and soon flesh eaters everywhere were called cannibals.''

"Ooh! That's disgusting!'' Darlene said.

"True story,'' Liam said, pleased that she was turning pale.

"How about another soda, honey? It'll calm your queasy stomach,'' Yancy suggested, rising and seeming to break the spell that had fallen over the group.

Sam rose, as well, slipping behind the bar with Yancy. As she did so, Judy and Lew Walker sauntered into the bar, arm in arm. They were starting to greet the others, but were interrupted when Darlene leaped up from her chair, ran to meet them and threw herself into her father's arms.

"Darlene, what on earth . . . ?''

"Do I have to dive, Daddy? Do I have to dive?''

Lew Walker stared at Sam, puzzled and indignant. "What have you told her, Sam?''

"Me? I haven't said a thing,'' she protested.

Adam was up, shaking his head apologetically. "I'm afraid that I'm at fault here,'' he began.

"Damned right,'' Liam muttered.

"Along with Mr. Hinnerman and Mr. Smith. I'm afraid I'm a bit skeptical regarding mysterious phenomena, and Mr. Smith and I indulged in a few historical tales. Sam had nothing to do with it.''

"Oh, Dad!" Brad said. "Mr. Smith and Mr. O'Connor know so much neat stuff! And Mr. Hinnerman's an expert on cannibals."

"Ooh!" Darlene moaned again.

"You've been telling my daughter about cannibals?"

"Right before supper, yum, yum," Yancy murmured.

Sam elbowed her in the ribs. Yancy sucked in a breath and shrugged innocently.

"The part about the cannibals was really cool!" Brad said.

Lew looked at his daughter, perplexed. "Honey, you're not going to meet any cannibals diving under the water," he assured her.

"Who knows? People seem to disappear so completely, they might have been eaten!" Darlene said.

Sam came around the bar, walked up to Darlene and took her by the hand. "Darlene, I've been out thousands of times, and I promise you, I've never lost a single diver to a cannibal."

"Have you lost any to anything else?" Adam inquired politely.

"No!" Sam snapped.

"Will you buddy up with me tomorrow?" Darlene asked her.

"Sure."

"What about me?" Jim Santino teased.

"It looks like it's going to be you and Liam tomorrow," Sam said evenly.

"What about Adam?" Liam demanded.

"Hey, Mr. O'Connor! How about being my buddy?" Brad asked excitedly.

"Sure."

"That leaves Sukee," Jim noted, eyes and smile flashing.

"Sukee can choose where she wants to make it a threesome," Sam said.

"Hands down, I'm going with the boys," Sukee said huskily.

"Which boys?" Yancy demanded.

"I haven't decided yet—they'll get to find out in the morning!" Sukee said, laughing.

Joey and Sue Emerson, the honeymooners, sauntered into the bar. "What's happening in the morning?" Sue asked.

"We were discussing tomorrow's dives," Jim said. "Don't worry—no one had any idea of splitting up the two of you."

"Or joining the two of you," Sukee murmured.

"Where are we diving tomorrow?" Sue asked.

"Away from the cannibals," Darlene said.

"Cannibals?" Joey repeated. "I know there are sharks out there, but cannibals?"

"Yes, there are sharks," Adam said idly.

"Sam?" Darlene said nervously.

"Darlene, I've been diving my entire life, and yes, I've seen sharks, but no, I've never been bothered by one." She cast a frown toward Adam, who had the grace to look instantly contrite. She knew that he hadn't been referring to Darlene's kind of shark, but the damage had been done.

Adam stood and came over to Darlene. "Did you know that swimmers and especially surfers are sometimes attacked, but that divers are almost never attacked?"

"Really?"

He nodded. "They've done extensive experiments out in California. A lot of scientists think that the sharks see people on surfboards and in their minds, the surfer looks like a sea lion, which is what the shark normally likes to eat. You've got much more of a chance of being struck by lightning than you do of being attacked by a shark."

"Really?"

"Really. Sharks are actually fascinating creatures. Many of them are quite harmless to man. And you know, they're related to skates and rays, like the giant mantas you see sometimes when you're down. You know, if you're careful and gentle, you can catch a ride on a big manta."

"Maybe you wouldn't be so bad to dive with, either, Mr. O'Connor."

"You can call me Adam."

She grinned at him slowly. "You could dive with Sam and me, you know."

"Hey!" her brother protested.

Sukee was quick to smooth his ruffled feathers. "Maybe I'd enjoy a younger man as a dive partner for the afternoon," she said.

"Oh!" Brad said. His mouth remained in a circular shape. Even his parents laughed.

"Why don't we work all this out in the morning?" Sam suggested, a brittle smile curving her lips. Leave it to Adam. He'd charmed Darlene. He still had the touch.

His eyes met hers. She realized that she still had questions for him. And apparently he still had questions for her.

Odd. She'd known him for only a few months, a very long time ago. She had changed since then, matured. Maybe. But everything about him was disturbingly familiar. Everything she should have forgotten. She knew just how determined he could be. That he had come for something. He wanted something.

And she knew that he would get what he wanted.

"Perhaps Miss Carlyle would be willing to show the dive party the Steps tomorrow," he said.

"The Steps?" Liam queried sharply.

Adam nodded, looking at Sam. Then he glanced at Darlene, smiling. "There are wonderful, fascinating things beneath the sea as well as the scary ones," he told her. "Off North Bimini Island, just a little more than thirty feet down, are huge blocks that form some kind of an ancient foundation. No one knows what civilization set them where they are now. A construction company used some of them in Miami in the 1920s, I think." He glanced over to Smith.

"Yes, it was the twenties."

"Anyway, scientists think that the blocks are definitely man-made, and that they may be over ten thousand years old."

"But we can't go to North Bimini, can we?" Brad asked.

"Not in a four-hour dive trip," Sam said tensely.

"But," Adam said, "Sam could take us to the Seafire Steps. Which are..."

He looked at Avery Smith.

Smith laughed. "There are a lot of strange man-made structures beneath the sea, and most of them make for fascinating mysteries," he said. "Just a bit northwest of Seafire Isle are a set of steps. They begin at a point that's just thirty feet beneath the sea, then they dive deeper until they suddenly just disappear."

"So where did they go?" Darlene asked.

"No one knows," Avery told her. "But, like the Bimini Blocks, they're supposed to be very ancient, and naturally, they're very intriguing. Maybe, if Miss Carlyle takes you out there, you can discover where they go and solve one of the great mysteries of the deep.''

"What do you say, Sam?'' Adam asked her.

She hesitated. She had been diving the Steps since she'd been a small child. She, Jem and even Yancy had made up stories about them when they were growing up. They led to Atlantis, or to a different, even higher civilization. On really whimsical days, they had imagined that they led to a secret doorway that would take them to a place where there were princes and princesses, maybe a magical bubble island in the sea, where pirates still ruled, or a unique island-within-the-sea where a Middle Eastern society flourished and all the tales told in the *Arabian Nights* came to life.

Of course, she'd been a child then.

She was older now, and looked at the world through eyes that had been narrowed greatly.

There was nothing all that mysterious about the Steps anymore.

She had avoided the Steps since her father's disappearance. He had loved them, had been fascinated by them. It hurt to go there. But though she no longer felt their enchantment, it did exist for children. Still...

"There are sometimes underwater currents there,'' she said, stalling.

"There are sometimes underwater currents almost everywhere,'' Liam said. "Would you actually consider it an unsafe dive?''

"No, no...."

"Sounds fun to me," Sukee said.

Sam still hesitated, uneasy, though she didn't know why.

Yes, she did.

She thought that her father might have been diving near them the day he had disappeared. He had been talking about them with so much excitement right before they had parted that day. He had been drawn to the damned Steps, almost as if both he and the Steps *had* been controlled by some strange magnetic force. Hank, too, had found them fascinating.

"The Steps sound cool," Brad said.

"I'd really love to see them, Sam," Darlene told her earnestly.

"I...well, sure. We'll dive the Steps tomorrow, then," Sam said.

"Not tomorrow," Yancy told her. "Not if the weathermen are right. They say it's going to rain all day."

"Well, then, we'll all sleep in tomorrow and dive the Seafire Isle Steps on Thursday."

"No diving tomorrow?" Brad said, disappointed.

"We'll just have to sleep late," Joey Emerson said to his wife. He spoke with such passion in his voice that Sam felt as if she was intruding on their privacy just by having heard him.

"A morning to sleep in," Sukee murmured.

"Then the Steps. Great!" Jim Santino applauded as he swished his long hair out of his face.

"Skol!" Liam Hinnerman said, lifting the Scotch he had just refreshened in a toast to the rest of them. "Know where that expression came from, young Mr. Walker? It's believed that the Vikings drank to victory from the skulls of their slain enemies, then raised those skulls in salute to one another."

"Oh, that is disgusting!" Darlene said.

"Neat, it's neat!" her brother insisted.

"Really, Mr. Hinnerman," Judy Walker admonished.

"Nothing he couldn't learn right in his own school, and not half as bad as the news these days," Hinnerman said.

Jerry North, at his side, was silent. She was staring at Sam, her lips taut. She appeared anxious. Unhappy, perhaps.

Suddenly Sam wondered why Jerry never went diving with them. Sam had never even asked her if she was certified, or if she wanted to take lessons on the island.

"Jerry, are you certified?" she asked.

"Certified? She's got certifications up the kazoo!" Liam said.

Sam arched a brow to Jerry, who nodded.

"Not just open water," Liam said. "She's an advanced diver. An expert with nitrox."

Nitrox allowed a diver to stay deeper for longer periods of time.

"Good for you. How come you haven't come diving with us?" Sam asked.

Jerry shrugged. "I lost my taste for the sea."

"She nearly drowned a few years ago," Liam said casually.

"Pretty serious," Adam said sympathetically.

Jerry offered him a broad smile of thanks.

"She's all right," Liam asserted.

"She doesn't have to dive if she doesn't want to," Sam said firmly.

Sam continued to watch Jerry, but she turned away quickly when she felt a little trickle of warmth along her spine. Adam's eyes, she thought. She looked toward him. She'd been right. He was studying her.

And he was smiling. Just slightly.

Adam had indeed come to Seafire Isle for something. And he was going to get what he wanted. In fact, he was already on the way to doing so, she realized.

Because Adam was just as eager as everyone else to dive the Seafire Isle Steps.

Why?

The question burned inside her.

5

"Ah, here comes Jem to lead us in to dinner!" Yancy exclaimed.

For another several seconds, Sam continued to stare at Adam. *What was he up to?*

And which one of her guests was dangerous? Who had been in her bathroom? Oddly enough, she realized, all of her male guests were of a similar height. Tall. Six-one, six-two. All about the same build.

She glanced quickly from Adam to Jim, then to Liam, before moving on to Joey Emerson and Lew Walker. Even Avery Smith stood a good six-one.

She looked at Adam. He was still watching her. Reading her thoughts. She turned quickly away from him, telling herself that she had a busy evening ahead. And in fact, for the next several hours she was so busy that she didn't dare take time to think.

Jacques summoned her to the kitchen, along with Yancy and Jem. She poured spoonfuls of the delicate white wine sauce on the dinner plates in an assembly line just before Jem slipped servings of the perfectly baked snapper Jacques had prepared atop them. Yancy served.

When it was actually time for her to sit down and eat, she found herself beside Jim Santino. As she ate, she couldn't help but notice that Sukee had maneuvered into position beside Adam.

The evening wound down slowly. The Walkers—all four of them—were the first to retire for the evening. Jerry seemed more interested in staying at the main house than in the concept of a return to her cottage— with Liam. Liam, however, seemed tired, irritable and ready to go, so Jerry went along.

The others slowly followed suit; Sukee, Jim and Adam holding out the longest. Sukee and Adam seemed to be getting along quite well.

Sam finally gave out herself, wondering if Adam would make an attempt to follow her.

Surely he'd feel compelled to keep her safe.

"Good night, all," she said, suppressing a yawn. "Don't forget, we all get to sleep in tomorrow. But for those who want to see the Steps on Thursday, remember that breakfast is from six-thirty to nine, and the dive boat leaves at nine-thirty sharp."

"I'll be there," Sukee promised. They were in the bar at that point, and she had a brandy snifter in her hand. She swirled the liquid in her snifter as she leaned close to Adam. Jim leaned closer, as well.

Pretty soon, Sam thought, the three of them would crash into each other and knock each other down.

The hell with them.

"Well, then . . . good night."

"G'night, Sam. Thanks for another great day," Jim told her, winking.

He tossed his hair back. She was sure that he saw it as some kind of a strange compliment to her.

She nodded.

"Good night, Miss Carlyle," Adam said. He, too, had a brandy. He lifted his glass to her.

She lifted a hand and exited the bar by the porch, muttering to herself as she started across the lawn toward her cottage.

"That rat bastard supposedly saves my life—years after destroying my heart and any belief I might have had in my own sex appeal—then drinks brandy with Sukee all night. Is this fair? Why is he back in my life? Dear God, is this necessary?"

She thought she heard a rustling in the hibiscus bush at her side. She spun around, staring into the shadows created by the blaze of night-lights on the paths around her.

She felt the whisper of the night breeze. Nothing more.

She started walking again, drawing her key from the slim pocket in her knit dress. When she reached her door, she opened it quickly, stepped inside, closed it, locked it, then leaned against it.

She walked through the living room, the kitchen, growing more nervous as she did so. She needed a weapon, she told herself. Just in case Ski Mask came back.

She opened the huge old secretary that stood beneath her father's treasure map. The secretary had once graced a captain's cabin on a ship; it had been one of her father's favorite pieces of furniture.

She found his Revolutionary War flintlock musket. No ammunition, of course—should she know how to manage the antique flintlock to begin with. Still, she could use it as a bludgeon to protect herself if necessary.

It would be better than nothing.

She opened closet doors. She went into her bedroom—then her bath.

Every window was still closed and locked. Her cottage, she was convinced, was empty.

She started turning off lights, then froze as she began to close the living room shutters.

There was a figure standing on the path that led to her cottage. Tall and dark. Watching her cottage.

Watching *her*.

She inhaled, exhaled. Then she lightly bit her lower lip. The figure was walking calmly down the path, making no secret of the fact that he was coming to the cottage.

Adam, she thought.

She half-smiled, leaning against the wall. She'd been right—he'd had to come back.

He had to protect her. He had come to her island. After someone or something, true, but he had managed to come into her cottage at just the right time.

And now he was coming back.

To protect her. He would insist, of course, that he couldn't leave her alone. That she had to be protected, and that there was no one who could protect her the way he could.

He would want to move in.

Well, she would tell him what was what. She would get him this time. He wasn't coming anywhere near her.

The knock she'd expected sounded on her door.

She threw it open.

And gaped.

It was Jem.

Tall, dark and handsome, all right.

"Jem!"

"Who were you expecting?"

"I, uh..."

"Adam, right?"

"Are you coming in or not?" she snapped. Adam, it seemed, was apparently spending the night with Su-kee.

He smiled. "You bet I'm coming in. I'm sleeping on the sofa."

"Oh, Jem, that's not necessary."

"It sure as hell is. You were attacked right here, and I didn't have the least idea."

"How could you have? Don't be silly."

"Adam suggested that you shouldn't be left alone. I agree."

"But, Jem . . ."

"I'll be on the sofa, Sam."

"Great. Make me feel guilty about you getting a sore back sleeping on my sofa."

"I can't sleep in the bedroom, Sam. Too kinky. It would be like sleeping with my own sister."

"Cute."

Jem grinned. "Go to bed, Sam. You have the opportunity to sleep in, thanks to the weatherman."

"That much will be nice. If I can get to sleep at all."

"You'll sleep. Go to bed."

She wouldn't sleep, though. She would lie there, wondering.

She smiled suddenly, ready to laugh at herself. Okay, so she'd wanted the chance to turn down Adam O'Connor and she hadn't gotten it. So what? Jem was just as good as a brother, and it was wonderful to have a friend who cared so much.

She kissed him on the cheek. "I'll get you a couple of pillows and some blankets."

She did so, then retired to bed herself, where she tried to sleep.

She kept tossing and turning, tossing and turning.

Adam was back in her life.

Back in her life. . . .

And it felt as if he'd never left. As if she knew him still.

She didn't know him at all! she reminded herself.

She jumped at a sudden shrill ringing, then realized stupidly that it was the telephone by her bedside. She lifted the receiver.

"Hello?"

"You're all right?"

Adam.

She was annoyed to feel a subtle warmth rise to her cheeks. "I was sleeping," she lied.

"Jem's there with you?"

"Yes. Where are you?"

"My cottage. I believe it's the one you call Paradise."

"Um."

"Want to know about your guests?"

"Are you . . . alone?"

"Checking up on me? Worried about me? Miss me?"

"Don't be absurd."

"Were you imagining that I had Sukee here beside me?"

"It would be completely your own affair if you did, Mr. O'Connor."

"Then why did you ask?"

She made certain that he could hear the depth of her very impatient sigh. "I was attacked this evening. Naturally I want to know as much as I can about who's where on the island."

"Interesting. Since you know so little."

"Thank you for that assessment."

"Do you want to know about your guests or not?"

"Do I?" she demanded. "You're not going to hang up on me if I say yes?"

He laughed softly. She gnawed on her lower lip. Just the sound of his laughter seemed to brush sensually into her soul.

And other places.

"Talk!" she told him.

Amazingly, he obliged. "Your Mr. Avery Smith isn't a Mr. Smith at all."

"What?"

"Mr. Smith isn't Mr. Smith."

"Then who is he?"

"James Jay Astin. Founder and chairman of the board of SeaLink."

Then, having made certain that Sam couldn't possibly sleep all night, Adam clicked off.

The Walkers had a two-bedroom cottage on the opposite side of the main house from Sam.

The kids were tucked into bed. Judy was being silent. The kind of silent Lew Walker just hated in his wife. Her lips were pursed. She'd changed into her nightgown, a long silky thing that should have been nice and sexy, just right for an island vacation for a man and his wife. However, as she pulled the covers neatly down on the bed, she kept up her silence—creating a killer chill within the room. Any excitement he might have been feeling withered in his BVDs as he watched her.

Finally the silence got to him.

He walked behind her and slipped his arms around her body. She stood very stiffly, not fighting him, just casting that awful chill.

"Judy—"

"It's not right," she said. "What we're doing—it's just not right."

"Judy, we need the money," he said.

"There are other ways to make money."

"We have two children. We have to survive."

"We have two children. We're supposed to teach them right from wrong."

"We're not really doing anything wrong."

"The hell we're not."

"The way you see it, maybe."

"Lew, just don't touch me right now, all right?"

He froze himself, then released her. He walked around to his own side of the bed and slid beneath the covers, keeping his back to her.

Judy turned off the lights. Once she got into bed, she kept her back to him, as well.

The chill, Lew thought, had turned into a regular ice storm.

He sighed and tried to sleep.

The day after tomorrow, the Steps.

Jerry North sat, legs curled beneath her, in a wicker rocking chair on the small porch that surrounded their bungalow. She looked out at the night. The sky was velvet black, dotted with unbelievably bright stars.

Beautiful.

The island was beautiful. Peaceful, elegant, casual. A perfect place to call home.

How ironic, how sad.

She felt Liam coming out to stand behind her. "You're going to have to go diving soon," he told her.

She shrugged.

"I can dive, but it won't help."

"You're the only one who really knows."

"I don't know anything. I didn't know what I was doing then, and I surely won't have the least idea now."

"Well, who knows? Anything is worth a try. Adam O'Connor is here. You know damned well he has to be working for someone."

"Maybe he's just after the truth," she murmured.

"What?"

She shook her head. "Nothing, really..."

Liam was silent, thoughtful. "You still haven't learned anything from Samantha?"

"Samantha doesn't know anything."

She heard him sigh. He was getting insistent. She bit her lower lip. *She could just leave now. Leave Liam. Surely he would let her go....*

And maybe not. Maybe what she did or didn't know, could or couldn't remember, mattered to him far more than she imagined. Well, almost everything else she'd ever done in life had been a mistake, why not this, too? Liam wasn't bad. He never pretended he didn't appreciate other women, nor did he ever pretend to love her. He was blunt, curt, rude, temperamental, aggressive. He could be violent—he was one of those men who believed a man had a right to knock a woman around a bit if she needed it—but never to the extent that he really hurt her.

And maybe she'd taken so many knocks in life that she'd grown to expect a few now and then.

Still, Liam had a strange honesty about him, at least where she was concerned, and she felt that if nothing else, at least she was playing the game with a full deck of cards. In that particular sense, she was getting more from him than he was getting from her.

She shivered suddenly, fiercely. No one could ever know the whole truth. No one. Partly it just hurt too damned badly. She couldn't bear to have the scar ripped open.

Not for Liam. Not for anyone.

"Samantha knows something," Liam insisted.

"She knows how to dive, and she knows the ship exists somewhere, and that's about it," Jerry insisted.

"You're wrong. She lived with her father. She listened to him day in and day out. She knows something."

"She doesn't even like to talk about the *Beldona.*" Jerry hesitated, then shook her head. "Don't you understand? She loved her father. He died because of that damn ship."

"He disappeared."

"He's dead."

"How do you know?"

"I don't know, I—I just don't believe he would ever have left his daughter intentionally."

Liam leaned over her. "You're alive," he said softly.

She shook her head, moistening her lips. "Justin Carlyle has to be dead. And you can't blame Sam for not wanting to talk about the ship."

"That's why she needs some gentle encouragement."

"Well, I've been encouraging her just as gently as I can," Jerry said. She rose, anxious to get away from him to recover her calm. She left him on the porch and walked on into the cottage. She headed straight for the bath, took off her makeup with petroleum jelly, then washed her face with cold cream. She'd performed the same acts religiously for years and believed with good reason that the very simplicity of her regime had kept her skin young and supple all these years.

She never told anyone quite how many.

She slipped into the slinky red nightgown hanging on the door hook. For a moment she studied her face in the mirror and wondered how she'd managed to make such a mess of things. Wondering wouldn't help. She'd already done it.

She left the bedroom. Liam was already in bed, in his boxers, staring up at the ceiling, his hands folded behind his head. He was in excellent shape—she had to hand him that.

She slid in beside him, her back to him.

"Tired?" he asked her.

"Mmm."

"Lounging around can be exhausting."

"The sun is hot. I spent the day at the pool."

"You're going to have to dive. Soon," he told her.

"All right, soon."

"You don't understand the stakes," he told her.

"No," she said quietly, "*you* don't understand the stakes."

She felt his hands on her shoulders, then his lips against her nape.

She didn't want him, but she didn't stop him. There had been too many men in her life. She stared at the wall in the darkness, felt his hands on her hips, heard his grunts. So much for romance. Liam had some mean appetites, and his idea of foreplay was a tap on a shoulder. Yet he was good to her, in his way....

Once upon a time there had been a good man in her life. One who cared, who laughed, who gave her flowers, who let her see the world through new eyes. But that had been long ago, when *things* had seemed important. Having things, going places, living the good life. She'd seen too late that one fresh flower could be worth a dozen diamonds, that one crooked smile could light up the world when the dazzle of gold failed.

She'd come so close to finding what was good again, only to have it grabbed from her hands. She'd come to know that love was precious, but life itself could be the grandest prize.

She felt silent tears forming in her eyes, sliding damply to her cheeks. Liam would never notice.

And even if he did, she wondered if he would care.

Jem had just settled down on the sofa when he heard a soft tapping at the door. For a moment he froze.

Already! he thought. *Already, already, already. The danger was coming already.*

Then he told himself it was unlikely that danger would knock on the door, and he rose, walking to the door, pausing just behind and to the side of it. He hesitated, but the caller on the other side apparently realized that he was standing there silently.

"Jem, it's Adam."

Jem opened the door, letting Adam O'Connor in. He grinned, shaking his head as he studied his old friend. "I still can't get over the fact that you're here. Of course, I'm damned glad, even if I have no idea what the hell is going on."

"Is she sleeping?" Adam asked, inclining his head toward the bedroom.

Jem shrugged. "I guess."

Adam walked in. He'd changed into swim trunks, a short-sleeved shirt and deck shoes.

"You can take the sofa," Jem offered, realizing that Adam had come to stay despite the fact that he had asked Jem to watch Sam. Jem wasn't insulted. Adam wasn't doubting his ability to keep Sam safe. In fact, Adam probably wasn't sure exactly why he was there himself.

Jem knew, but he sure wasn't going to try to tell Adam.

"No, no. I'll be fine on the chair."

Jem tossed him a pillow. "You really think Sam's still in danger? I mean, this guy must know you're looking after her now."

"Someone wants her, at almost any price. Someone who thinks she knows something."

"About what?"

"The *Beldona*."

"Damned old shipwreck! What could she know about it?"

"Where it is, for one thing."

"There could be more?"

"I think there's got to be more," Adam said.

Jem cocked his head, watching Adam. "You know, I'm damned glad to see you. I was sorry when you left. I thought you and Sam both lost something really good. But I'll tell you bluntly, I can't quite figure out how the hell you managed to come back at just the right time."

"I didn't manage to come back at the right time," Adam said flatly, lifting his hands, palms up, to Jem. "Sam's father disappeared, then that researcher out of Massachusetts she was involved with."

"Hank," Jem said softly. But he wasn't going to be sidetracked. He and Sam and Yancy had been friends for too long. They were family. "So how'd you happen to be back here tonight?"

"That I was here at exactly the right time—luck," Adam said grimly. "That I'm on the island now... well, I'm after the *Beldona,* as well, I guess. I'm working privately. Following in the footsteps of other divers who've been after the ship. And there are several people on the island now who are also working for people interested in the *Beldona.*"

"First things first," Jem said. "Who are you working for?"

Adam stared him in the eyes, but hesitated. "Jem, I'm not in a position to tell you that yet. If it becomes necessary, I will tell you. That's a promise."

"All right, then what the hell is happening on the island?" Jem demanded.

Again Adam hesitated.

"Adam, you've gotta give me something," Jem insisted.

Adam grinned suddenly. "Frankly, I don't quite know where the hell to start!"

"We've got a long night ahead of us," Jem said, crossing his muscled ebony arms over his chest.

Adam smiled and took a seat in one of the big Victorian chairs. He folded his hands behind his head and settled back. "Yeah, I guess we do. Does she keep any brandy around?"

"I imagine," Jem said.

"Well, go get it. I'll do my best to start at the beginning. And I'll tell you what I can."

6

The promised rain started very early, at about five o'clock in the morning.

Adam awoke when the rain began.

He sat in the chair where he had slept, listening to it pound against the roof of Sam's cottage. Then he tried to move. He winced, feeling a dozen cricks in the back of his neck. He stretched, then rose, walking awkwardly around the room, glad that Jem wasn't awake yet. Chairs were just not the way to go.

He moved silently down the hallway, slipping into Sam's room.

She was sleeping. Soundly, or so it seemed.

She was curled on her side, hands folded prayer fashion before her, her profile against the pillow, her hair splayed out like wild tongues of fire upon it. She had fantastic hair. So deep a red. It matched her so completely.

The covers were mostly over her. Not completely. One long leg lay exposed all the way up to the thigh. So what? he taunted himself.

He'd rescued her stark naked. Held her naked in his arms.

It had been a mistake to come here, God knew. A mistake to come back. He'd left, Hank had come, and now...

No, it hadn't been a mistake. She might have been killed last night.

Or taken. But where?

He didn't know yet.

By whom?

He couldn't answer that one, either, even though he had a few suspicions.

For what reason?

Well, he had no guaranteed answer to that one, either, but he would damned well be willing to bet that someone wanted to find the *Beldona* badly enough to kill.

It seemed, however, that someone must have found it already. Someone who'd caused the disappearance of anyone else who came anywhere near it.

No, it hadn't been a mistake to come. He had to be here. And he had to find the answers.

It was, however, a mistake to stand here, watching her sleep. It caused knots inside of him. It caused...

He muttered an expletive beneath his breath and turned away, starting down the hallway. Jem woke when he returned to the living room, and started to rise from the sofa.

Adam brought a finger to his lips. "I'm out of here," he murmured.

"It's pouring."

"I know. I'll dry."

Jem grinned.

"Stay with her?"

"You bet."

"I'm going to wash up, then I'll be at the main house, studying in Justin's library."

The rain came in buckets.

It was pleasant, Jim Santino thought. He'd slept deeply, in absolute comfort.

Of course, the fact that Sukee had arrived somewhere around two o'clock had added to that comfort. He hadn't been expecting her; she made no bones about the fact that she was a woman with her own mind, a woman of the world. She'd been with O'Connor when he'd last seen her.

But apparently, Jim thought with amusement, that hadn't quite worked out. O'Connor was interested in their hostess, it seemed. Not a bad idea. She'd intrigued Jim, the more so the more he saw of her. He grinned. Maybe it was just the challenge that made her so darned appealing. He was a good-looking guy himself, young, in good shape. And if that wasn't enough, he was as rich as Midas—as long as he remained red-blooded, heterosexual and loyal to his father, that was. Not a bad bargain. His father could buy him anything he wanted in life, and so far, Dad had bought him quite a bit. Things—and people.

It was amazing. Lots of people were for sale.

Like Sukee.

Not that she would ever admit it.

Sukee was something—just no challenge. She left nothing to the imagination. Nothing whatsoever.

But as the rain continued to pour down outside his cottage, Jim was glad of the musky warmth of her body next to his. She was insatiable. And she would do damn near anything.

Anything at all.

With that in mind, he turned toward her. She was slim and sensual, a small package, but a good one. He ran his finger down her back, rounded his hand over her tight buttocks. She moved nicely at his touch.

Sukee stretched and yawned, her back still to him. She turned then, her small hand reaching straight for his aroused sex organ in a no-nonsense fashion.

"Mmm. Not bad," she murmured.

"I am accustomed to a bit more enthusiasm than that," he told her.

She rolled on top of him, resting her hands on his chest and her chin on her hands as she stared into his eyes. "That's because you're a deviant and you're hearing whatever you've paid some poor whore to say."

He laughed, unoffended. "And you're not a well-paid whore?"

She crawled against him, straddling his hips, rubbing her sex against his.

"I'm a whole lot more than that. A whole hell of a lot more." She leaned against him. Licked his lips. Rose again, staring into his eyes. "And you know it." She smiled, feeling the growth of his arousal. "Just think, we ought to be out on those Steps today, sniffing around every move made by everyone. Of course, I know where you'd like to be sniffing," she murmured.

He laced his fingers behind his head, amused. "Cleaner scent than what I'm accustomed to," he told her.

"Personally, I think you like dirt," Sukee told him.

"Every boy likes to play in the dirt," he told her. "But then, you know, come mealtime, he usually likes to clean up."

"Maybe, maybe not," Sukee told him. She leaned down again, pressing her lips to his, running her tongue over them. "And maybe that redheaded fantasy of yours is doing just what I'm doing, and more, with O'Connor."

"Yeah, maybe."

"With all the same body parts."

"More or less the same," he said flatly. "I don't imagine hers have been quite so widely used."

Sukee laughed; he thought, though, that he might have struck a nerve.

"That was nasty," she told him.

"Sorry."

"It's all right. I like nasty. I even like your red-haired fantasy. We could make it a threesome."

He cocked his head. "Actually, I think you like my red-haired fantasy's gray-eyed macho man."

"Okay, we can make it a foursome," Sukee said.

"Over their dead bodies," Jim said.

Sukee shrugged. "That can probably be arranged," she said. She arched her back, stretching against him, using him like a post against which to sleekly rub her body. Just like a cat.

"You're all mouth, Sukee," he told her.

"That can be arranged, too," she whispered. She pouted suddenly. "Tomorrow, the Steps. Diving with all the little darlings, searching out their secrets. But today, stud, it's breakfast in bed."

"Ooh. Feed me, baby."

Sukee smiled. And obliged.

At noon the rain was still falling. And they were still lying in bed.

And no matter how damned good—or bad—Sukee was, he still found himself wondering if Samantha Carlyle and the newly arrived Adam O'Connor were shacked up out of the rain, as well.

There were things he needed to know about O'Connor.

Easy enough. He knew the right people to ask to find out just about anything. Anything at all.

Even if he'd finally found a fantasy he couldn't quite fulfill, Jim determined, it was good being who he was.

He'd almost had her, he told himself. Almost. And besides, like Sukee was so fond of saying...

Things could be arranged.

Sam had been sure that she was never going to sleep. And yet she did. Very deeply.

When she awoke, her room was filled with gray light. She lay in her bed, stretched and thought that the weathermen had been right on the money this time—it was definitely raining.

She rolled over, looked at her watch and saw that it was past noon. Startled, she crawled out of bed and quietly inched her way down the hall, curious to discover what was going on in her house.

Jem was in the living room, engrossed in a magazine. He looked up as she came down the hallway, and Sam was touched to realize that he was listening for every move that was made within the house. He meant to protect her.

"You must be bored silly, waiting around all day for me to wake up."

"You did sleep in," he commented dryly.

She grinned. "Sorry." She wandered into the kitchen. It was noon, but it felt like morning. She needed coffee. High-test coffee. Sleeping late hadn't made her bound right out of bed. She felt as gray and misted-over as the day.

"You know," she called to Jem, "it *is* noon. I'm probably quite safe now." When the coffee was starting to brew, she came into the living room, walking over to where Jem sat on the sofa and looking down at him. "Jem, I'm sure it would be okay if you got on with your own life—"

She broke off, because he suddenly lifted a hand, pointing toward the door.

She stared. The knob was turning, being tested.

"Jem . . ."

He stood, lifted a finger to his lips and mouthed, "It's locked." He motioned her to move out of the way. She did so, flattening herself against the wall as he strode to the door and flung it open.

He stood dead still. His shoulders slumped.

"Jem?" she whispered.

He shook his head. "No one there. I could have sworn I saw . . ." He shrugged again. "I'm going out."

"In this rain?"

"It's a trickle now."

"Jem, don't—"

But he was already gone.

* * *

Yancy sat in front of the fireplace in the bar. The fire was blazing beautifully. The rain hadn't actually made the day cold, but the fire took the dampness away.

Adam had lit it for her when he'd come in this morning. Despite the fact that the majority of the guests would sleep in and have something to eat in their own cottages, Yancy had been down early to set out the buffet. Breakfast in the main house happened even if the staff were the only people on the island.

Jacques had come down to cook, then retired. Adam had built the fire, gone for coffee and an egg sandwich and disappeared into Justin Carlyle's old office.

Lots of guests liked the office. Justin had collected all sorts of books about the ocean, books on shipwrecks, diving, wind patterns, geography, natural phenomena, the Devil's Triangle and more. He kept a beautiful antique globe in his office, and deep comfortable leather chairs. It was a natural enough place for guests to go.

The fire snapped and crackled. She suddenly had the strange feeling that someone was behind her. For a moment she froze, feeling as if the damp, gray mist of the stormy day held something mysterious. As if sodden ghosts could rise from the sea and swirl into the dampness of the day to face her there in the bar. She jumped up defensively, turning around.

She was alone.

Uneasy, she left the room. The registration area and parlor were joined to the dining area and bar by symmetrical doors. She passed through the dining area and down the opposite hall, toward the door to Justin's office.

Adam O'Connor was there, his handsome dark head bent over a journal. He heard her, though, and looked up. "Hi, Yancy."

"Hi. Need anything?"

He shook his head. "I'm fine." He leaned back. "Have you seen any other guests this morning?"

"Avery Smith had coffee, then left."

"Bad weather for an elderly gentleman," Adam commented.

Yancy shrugged, then heard Lillie calling her name from upstairs. Lillie had stayed over because of the dinner party. She'd been happy to play with the baby all morning, since she couldn't get into the cottages to clean with everyone sleeping in.

"Why don't you get some coffee and join me for a while?" Adam suggested.

"I..." Yancy hesitated. Not this morning. Lillie must be calling her because she needed a break from baby Brian.

And something more than he was telling them had brought Adam here, Yancy thought. She didn't understand it yet, but she was certain Adam was going to want an explanation for Brian as soon as he knew of the child's existence.

She bit her lip.

He would see Brian eventually. She would just put that moment off as long as she could. She wasn't emotionally prepared to explain Brian to him this morning.

"Maybe I'll join you soon," she said. "I've got a few things to see to upstairs."

"Okay."

She turned to leave, then paused and told him honestly, "It's really good to see you again, Adam."

He smiled. "Thanks, Yancy. Thanks a lot. It's good to see you, too."

She nodded. There was more to say, but it wasn't time yet. She smiled, waved and left him to the journal.

Great. Jem had left her. If there was one thing Sam had learned from her father's love of the old black-and-white horror flicks, it was that you never left the girl alone.

Never mind the fact that the girl was a screaming idiot who would watch bony fingers reach for her or a hatchet fall and not even make a move to get away. You weren't supposed to leave the girl alone.

She stepped onto the porch. It wasn't exactly raining, but the moisture in the air was so heavy it seemed that the entire island was blanketed in fog. It wasn't an unusual weather pattern here. Most of the time the sun was shining and the weather was beautiful. A storm came, it got gray, it rained—and the next day, the sun came back.

She wished it was the next day.

"Jem?" she called.

She'd just made another mistake. The stupid girl always left behind a place of safety and walked right out where she would be most vulnerable.

What to do? Turn around and walk into the cottage? What if her attacker had slipped in behind her back and was now waiting for her to return to what she hoped would be safety, where she would lock herself in with the danger?

"You're taking to flights of fancy, Samantha Carlyle!" she murmured out loud. "It's this island living. Surely I wouldn't be quite so influenced by Mr. Adam O'Connor if there was a normal amount of healthy young males in my life. Not that men don't come here. They just come and go so quickly. Never a chance to get to know them. Never a chance to ask pertinent questions, like you are in good health, right? The men I do know are like relatives. Jem is like a brother, and where the hell are you, Jem! Jem!" She screamed his name.

Then she spun around, hearing a rustling in the hibiscus bush flanking the cottage to her left. She opened her mouth to scream. Something—some-one—large, very large, was coming out from behind the bush.

"Oh, my—Jem!"

He stood up, pressing his palm to his forehead. A small trickle of blood ran down from his scalp.

"My God, Jem, what happened? If someone hurt you, he'll pay. I'll—"

"Sam, I'm supposed to be protecting you, remember? And besides, there was no one out here. I ran into the privacy fence around your bathroom while I was trying to be quiet and sneaky," he said ruefully.

She stood back, frowning. "But you're hurt."

"It's just a scratch. I'll wash it off. If you want to go over to the main house, I'll walk you over, then go to my own cottage and get some sleep."

She smiled, got him a clean washcloth with ice to hold against the bump and quickly changed into jeans and a T-shirt. They started to walk to the main house together. Jem paused as they left her cottage behind, studying the ground by the bushes.

"What's the matter?"

"Look at all these footprints," he said. "Some of them are mine, and some are probably yours," he added with disgust. He shook his head. "Did that doorknob really turn? I'm feeling like an idiot. There was definitely no one there."

"Maybe not," Sam said.

"Let's not mention this, huh?"

She agreed. "Let's not."

He left her at the door to the main house. She went in and found the living room, dining room, kitchen and bar all empty. She hesitated, wondering how the entire house could be empty, then wandered into her father's office.

Adam looked up as she entered. He was in black jeans and a black T-shirt. The color complemented his dark good looks, the ebony sleekness of his hair, the gray of his eyes. The shirt even seemed to make the muscled bronze of his arms more appealing.

"Dismal day, huh?" he said.

She nodded.

He stretched out an arm. "Come in and join me. I don't bite."

"Really?"

"Not unless I'm invited to."

She would have liked to dispute those words, but he was telling the truth—she knew from experience. It would be a lie to suggest that she hadn't invited what had happened between them when they first met.

"What are you doing?" she asked him. He was seated at the big old seafarer's desk. She chose one of the big leather upholstered chairs on the other side of it, curling her feet beneath her as she sat.

"Studying charts, notes, references."

"Find anything?"

"Lots of things."

She folded her arms over her chest. "I've studied almost everything in this room, and I never found anything. Except the obvious. Charts—dozens of charts. Books on the building of the *Beldona,* her cargo, her crew, her purpose in the New World. Speculation on the Steps. Advice on sailing through storms. Theories on the disappearances in the triangle."

"Your father's notes?" he suggested.

"I've read them."

"Hank's notes, as well?"

She nodded.

He stood, pushing a journal toward her. It was written in her father's handwriting. He tapped an entry made the morning Justin had disappeared. Sam leaned close to read the scrawl her father had left in the book. She squinted. It read, *Study ocean floor.*

She sat back, shrugging. "I know all the dive sites. I've visited them all my life. I can see the 'ocean floor' at all those sites with my eyes closed."

Adam seemed disappointed. "All right," he said, after a moment. "I've got another one for you." He stood, taking another ledger from behind the desk, setting it down.

She thought that his fingers trembled slightly as he turned the pages of the book.

Hank's book. A diary he'd kept on his research. Every page seemed to be filled. He'd listed crew members by name, sails, masts, guns, ship's silver and china, glassware, cutlery. Then suddenly, as if it had been an afterthought, he'd written, *Things not what they seem?*

"What do you make of that?"

"I don't know. Hank was... obsessed."

Adam closed both books, staring at her. She wanted to return his stare, but she felt her gaze falling. She studied her hands. "It's a dismal day. Jem has gone back to his place to sleep. Jacques will be starting dinner soon. I wonder if anyone will even make it in to eat. I hope the weather clears for the morning."

"Do you?"

"Of course. Everyone is so anxious to dive."

"You're not."

She shrugged, suddenly wishing she hadn't come in here. It was disconcerting to be here. On the one hand, it was oddly comfortable to be alone with Adam. On the other... It was torture.

Adam leaned forward suddenly. "Sam, you're like an ostrich. You want to hide your head in the sand so you won't have to realize that your father is dead."

Tears pricked her eyes. She blinked them back. "You're wrong. I do realize my father is dead. I know it all too well."

He stared at her, shaking his head sadly. "All right. You accept that he's dead. But you don't want to know *how* he died. You don't want to think that Hank Jennings found the same brutal end."

She lifted her hands in a dismissive gesture. "You're wrong. No matter how they died, it had to be brutal. Drowning can't be easy. A heart attack, a—"

"It would be a little too convenient for both men to die of undersea heart attacks, don't you think?"

She sat very still, then closed her eyes for a moment, leaning back. She looked at him again. "When my father disappeared, I spent a week sleeping out on the dock, praying that he'd come back. Yancy and Jem finally convinced me that my sleeping on damp wood wasn't going to help anything. I still spent the majority of my time on the dock. I stood there, I sat there, I waited. I took the *Sloop Bee* out day after day. I talked to the Bahamian police, the Coast Guard, the FBI—divers, salvagers, you name it. I—"

"You wrote to me."

She nodded, looking away. "Yeah."

"I'm sorry, Sam. So sorry."

She shrugged. "It's been a long time now."

"Not so long since Hank disappeared."

She shook her head, wishing he would go away. She didn't want to think about things that hurt so badly.

"The point is, Sam, something happened to them. You've got to come out of your shell. We owe it to them to find out what the hell happened."

She hesitated, then leaned over the desk. "Give me a journal."

"You said you've read them both."

"I have, but..." She shrugged and admitted, "I missed both those entries you just showed me. Or, if I saw them, I didn't think anything of them. And it's a rainy afternoon. What the hell else is there to do?"

Adam passed her a journal, arching a brow, but her head was already lowered over the book he had passed her.

He smiled anyway, lowered his own head and tried to concentrate once again.

At around six Yancy came in. She'd made them Jamaican coffee, rich with sugar and whipped cream. She wound up staying, perched on another chair, and reading about the Spanish prisoners taken aboard the *Beldona.*

Jem joined them at six-thirty, having gotten some sleep. The bump on his head was all but invisible. Sam kept her head studiously in her book while he explained that he'd gotten the bump from the medicine chest over his sink.

Jem read with them for a while. They exchanged books and read some more.

At seven-thirty Jacques—his chef's hat perfectly in place, his mustache perfectly twirled—stuck his head in. He cleared his throat, winking at Adam. *"Mon Dieu, ma cherie!* There are real guests here, as well, you know."

Sam looked up, startled. She glanced at her watch. "My Lord, I've forgotten—"

"Mais oui! But *I* have not!" Jacques said proudly. "Your guests have made themselves drinks and are now in the midst of an Italian buffet."

"Oh. Pizza night," Yancy said.

Jacques rolled his eyes. "Pizza night! Where is the respect due?" he moaned.

"Thanks, Jacques. You're great!" Sam called as he disappeared down the hallway. "Well, I guess I'll see to the guests," she said, rising.

Yancy followed her. "Can you help Jacques? I left Brian asleep. He'll probably be waking up soon, and Lillie went back on the mail boat this afternoon despite the rain."

"I'll do dinner. Take a break if you want."

"Thanks." Yancy went upstairs.

Neither Jem nor Adam emerged from her father's office. Sam found the Emersons, the Walkers and Liam and Jerry munching on pizza, pasta and salad in the dining room. She joined them, noting that neither Avery Smith nor Jim or Sukee had chosen to come to dinner. All the cottages had little kitchenettes, and they were kept stocked with the basics. No one had to come to a meal if he didn't choose to. Sam imagined that Sukee and Jim were together and had things other than food on their minds. What Mr. so-called Avery Smith might be up to, she didn't know.

"I'm sorry we had such bad weather today," she apologized in general, pouring wine for her adult guests.

"It wasn't so bad," Sue Emerson said with a wink for her husband.

He slipped an arm around her adoringly. "Not bad at all."

"It sucked," Brad assured her.

"Brad!" his parents gasped in unison.

"We'll make tomorrow extra special," Sam promised.

"Do you ever feel you've missed a lot—living on the island all your life?" Jerry North asked her suddenly.

Sam looked across at the blond woman who was studying her so intently. She shrugged. "I love the island. What could I have missed? Besides, I did go to college on the mainland. And any time I want to see it, a few hours will get me there."

Jerry nodded, still watching her.

Liam didn't seem to notice. "Pizza's good," he said with a grunt.

"The chef will be pleased that you're so satisfied," Sam assured him.

Jerry smiled and looked at her own plate at last.

No one seemed of a mind to linger long over coffee. Dessert—delicious tiramisu—had scarcely been served before Darlene yawned, anxious to go to bed so she would be wide awake for diving the next day.

The Emersons had skipped dessert entirely, leaving hand in hand the moment they'd finished their meal.

Even Liam seemed quiet. He and Jerry left the main house right after the Walkers. Sam still hadn't seen Jem or Adam emerge from the office. While she was helping to clear the last of the plates, Jacques informed her that he had brought dinner to the men in the study.

Nice, Sam thought, irritated that Adam had taken over to the point that Jem had decided to keep studying with him rather than help her run the evening meal.

The hell with them both, she decided.

She told Jacques good-night, determined to reach her own cottage and lock herself in.

She departed by way of the porch once again, cutting across the lawn to her cottage.

The key was in the pocket of her jeans. She reached for it as she neared her door.

Judy Walker had watched the news, and she'd assured Sam that it was going to be a bright, hot day tomorrow. It was hard to believe right now, when clouds were obscuring the moon. Despite the lights on the island, it was a dark, misty night. She hadn't gone far from the main house before it was nearly swallowed up in the mist.

Damn! she told herself. But she was nearly at her own cottage. Too close to it to run back to the main house. Why was she suddenly frightened? She'd never been afraid on the island before.

But then, she'd never been attacked in her own bathroom before, either.

Well, this is it, stupid, she warned herself. Hadn't she been thinking about old horror movies earlier? Wasn't it true that only really stupid heroines managed to find themselves alone with the murderer?

And not just alone. Alone in the mist. In the darkness.

Oh, great.

And all because she was irritated by Adam. Because he was as appealing as he had ever been. As aggressive. As dominating. Never mind that his decision that she shouldn't be left alone was for her own good.

She'd just been so damned hurt. Because she'd been so infatuated. Young, and so in love.

And now...

Now the night seemed alive. Everywhere she looked, the mist-enshrouded tropical beauty of the island seemed to harbor danger.

She quickened her pace and reached her door. Nervously, she tried to slip her key into the lock.

The bushes rustled behind her, startling her into dropping the key. It fell to the concrete with a sharp ping. As she reached for it, a shadow fell over her. Huge, dark, looming over her like wings of death in the night.

Then hands came down on her, biting into her shoulders.

And she started to scream.

7

Sue Emerson stared at her reflection in the bathroom mirror and smiled. Her hair was brushed to a high gloss. God, she had good teeth. And good skin. She frowned slightly, then rubbed a little more lotion into her cheeks and under her eyes. No premature aging for her. The sun could be vicious. She didn't intend to allow it. One day, she meant to be very rich.

She didn't want to decay before that day came.

She stepped back to give herself a fuller view of her body. Her outfit was sexy. In fact, it was downright decadent. A black creation that covered her whole body while leaving strategic locations covered in nothing but gauze. She smiled again. She should grace the pages of a men's magazine, she thought. She pouted, practicing for an imaginary camera.

Lucky, lucky Joey.

She stepped out of the bathroom.

The lighting was low. A fire burned in the hearth. Joey had opened a bottle of wine and poured them each a glass. He sipped burgundy from his, sitting in his briefs on the edge of the bed, the telephone receiver in his hand.

Sue picked up her wine, smiling.

He waved a hand at her to wait a minute.

Wait, hell.

She struck a pose by the bathroom door, sipping the wine artfully. Running the tip of her tongue over her lips. Wiggling it in his direction.

He should be drooling by now. Instead he just stared at her.

"Hey, stud!" she whispered, running a hand down the length of her body.

"Yeah," he said to whoever was on the telephone. "I can hold a second."

Joey was young and very good-looking, with a strong body, blond hair and good features. Not bad at all.

If only he would learn to listen to her a little more.

She left the doorway and walked over to him. Lowered herself to her knees between his thighs. Ran her hands along them. "Ooh," she murmured. "Want to fool around, lover?"

He covered the receiver with his hand. "Will you cut out the honeymoon crap for a while?" he demanded irritably. "Can't you see I'm busy?"

Sue rose, her jaw locked in anger as she stared at him. "Fuck you, asshole," she said sweetly, then turned and strode out of the bedroom.

Joey looked after her broodingly. Women. Now he would be apologizing for the better half of the night.

Didn't matter. Maybe he wouldn't bother. Maybe she would just have to come back on her own. He smiled slightly. She was enough of a nympho that she would be back. She had no right to be acting like such a bitch.

After all, she was the one who liked money so much, he reminded himself angrily.

Then he heard a voice talking to him on the phone, and he gave his mind over to the business at hand.

"It's me! Will you please shut up!"

Sam gasped, aware even as she was spun around that Adam was the hulking shadow behind her.

"You scared me to death."

"Well, what the hell was the matter with you, walking out like that?"

"I was ready to go."

"Are you anxious to meet that guy again? Hoping he'll be in your bathroom again?"

"Oh, will you go to hell!"

"Then what were you doing?"

"You two were still busy, so—"

"Get inside. I'm not going to argue out here."

She had little choice. Adam had the key and turned it in the lock. He propelled her inside.

She kept moving, heading for the side of the room opposite him.

"Damn you, Sam, it should be obvious to you that you're not safe."

"All right! I'm sorry."

"You damned well should be. You—"

The door was shaken by a hard knock. Sam jumped. Adam instantly flung it open. She started to cry out in protest, then saw that it was Jem on the other side.

"Great, I'm in danger, and you just fling the door open," she said.

"I knew he was right behind me."

"I, uh, don't mean to be interrupting anything here," Jem began.

"You're not!" they both swore in vehement unison.

Adam lowered his head slightly, lifting his hands. "You're here, Jem, so I'm out of here. See you both in the morning." He stared at Sam. "Bright and early. We're diving the Steps."

"Good night to you both!" Sam snapped, heading for her bedroom. It seemed important for some reason to make her exit before Adam made his.

But once she was gone, he didn't rush to go. Jem looked at him. "Sofa is yours tonight," he said.

"You don't need to—"

"Fair is fair," Jem said.

Adam shrugged. "Okay. I've got to get a few things. I'll be back in about thirty minutes. I'll knock twice."

"Gotcha."

The baby started crying in the middle of the night. Yancy bolted up, hurried to the crib and looked at the infant. She had to smile as she reached for him. What a temper! His little fists were balled and waving, his mouth opened wide to give his angry screams full volume.

"You know, young man, you're supposed to start sleeping through the night one of these days," she said, picking him up and patting his back as she held him comfortingly against her shoulder. His screams turned to sniffles. "That's what the baby books say, anyway. But you're hungry, and if you're hungry..."

She walked to the dressing table and cracked the cap on a sealed, disposable bottle of formula, balancing the baby on her shoulder as she screwed on a sterilized disposable nipple. All the prepared stuff was expensive, but worth it in the middle of the night. She adored the baby. There was absolutely nothing about him, nothing he could do, that would be too much trouble for her, but still, she was certain that even the very best parent in the entire world had to stumble around a bit in the middle of the night.

"Don't be a little piglet. You'll wind up with a stomachache," she warned him, settling in the rocker to feed the baby.

Oh, God, yes, she adored him. He looked so much like his father. Thank God for Sam's belief that human life was precious, no matter what! Thank God the baby existed. He was hers now, no matter what the situation that had brought him into the world. He was precious. Those blue eyes, that soft, soft, light brown hair.

Those eyes on her. So trustingly.

He suddenly smiled around the nipple in his mouth. Reached out little fingers toward her.

That smile, so much like his father's . . .

She rocked, thinking, reminiscing. Wondering.

She realized that the baby had closed his eyes. She took the bottle from his mouth, set him over her shoulder and burped him. Then she rose and began to walk idly around the room.

She paused, certain that she had heard a sound from downstairs.

She stood dead still.

Yes . . .

Someone was downstairs. Someone moving around in what had been Justin Carlyle's office.

She hesitated, feeling the thunder of her heart. It was just Jacques, she told herself.

Never, he had no interest in the office.

Should she go down?

No, definitely not! Sam would send her right off the island with the baby if she thought that Yancy had risked him in any way.

It was just Adam, she told herself. Adam had spent the entire day in the office, going through books, charts and papers. They'd all been with him. No secrecy there.

She'd heard Adam leave in a hurry earlier. She'd heard Jem follow him out. But he might have come back.

But if it wasn't Adam . . .

What should she do?

Her agony of indecision was short-lived, at least. She heard a click and realized that someone had exited by the bar door onto the porch.

She pulled out the little lamb night-light that had softly illuminated her room, casting it into total darkness, then flattened herself against the wall, staring over the lawn area that led down to the docks.

She saw . . . nothing.

No, a figure.

But just as she caught sight of the figure on the lawn, a cloud covered the moon completely.

The figure stood just between the pools of illumination cast by the island's night-lights. In darkness.

She could see very little. The figure was tall. . . . Dark. . . . Nothing more.

Shaking, she set the sleeping baby into his crib. Then she checked her door. Locked. Securely locked.

She set a chair in front of it anyway.

Whoever she'd seen, they weren't coming back tonight, she assured herself as she lay down. But she didn't sleep.

She was suddenly certain that neither Justin Carlyle nor Hank Jennings had died by any trick of nature or by accident. Both men had been murdered.

And now the murderer had come to the island to strike again.

There was a very strange place between sleeping and waking, a place where memories came to haunt her sweetly in a pleasant mist.

The day was perfect. The sun was high, strong, the air touched by the perfect breeze, keeping the summer's heat palatable. They'd spent the day on the *Sloop Bee,* her father on deck, reading another of his "sources." She'd been diving, buddied up with Adam, since it had been just the three of them out for the afternoon. They'd come across the huge manta ray that afternoon. Adam had pointed out the creature to her. She'd been determined to befriend it, to take a ride on its mighty wings. The manta had been obliging, allowing her to close her fingers over its wings, to feel its power as it whipped through the water. Soon after, Adam had joined her, laughing behind his mask. It had been the perfect dive. They'd been near the Steps, and the sea had come alive for them. Barracuda had skulked about, offering up their wicked-looking grins but keeping their distance. Brilliant yellow tangs had darted about the reefs to the southwest of the Steps, along with clowns and angelfish. The colors had been so vibrant and magnificent, the sea so excitingly alive....

She had seen everything by his side. Shared the visions, loved the underwater world with someone who loved it equally well. Back aboard the *Sloop Bee*, she'd described it all for her father, who had laughed, bright-eyed himself, because he understood their feelings so well. Justin had tried to tell her then what he had been working on, but she hadn't really been listening that day.

She'd just watched him with Adam. Seen Adam's interest. His enthusiasm. Seen Adam smile. Seen his dimple. Seen him move. Her heart had thudded with exquisite pleasure to see the two men in her life find such a satisfying friendship. One of them, however, hadn't realized that he was one of the men in her life....

Until later.

Running down the beach on Drop Island. The white sand beneath her feet, the setting sun crashing down around them in shades of bloodred crimson. She'd doused him in cold water when he hadn't listened quickly enough to what she'd been saying. Running had seemed the most prudent action.

Until he caught her. Until they tripped in the sand. Until she looked into his eyes while feeling the sun-fevered smoothness of his flesh, the power of his muscles pressed against her.

Tasted his lips, the salt, the sea . . .

Every young girl dreamed about her first time making love. Planned it, perhaps. Yet nothing in Sam's imagination had been so sweet, so smooth, so perfect. Words had failed her, but actions hadn't. He was so experienced; she was simply so in love. The crimson-streaked sky was the perfect canopy, the sun-baked sand the perfect bed. God! Even now, she could almost *feel* his lips against her flesh, tantalizing her, the way he could move his mouth against her, cir-cling, barely touching, making her want to scream to feel his caress just where it wasn't, scream again when it came against her flesh just where she had yearned for it to be. He seduced, awakened, evoked. By the time he actually entered her, she was half-crazed with wanting him. If there was pain, it was fleeting. It was the wonder that remained with her, the warmth, the feeling of intimacy, the awe. . . .

The silver touch of his eyes. . . .

She shifted, smiling slightly, remembering. He was older, mature, responsible. Magnetic. Experienced, aware, fascinating.

She was . . . distracted.

The morning light was coming into her bedroom. She blinked against it, groggy as she awoke. Blinked again.

Those eyes. Silver eyes, watching her still.

Sam bolted up in bed, dragging her covers with her as she stared at the man seated in the Victorian rocker at her bedside, a big mug of coffee in his hands as he stared at her. She clenched her teeth, hoping to hell that she had been sleeping soundly and that nothing had escaped her lips while she drifted in her semiwaking state.

"Damn it, what the hell are you doing in my bedroom?"

He shrugged, leaning forward, offering her the coffee. She ignored the mug and continued to stare at him, outraged.

"Don't bring that too close to me. I'll dump it over your damned head."

"Still hostile in the morning, I see. I couldn't imagine that you'd changed that much. Take the coffee. You're usually much nicer after a cup."

"What are you doing in here?"

"Jem suggested I wake you."

The coffee smelled delicious. And it would be just the way she liked it, black and steaming. She'd learned to like it that way from him.

No, she wasn't going to give in to temptation.

"If you were supposed to wake me, why were you sitting there staring at me?"

"Take the damned coffee."

She accepted the mug. It was just coffee. She wouldn't be making any kind of commitment. She sipped it and it was as good as she'd imagined. She had a feeling he'd made it. Jem couldn't even boil water properly.

"Why didn't you wake me?"

"Because you were smiling in your sleep. I didn't feel like ruining your dream."

"No, you decided to be a damned voyeur."

A wicked half-smile curved his lips. "I was waiting to see if you'd whisper my name."

"After this much time? You, Adam O'Connor, are the dreamer."

"Well, whoever caused that smile also caused you to oversleep. It's almost eight."

"Eight?" Sam glanced at her watch, saw that he was telling the truth and thrust the coffee mug at him. She leaped out of bed—careful to bound up on the side opposite where he had drawn up his chair. She raced to the bathroom—carefully locking the door with an audible click.

She brushed her teeth with a fury, washed her face, then stared at herself in the mirror. God, she was a sorry sight.

Her hair was everywhere, even standing straight up. She looked like Alfalfa from the original "Little Rascals."

It also might have been nice, she told herself, if he'd caught her in something more appealing. She did own a few silk and satin nightgowns, but she had a tendency to sleep in oversize T-shirts. This was a sad one. Huge and red, with a picture of Audrey from *Little Shop of Horrors* on it.

She pulled off the shirt and hopped in the shower— nice cold water to wake her up. When she came out she wrapped herself in a large bath towel, realizing that she'd made a mistake coming in here without any clothes. Now she was going to have to go out there in a towel to find her bathing suit and cover-up.

The hell with it. She didn't give a damn about Adam. He was ancient history. It would just be nice for him to find her so appealing that he would feel like dying for having thrown her over. It was exactly the way most women would feel about an ex-lover, wasn't it? Especially when that ex-lover had lost none of his own appeal.

She rewrapped the towel, wanting to be appealing but certain she would die if she lost the damned thing in front of him. Just when she was about to open the door, she realized that he was waiting for her just on the other side of it when she heard him speaking, his voice deep, husky and provocative.

"Sam?"

"Are you still there?" she demanded. "Will you please get out of my room?"

"Testy, testy."

"Damn you, go."

"And just as I was about to give you more information."

"About what?"

"You do know who your heartthrob is, don't you?"

"What?" she demanded, throwing the door open.

Silver eyes swept her up and down. "Santino."

"What?" she repeated, completely confused.

He sighed. "Jim Santino. The guy with the cover-boy hair."

She crossed her arms over her chest. It would help keep the towel in place. "Damn you, Adam."

"Never mind, then. Still want me to leave?"

"Adam, if you walk out of here..."

He smiled slowly. "If I walk out of here, what?"

"You'll be sorry," she promised.

His smile deepened as he turned and started walking down the hallway.

"Adam! Will you come back here! Adam, I'm threatening you, damn it!"

He kept walking.

"I'll throw you off my island with my own damned hands!" she called after him.

He didn't reply.

Keep this on an adult level, she warned herself. It was no good.

She started running, then slid on her bare feet and crashed into his back, slamming her fists against it. "I mean it. Damn you, Adam!"

She broke off when she realized she was losing her towel. She quit thundering against him just in time to catch it, managing to hold it to her chest. Her rump was exposed, but at least she managed to cover up the valley *between* her breasts.

Jem was in the kitchen, a coffee cup halfway to his lips. He arched a brow. Adam turned to her at last. "Well, if you really want to talk . . ."

"You two can both go straight to hell!" she snapped.

She swished the towel around her. Furious, planning every devious revenge known to man, she swirled on one heel and strode toward her bedroom. It was a tremendously dignified exit, or so she told herself.

Except that she could hear them laughing in her wake.

The hell with them both. She spun around and strode to the kitchen.

They both started. Jem spilled his coffee.

"All right, Adam. Who the hell is Jim Santino?"

8

Adam looked at Jem. "I guess she wants to talk."

"Yeah. Looks like that to me."

"She keeps trying to throw me out, though."

"Women," Jem agreed.

"I'm going to throw you both into the sea in about two minutes," Sam warned. "Adam O'Connor, we had hours alone together yesterday. You could have spent all that time talking to me, answering questions."

"You didn't ask me any questions yesterday."

She swore beneath her breath. "You knew whatever you're going to tell me now yesterday. You didn't tell me then."

"I'm telling you now."

"But you should have—"

"Yes, and you should have had the decency to let Jem or me know that you were leaving the main house and coming here so I didn't have to nearly suffer heart failure racing after you!"

"Oh, really?"

"I'm right, and you know it."

"Fine. You're right. Now talk to me."

He met her determined stare and smiled grudgingly. "Your young friend Jim is the son of Robert Santino."

Sam shook her head, not recognizing the name. "So?"

Adam continued. "Organized crime boss, reputedly responsible for a good hundred murders—though he customarily keeps his killing in the business. He's known for murder, theft, racketeering, drugs and prostitution."

"I don't mean to belittle the man's terrible deeds," Sam said evenly, "but what the hell do any of them have to do with me or this island?"

Adam watched her. "He's also reputed to have one of the most comprehensive collections of sixteenth-century Spanish jewels and relics."

"The *Beldona* was an English ship."

"Carrying Spanish prisoners. And Spanish treasure. You know that."

"So is everyone on the island suspected of something in one way or another?"

"Just about," Adam said.

"Including you?" Sam suggested. "You did say that you were working for a private concern."

He was silent for a few minutes. "Yeah, I'm a suspect in a way, too."

"Any more surprises?" she demanded.

He shrugged. "Nothing I know for certain."

"Anything else you care to share with me?"

Clouds obscured the sharp silver of his eyes. "Not quite yet."

"Well, then, Adam, you can go right to hell."

She turned away from him, but he caught her arm, drawing her back. She stared at his hand on her arm, then looked into his eyes. He had to let her go. She didn't like being so close to him. She didn't know how it was possible that so much time could pass, and yet she could still feel such a strange, familiar warmth when he touched her.

"As soon as I feel I can say anything else, I will. I swear it."

Wrench free, she told herself. Instead she stood very still and returned his stare, trying to read his unfathomable eyes, but he was giving nothing away.

"Well, tell me this, at least. You seemed to be on the same wavelength as Avery Smith when you were talking to him the other night. Does he know that you're aware he isn't Avery Smith?"

"He must."

"You're certain?"

He nodded. "We've met before. He remembers me—I could tell when we met the other night."

"Has he attempted to explain his alias to you?"

"Not yet."

"Isn't he afraid of you?"

"Why would he be afraid of me? I was a cop when we met. A good guy."

"Yes, but if he's here under an alias . . ."

"It doesn't necessarily mean that he's up to something evil."

"You're the one who made a point of the fact that the man is not who he says he is."

"Yes, because it could be important."

"Because although he may not necessarily be up to something devious, there's a chance that he might be."

"Right."

"But if he *is* up to something illegal, shouldn't he be afraid of you, since you know he isn't who he says he is?"

Adam shrugged. He still had his hand on her, and she stood very still, not wanting to feel the electric waves of energy that emanated from him and swirled distractedly around her.

"James Jay Astin is a very wealthy man, always being pursued in the world of business. Naturally such a man might want to escape to a private getaway. And Seafire Isle is advertised as a very private getaway."

She thought that, if nothing else, he was offering her sound logic. Either that, or the feel of his hand on her was making her want to believe anything he said. Anything.

It was time to escape with dignity.

She tugged free from his hold and headed to her bedroom, where she dressed quickly in a sky blue tank-style swim suit, terry shorts and a matching shirt, and her deck shoes. She came to the kitchen to find both men waiting for her.

"Breakfast?" Jem suggested with a hopeful smile.

She stared at him tight-lipped, refusing to reply. She started out of the cottage, and the two men followed behind her. She walked quickly, as if hoping she could shake them.

Silly thought. They were on an island. There really was no escape.

The others were all gathered in the dining room of the main lodge. Except for Mr. James Jay Astin Avery Smith—who was reading a magazine while he sipped his coffee, dressed in Dockers and a denim shirt— everyone appeared to be ready to go diving. Even Jerry North was wearing terry cover-ups over her bathing suit, or so it appeared.

"You're diving?" Sam asked her, surprised.

"I'm going to bubble watch," Jerry said, smiling wanly.

She looked tired, Sam thought. "Jem will like the company on the boat."

Jerry nodded. "I hope so."

Sam moved to the buffet table, helping herself to coffee and a corn muffin. She heard a commotion, then saw that Brian had apparently escaped Yancy's

care in the kitchen and was crawling out to the breakfast area as fast as his little hands and knees would
take him. He paused right by her leg, looking at her
with his broad, toothless smile. She stooped down and
scooped him up, laughing, giving him a hug.

"You want my muffin, huh, kid?" She laughed,
nuzzling his little neck. She loved the clean, baby-
powder-sweet smell of him, loved the way his huge
blue eyes stared so trustingly into hers. He reached out
a hand toward the buffet table. Sam broke off a piece
of her muffin, offering it to him just as Yancy made
it over to her.

"I set the little rascal down beside his high chair for
a whole two seconds before he was gone!" Yancy said.

"He just wants to go diving with us, Yancy!" Brad
said.

"Well, he'll have to wait a few years for that, I'm
afraid," Yancy said. She seemed uneasy, determined
to get the baby back speedily. "Here, Sammy, I'll take
him. You eat so you can get your party started."
Yancy lowered her voice. "I need to talk to you."

Sam arched a brow to her.

"In the pantry, for just a minute, when you get the
chance."

As Sam gave up the baby, she turned slightly. Adam
was standing about five feet away from her. Dead still.
Had he heard what Yancy had said to her? Did he in-

tend to be in the kitchen, listening to whatever Yancy had to say, as well?

Then she realized that Adam wasn't looking at her. He was staring at the baby. Hard. As if he was witnessing some kind of unexplained phenomenon. He was very pale. No, he was actually more a soft shade of green.

"Adam?"

He seemed to give himself a shake. Then he turned away from her, pouring himself a cup of coffee. His hands were shaking slightly.

She walked up behind him. "I know, the baby isn't really a baby. He's a multimillionaire collector of ancient documents, and he's here—"

He swung on her. She was startled by the violence in him and started to back away. His fingers settled around her elbow like steel grips. "I'm wondering where the hell you'd be right now if that visitor of yours the other night had managed to snap that cloth over your face a few minutes earlier."

"Would you let go of me? You're making a scene!"

"How old is that baby?"

"He's six months. Jesus, let me go! You're about to break my arm."

His mouth worked as if he was about to say something. Then he released her arm as if it had suddenly caught fire and turned away from her, walking across the room to enter into conversation with Jim Santino and Sukee.

Sam hurried into the pantry, where Yancy was waiting for her.

"Someone was in the house last night," Yancy said.

"What?"

"I heard someone in your father's office."

"Adam?"

Yancy shook her head. "I don't think so."

"Oh, God, Yancy, I should have called the police when this first started."

"No, no, Sam. I was never in danger. No one came near me or the baby. I wouldn't even have known except that Brian woke up, crying for a bottle. While I was feeding him, I heard someone downstairs. Then I looked out and saw someone leaving the house. Sam, if you'd called the police, it wouldn't have done anything. Adam is right. Unless you want to just close the island and give up the business, we've got to figure out what's going on ourselves."

"But if anything happened to the baby..."

"The baby is with me! No one is threatening him in any way. I wasn't threatened. I don't know anything at all about the damned *Beldona*. I'm a barely competent diver. No one is going to give a damn about me. You're the one in trouble here, Sam, and I'm scared for *you*. You've got to be careful. Really careful."

"I will be. But I don't want you and the baby to be alone—"

"Jacques was in the house. If I had really been afraid, I would have called him."

"He was probably snoring through the whole thing," Sam said. Jacques was a wonderful chef, but he was also a cheerful man with tunnel vision. He would have been dreaming of the next day's soufflé while the house caved down around him.

"I'm certain I'll be okay," Yancy said.

"We can't be certain of anything. I don't want you to be so alone."

"Matthew will be over for the weekend tomorrow night. He can take the room next to mine."

"That will be better. For tonight—"

"We can figure out tonight when you get back. This is what's scaring me—don't you even think about diving alone anywhere," she said passionately. "Don't you be alone under the water—not for a minute, not for a second!"

"She won't be," a deep, angry voice suddenly assured them both.

Sam swung around. Adam. He'd followed her. Come up behind her, and heard every word. And he still seemed angry.

She gritted her teeth, folding her arms over her chest. "Imagine! He's been back a day and already he's taking charge. I don't think he can do that, do you, Yancy?''

Yancy glanced over Sam's shoulder to Adam. "Yes, Sammy, I do. I think you have to listen to him.''

"Really? Well, you know, Yancy, he's working for some private concern. Why should I trust him more than anyone else?''

"Sam, he was a cop—''

"Not anymore.''

"Sam—''

"Thanks for the warning, Yancy. I have a dive party to take out,'' Sam said. She turned and started walking past Adam, but she should have known it wasn't going to happen. He took a step, which brought him in front of her. His hands bit into her shoulders. "You can be as much of a bitch as you want, but I owe it to your father not to let anything happen to you, and I'm not going to.''

"Really? If you owe my father, it took you one hell of a long time to decide to pay the debt!''

"I explained to you what happened!''

"Well, it wasn't good enough!'' she whispered, furious at realizing that she was close to tears. "It just wasn't good enough!''

She pushed her way past him, determined to regain control as she returned to the living room. She poured herself another cup of coffee and spoke loudly to everyone in the room.

"I'm heading down to the *Sloop Bee*. We'll try to cast off in twenty minutes, for those of you who are coming along."

She started down the path from the house to the docks, then realized that Adam was following right behind her. She stopped, letting him catch up. "This isn't going to work."

"What?"

"You being there every time I try to breathe."

"Well, just what are you going to do, then?" he demanded.

She opened her mouth to answer him, then realized that she really was in some kind of danger and that she might be jeopardizing her livelihood and her life—not to mention the lives of Jem, Yancy, Jacques, Brian and even others—if she didn't try to discover what was going on without having to close down the island. She hated it, but he was her best bet.

"You're a bastard, and I really hate you, you know that?" she said to him.

"So you informed me the day you asked me to leave."

"I haven't changed my mind."

"Well, you know what? You're still a little brat."

"Am I? I thought I was a bitch."

"You're a woman of many moods, Miss Carlyle."

She wanted to hit him. Nearly five years since she had seen him! she told herself desperately. She shouldn't still be so furious. So hurt.

She'd been so damned naive! When she'd first seen him, she'd thought he was wonderful. So tall, so handsome and so at home in the water. A noble type of guy. His dad had been a cop; he'd wanted to be a cop. His skill in the water had allowed him to be a different kind of cop. He'd almost instantly formed a bond of friendship with her father.

And he'd been so determined to keep his distance from her, to be a professional.

It didn't help any to know now, to admit to herself, that she'd been determined to seduce him. Determined that if she could get him, she could hold him. She'd never wanted anything with such blind, reckless desire. She'd plotted, planned, been bold, argumentative, mocking.

She'd done her best to torment him. She'd fought with him. If he was interested in a sunken ship, she mocked his knowledge of it. He argued that divers were basically safe against shark attack; she recited incidents of sharks attacking divers. He argued back.

She brushed against him every time she passed him.

She wore his patience down. She wore his resistance down, as well.

She challenged him in the water, and he met her every challenge. His smile, his laughter, captured her heart.

But whether they fought or found common ground, he'd talked to her. By the fireside at night, he'd talked to her about his job, about the bad guys who led kids astray, about the kids in the ghettos who somehow had a sense of right and wrong no matter what ugliness they saw in their lives. He'd come undercover, but, like her father, she'd been informed right away who he was. She was a nice adornment for the role he was playing, though. Naturally his nobility had extended to his determination to protect her, but then, his drug smugglers weren't hardened criminals, just rather stupid ones.

He'd had an aura of danger, of excitement, that had been irresistible to her. And they'd had lots of time together. Time beneath the sun, sailing on the *Sloop Bee*. By the fire.

In bed.

Talking, laughing, arguing.

Making love.

How many times, she wondered, in that span of a few months? Thirty? Forty? Fifty? Enough to remember so clearly that she couldn't forget now, even when she prayed to.

The last thing she wanted to do was remember being with him while she was standing there on the pathway being told that she was a brat and a bitch.

"Fine!" she snapped, staring at him, her hands clenched into fists at her side. "Follow me from here to Kingdom Come if that's what you want, but I warn you, stay the hell out of my way."

He didn't reply, so she started walking again. He followed.

She leaped aboard the *Sloop Bee*. The day seemed exceptionally hot. The sun was already shimmering down, so she stripped off her shirt and shorts and mechanically began to check their supplies, though Jem was so efficient that it was scarcely necessary. The air cylinders had all been filled and stored in their slots; the ice chest had been loaded with sodas and water and a few beers and wine coolers for the drinkers on the way back in. There was absolutely no drinking on the way to the dive sites.

The *Sloop Bee* was forty-two feet long and carried twenty divers and their supplies comfortably, two cylinders per diver for plenty of air for two dives per trip. She ignored Adam while she continued to check the supplies. She went on ignoring him as she sat down to draw up her dive plan, painfully aware that he was still watching her, tension drawing his face taut.

"My turn," he said suddenly.

She looked up, almost jumping when she found him hunched down in front of her, a finger sternly planted beneath her nose. He, too, had stripped off his shirt. The muscles of his chest were already glistening from the warmth of the sun. His features were tense, eyes hard and bright, voice harsh as he spoke. "You made up your mind about things, told me what I was thinking and feeling. You had it all decided, and you weren't willing to listen to a word I said. Say what you want now—you acted like a wretched little brat back then. Maybe I didn't respond well, but you insisted I get off your island, and I did it. I was probably an idiot to let you act like a queen to begin with, but I won't make that mistake again, so you get this. We have a situation here. Your father was almost certainly murdered. Hank Jennings, as well. You can ignore those facts if you want to—but I can't.

"So you get this straight—accept the fact that I'm here for the duration, and don't you dare get your little butt in my way!"

"Why, you—" She stared.

"And who the hell does that baby belong to?"

"*What?*"

"Whose baby is it?"

"What business is it—"

"Whose is it?"

He was so insistent that she found herself answering him when she longed to slap him. "Brian is Yancy's baby, obviously."

"Obviously? Yancy is black, and that baby is white. And he—"

"He *what*?"

"Who does that baby belong to?"

"Take another look. Yancy's heritage is mixed. Brian is her son."

"Is that what you're hoping people will believe?"

She eased back, incredulous. "Yancy is the color of café au lait. She—"

"Yancy is beautiful," he said impatiently. "That isn't the point."

"Then what is?"

"Sam, tell me! Who is that baby's father?"

"Well, let's see—you're definitely not. Since you're insinuating that the child is mine and we haven't had relations in almost five years. Wow. Long pregnancy."

She was amazed to see the depths of his anger. But it wasn't her place to share what had gone on with anyone else.

"Who does that baby belong to?" he demanded again.

She stared hard at him. "Yancy."

"Let's try again. Who is that baby's father?"

"You can try from now until hell freezes over. What you're asking is none of your concern." His fingers suddenly closed over her knees. His eyes were hot and level with hers. "Damn you, Sam, you're going to tell me."

"Damn *you,* Adam. I'm not."

She looked over his shoulder. The others were coming down the path toward the *Sloop Bee.*

"People are coming, right?" he said.

She felt his hands on her bare knees. Her heart hammered furiously, and blood was rushing to her cheeks.

She wanted so badly to lash out at him. Instead she tried to rise. She bumped against him, felt his breath against her bare thighs, felt something wickedly hot within her begin to burn. Why didn't arguing with him cool the fever inside her instead of making it worse?

"Excuse me," she muttered.

He set his hands on her waist. To keep her balance, she was forced to clutch his shoulders.

His eyes met hers, and she couldn't seem to draw her gaze away from him. She was still furious, yet she suddenly wanted in the worst way to know just what had happened, how the hell they had messed everything.

He shook his head, steadying her as he rose. Aware that the others were nearly upon them, he lowered his lips to her ear. "Damn it, Sam, I swear to God, you are going to give me answers."

She pulled back, freeing herself from his hold before she replied. "The hell I will!" she promised vehemently, sweeping by him. And then she added for good measure, "The absolute hell I will!"

9

Jerry North, exquisite, blond and beautiful, was the first to reach the *Sloop Bee,* arriving just as Sam escaped Adam.

"Jerry, come on board and give me a hand," Sam called cheerfully.

"Of course!" Jerry said.

Jerry was wearing dark glasses, and Sam couldn't see her eyes. The woman was smiling, but it seemed tense, as if she wanted to be just about anywhere rather than where she was.

"You're not afraid of boats, are you, or of being out on the water?" Sam asked, concerned.

"Bless you, no," Jerry said. "But thanks for asking. You're a dear."

"I just don't want you to be unhappy."

"I'm not unhappy. I'm thrilled. Just thrilled."

But she *was* unhappy, Sam was certain of it. Liam hopped on board just behind her, and Sam thought that Jerry jumped a mile high when Liam set his arms on her shoulders.

"I can't wait to see these Steps," Liam said enthusiastically.

Jim Santino jumped aboard, flinging his head to toss his hair out of his face. "Ah, yes! The mysterious Steps."

"They're not so mysterious," Darlene announced, hopping aboard. "I mean, obviously they were carved by someone a million years ago, and once upon a time, they actually went somewhere."

Adam laughed outright, and the others chuckled, as well. Except for poor Darlene, who looked offended. "Really, that's a perfectly logical—"

"Yes, dear, of course it is," her mother told her. "That's why they're all laughing."

"At ourselves," Adam assured her, "for not being so quick to point out the obvious!"

In another few minutes everyone had boarded. Jem was at the wheel, and Sam showed him her dive plan. A moment later, they were under way.

Their first site for the day was going to be the Steps. Sam had planned a thirty-minute dive to fifty-five feet. While Jem motored them out to the site, she sat with the children, going over the dive tables with them again so they would know how deep they could stay down and how much air they would use. Children were usually better dive students, in Sam's opinion. Adults were too quick to assume they could stretch the safety factors built into the dive tables. Oddly enough, young divers also tended to be more careful with their equipment. She stressed to them how important that was—if someone had a hole in his tennis racket, he would be unhappy and might lose a match, but he would survive it. An improper mixture of air in a cylinder would not just be inconvenient—it could kill.

Sam had been determined to stay away from Adam on the way out, but Darlene had stars in her eyes where the man was concerned, and Brad found him just as interesting. Even when Sam had purposely gathered them around her to work on the tables, they had enthusiastically called Adam over, suddenly seeming to need him to confirm all her lessons.

"Nearly there, if you all want to start suiting up!" Jem called.

Sam slid into her own environmental protection suit, a light "skin," since the water temperature around the island tended to remain warm, even in winter. She was an advocate of suits, though, simply because they did what their name implied—protected divers from the environment. She'd been hit a few times by the tentacles of jellyfish—with and without protection—and it was much, much better to have protection, she had discovered.

Liam Hinnerman was an old-time diver. He hated wearing a suit, but he did for her dives. He'd begun diving, he'd told her, before many of the associations that now certified divers had existed. Liam liked being a teacher. He'd wagged a finger beneath her nose, telling her, "You forget, young lady, that this *certification* thing is all comparatively new. I was diving when they still called a damn tank a tank instead of a *cylinder*. All this book learning and computers!"

She'd very patiently reminded him that with the number of sports divers that had begun enjoying the sea in the last few decades, it was necessary to train people in order to save lives.

"Humph!" he had told her. "Stupid people shouldn't dive."

It was difficult arguing with Liam Hinnerman. He had his own brand of logic.

Jem dropped anchor and came around to help the divers into their buoyancy control vests, weights and cylinders. Sam went through her speech, automatically slipping into her own vest and cylinder as Jem came up behind her to help her. Her speech was about taking care of coral, reminding them that it was actually alive. She also warned them that buddies needed to stay together and watch out for one another.

"We're making this one a thirty-minute dive, folks, so enjoy the Steps, and if you take it all the way down to fifty-five feet, remember to watch yourselves coming up."

"Watch out for our buddies—did we decide who our buddies are going to be?" Liam asked.

"Can't be me today," Jerry North said, waving a hand in the air. "I'll be up here, sunning with Jem."

"I'm with short stuff over there," Sukee said, winking at Brad. "A promise is a promise."

"I'm a threesome with Sam and Adam," Darlene said, afraid that someone might try to change the previous night's arrangements.

"I've got my wife!" Joey Emerson announced, smiling adoringly at Sue.

"And I've got my *husband*," Sue said.

"Is that mushy, or what?" Brad muttered.

"Hey, kid, mind your manners!" Sukee suggested.

"Oh, I, er, I didn't mean anything," Brad moaned.

Adam tousled his hair. "She knows that. Women just like to give men a hard time."

"I think it's the other way around," Sukee murmured suggestively.

Adam laughed, a smile on his face as he returned Sukee's stare. The air seemed to sizzle between them.

Irritating as hell, Sam decided.

"Well, mushy or not, son, I've got your mother," Lew Walker said.

"Oh, you guys aren't mushy anymore," Brad said.

"Ouch!" Judy murmured.

"Young man, you'd better mind your manners!" Sukee told him. Brad grinned.

"That means we're stuck with one another," Jim Santino told Liam, who nodded glumly in return.

"I can already tell that the dive we made the day before yesterday is going to prove to be the better of the two," Jim said.

"But today we're diving the Steps," Sukee said. "Come on, short stuff, let's get in the water. I want to see these magnificent relics."

In twos and threes, the divers went off the back platform of the *Sloop Bee*. Sam held her mask to her face as she plunged in, checked to make sure that all her divers gave her an okay sign, then joined Darlene and Adam.

It was odd. Adam's eyes, completely silver in the watery silence surrounding them, seemed very large behind his mask. He still seemed tense, watching her with the same anger he had shown her ever since they'd been at the breakfast buffet when Brian had come trundling out to demand a piece of corn muffin.

The hell with him, she decided. She pointed downward and began a slow descent, making sure that Darlene was following without suffering from any of the squeezes that could occur due to increasing water pressure.

It was a beautiful portion of the sea in which to dive. A coral slope fell slowly into the sea right by the sandy floor where the Steps plummeted downward. The Steps themselves were very large, a good foot thick, and approximately four feet by four feet wide.

Following them downward, Sam and her party passed by a school of amberjack, a half dozen pretty yellow tangs, one massive grouper—a fish that weighed about five hundred pounds—and a curious barracuda. Darlene cringed at the sight of the multitoothed sea dweller. As Adam drifted by Sam to reach Darlene, it felt to Sam as if he touched the entire length of her body.

He seemed to realize the stirring he had caused and paused, staring at her.

She had to remind herself to breathe. This was ridiculous. He was behaving even more oddly than he had been now that he knew about Brian. Why? What difference did it make to him? He seemed convinced that Brian had to be hers, and angry about the baby's father, which was absolutely ridiculous. Wasn't it?

She was furious herself, dying to send him off the island. No, dying to hurt him the way he had hurt her. Then she had to admit that it wasn't really the truth. The truth was, she was...

Dying to touch him. In the middle of the water. To reach out, take his hand.

No! She wanted to tear his hair out.

At least, that was what she *should* want, and she told herself it was what she did want. Wrong. She wanted to... just touch his hand....

Run her nails down his back....

No, just her fingertips....

She wasn't breathing! she reminded herself. The first rule of diving was to breathe continuously. She tore her eyes from his. Darlene was still staring at the barracuda. At last Adam set a hand on Darlene's shoulder and gave her the thumbs-up sign.

They moved by the barracuda without incident.

Sukee and Brad were just ahead of them. Sukee motioned them over, and they all watched a ray try to cover itself with the sand to escape their curious eyes. Sukee shot down lower, following the Steps. They followed.

It was a beautiful dive. They followed the Steps until they suddenly disappeared into the ocean floor, pointing out fish and sea fans and exceptional pieces of coral along the way.

At fifty-five feet the group was still basically together. The Emersons—hand in hand as they floated through the water—studied the ground. Brad and Sukee remained near. Lew and Judy Walker, too, seemed happy to stay hand in hand, cruising along the bottom.

Both Jim Santino and Liam Hinnerman seemed to be studying the stones.

Well, they had all wanted to see the Seafire Isle Steps. Everyone had seemed avidly determined, beyond eager. Now they were here. *So just what in God's name were they all looking for?* she wondered.

Something. All of them.

And all of them somehow suspect.

Even if her father—and Hank—*had* met with foul play, she told herself sternly, it was only Adam's presence making her feel that her father's enemy was now among the guests on Seafire Isle.

Sam found herself studying the stones, seeking some elusive answer herself. Here, at the fifty-five-foot mark, they didn't create a clean trail as they did at the lesser depths. It seemed that someone had tired of his task and thrown the last few any which way.

Ahead was an ocean ledge, leading to deeper water. Sam, with Darlene right beside her, was still staring at one of the Steps, studying the craftsmanship, when she realized that Adam had gone ahead of them.

He had disappeared over the ocean ledge.

Curious, she caught Darlene's hand and shot after him. When they reached the drop-off, he was already returning.

His right hand was clenched, as if he was carrying something. She stared at him questioningly, but he pretended not to notice and tapped his watch. It was time to go up.

Back on the *Sloop Bee,* the guests all talked excitedly about the Steps. Sam was quiet.

She'd tried very hard to watch Adam, to see what he was up to. But he'd never let her see what he had been carrying, and when she'd asked him outright, he denied that he had found anything, and the hostility between them made it difficult to insist he tell her the truth.

"Where next?" Liam Hinnerman demanded.

"Nellie's Reef," Sam said, forcing herself to forget Adam and whatever he was up to. "Our second dive of the day will be at a small outcropping of coral we call Nellie's Reef—supposedly because a girl named Nellie chose it as a place to throw herself into the sea to drown."

"Did she? Drown?" Darlene asked.

Sam smiled, shaking her head. "When she threw herself in it was low tide, and the coral was so high that she ended up standing on it—and then she was rescued by the young man she had thought had forsaken her."

"That's nice," Darlene decided.

"Don't tell her the rest of it!" Adam warned.

"The rest of it?" Darlene said.

Sam shrugged. "Some people say there's more to the story. And it's really not bad. Actually, it's kind of nice."

"Then tell me," Darlene insisted.

Adam did the telling. "Nellie and her beau had a wonderful wedding, a half dozen children and lived happily ever after."

"That's still nice," Darlene said.

He shrugged.

"Yes, they lived to ripe old ages—then had themselves buried at sea on Nellie's Reef," Sam said.

"Oh," Darlene murmured. "So do they haunt the reef?"

"Well, only as really nice ghosts," Adam assured her.

"Even if they *were* thrown in here," Liam Hinnerman said, "the currents probably carried them elsewhere, and then the sharks probably ate them up right after their carcasses got tossed into the drink anyway."

"Liam!" Jerry North—slicked down beautifully in suntan oil—moaned.

But Darlene laughed. "Mr. Hinnerman, you are *very* pessimistic!"

Nellie's Reef was a nice dive, but it seemed almost anticlimactic after the Steps.

When the divers were all aboard the *Sloop Bee* after their second dive of the day, Sam realized just *how* compelling the Steps had been when Jim Santino said, "Great day, dive mistress! But let's do the Steps longer, maybe tomorrow or the day after? That was the most fascinating dive I've had in a long time. Don't you all agree?"

A chorus answered him affirmatively.

"Jerry will even go in if we go back," Liam said.

Sam glanced at the blonde, who looked miserable. "Jerry, if you hate to dive—"

"I don't hate to dive. And if you decide to go back to the Steps..." She shrugged. "I guess I'll join the party."

"See, Sam!" Joey Emerson said, his arm around his wife. "Even Jerry will dive."

"Well, we'll see," she murmured.

Adam was staring at her. She returned his stare. What the hell had he been holding in his hand?

When the *Sloop Bee* returned at last to Seafire Isle, the guests were quick to disembark and disappear.

Except for Adam. He helped Jem rinse down equipment as if he'd been doing it every day for years. The two men worked naturally and well together. Sam watched them broodingly for a while, then felt Adam's eyes on her.

Like a touch. Just like a damned touch.

She turned away, then started along the path to the main house and her own cottage.

"Hey! Where are you going?"

She turned to see him standing on the dock, his hands on his hips. He was barefoot, wearing just his swim trunks.

Damn. She wasn't breathing again.

He was sleek and toned. Bronze muscles rippled along every hard inch of his body.

She threw up her hands, exasperated with him and with herself. "To bathe and change," she said.

"Not alone, you're not," he told her.

She arched a brow. "Oh?"

"Damned right, oh."

"Well, I'm going. So if you're coming..."

She turned and started along the path again. Fine, she decided. If he was going to follow her, he could tell her what he'd had in his hand.

She didn't look back, but she was certain that Adam and Jem had exchanged a look assuring one another that women were indeed cantankerous creatures. A man couldn't live with one, but then, he couldn't shoot her, either.

It didn't matter. She knew he was behind her. She could almost feel his breath, sense his warmth.

She unlocked the door to her cottage and stepped inside. She left the door open.

She knew that he had followed her into the living room of her cottage, that he'd closed the door behind himself and carefully locked it. All too aware of him, she started down the hallway to the bathroom.

"Sam—"

She stopped, dead still, staring at him. "What?"

"Sam, you can't stay alone."

"What did you find at the Steps, Adam?"

"Nothing."

"You're a liar, Adam."

"I can't leave you alone, Sam."

Can't leave you alone.... What exactly did that mean? He couldn't leave her alone because she might be in danger, or he couldn't leave her alone because he was caught in the same tangle of emotion—and lust?

Maybe it was a little bit of both.

It didn't really matter. She had lost. Lost what, though, she wasn't quite certain. A battle with herself, she supposed. Longing was rising over dignity.

"Sam, you've got to realize, I can't leave you—"

"Fine." She turned again, peeling down the straps of her damp blue bathing suit as she went.

She stepped out of it completely in front of the bathroom door and left it lying in the hall.

He couldn't leave her alone. Well, if he was going to be with her constantly, she couldn't bear it if he left her alone.

He never attacked without an invitation. Well, now he had his damned invitation. She stood in the hallway for a moment with her naked back to him.

Then she walked into the bathroom and into the shower, turning the spray on full, allowing it to sluice through her hair. She moved mechanically, scrubbing her body, then her hair, rinsing, not opening her eyes, hearing only the thunder of the water.

He was there, she thought. He'd followed her. Into the bathroom. He was near her, now.

Because he couldn't stay away.

Because he'd been invited....

And any minute, he would step in beside her. He would touch her.

He was near.

Wasn't.

Was....

Oh, God...it was wrong, she tried to tell herself. What she was doing was wrong. Justin Carlyle had taught her all the right things about life. He had taught her that love was the greatest emotion. He had taught her to be considerate, caring, fair and honest. He had taught her to see the world through the eyes of others, to be just and understanding. He had taught her that sex wasn't something to be engaged in lightly. He had taught her that it was an expression of love to be shared between two individuals when there was commitment and caring between them.

She had believed him. And she had been deeply in love with Adam O'Connor the first time she had ever made love with him.

Now...

Now, she just remembered.

The way he'd touched her.

The way he'd made her feel.

Now...

Now the man had scarcely come back in her life, and here she was, fantasizing. He didn't know what her past few years had been like, and she didn't know about his.

Of course, she could guess....

But that didn't matter. The things her father had taught her didn't matter. The look Adam had given her in the water did.

Just as her early years had been too sheltered, her last years had been too isolated. She wanted Adam. She didn't want to think about right or wrong. She didn't want to assess her feelings for him, and she most certainly didn't want to think about the emotional hell she would endure once things were over. Her every action seemed to be ruled by her nearly desperate desire for him. She wanted to be held. Touched, stroked. More. . . .

She opened her eyes at last, feeling the water pouring over her head and hair and shoulders.

He was there, standing just outside the shower door, arms crossed over his chest, silver-gray eyes hard on her. She stared at him. He opened the shower door, still in his trunks, stepped into the stall and stood before her. For long moments the water splashed and poured and rioted around them as he continued to stare at her.

She could tell him to get the hell out, and he would go.

But she had nothing to say.

Neither did he.

Suddenly he pulled her into his arms. His lips ground down on hers, hard, with the same anger that had radiated from him all day. It didn't matter. She was just as angry. And she was glad of the rough feel of him, of his hands, hard as they moved down her back, crushing her shoulders closer, then her hips, then rounding over her buttocks until she was so intimately close against him that she could feel the rise of his erection through the material of his bathing briefs. He drew her even closer, kissing her all the while, openmouthed kisses, as hot and wet as the water streaming around them. Finally he stepped back ever so slightly, and his hand slipped between them to thrust her thighs apart, his fingers moving supplely over the riot of short red hair at her pubis, then drawing a gasp from her as they thrust inside. His lips remained on hers, his tongue moving within her mouth, his fingers within her, his thumb rubbing a tender nub of outer flesh. Weakness pervaded her, sensation spilling through her like the burning rays of the sun. She clung to his shoulders, nearly shrieking aloud.

His lips parted from hers, but his hands remained on her.

His eyes demanded, challenged or mocked, she wasn't sure which. It didn't matter. She still didn't have anything to say.

Neither did he.

She leaned her head against his soaking chest, afraid that she was going to fall.

He whispered to her at last. "How many times do you think we made love?"

"I don't know . . . maybe thirty, maybe—"

"Let's make it thirty-one."

"I . . ."

"Yes?"

"I thought we were already doing that."

"Getting there," he murmured. He slammed the faucet, and the cascade of water came to an abrupt stop.

She stared at him, hoping she wasn't going to have to stand too much longer. She couldn't breathe at all. Rivers of liquid heat were flooding her limbs. Her throat was dry, her knees incredibly weak.

Pathetic! she taunted herself.

Seduced. *Needy.*

"I thought—" she began.

"We're both just too damned tall for a shower stall," he said.

And then she didn't have to stand any longer, because he picked her up.

And she was in his arms, her eyes on his. . . .

Pathetic behavior, she warned herself.

No. Just . . . *hungry.*

God, yes.

Just so *hungry.* . . .

10

There was absolutely no question of thinking about what she was doing.

Maybe she had already done all the thinking.

And maybe all the thinking and logic in the world didn't mean anything now.

Adam had returned to her life just the way he had come the first time, becoming the very center of it simply by being there. Adam was here, and she wanted him. Just as she had before. And his touch...

Just as she had wanted it before.

She was barely aware of being carried from the shower to her bedroom. Peripheral perceptions of tile, then carpet, as he moved, and nothing more. They were both still wet when he came down beside her on her bed, the room in shadow because the sun was starting its crimson fall into the west, and she'd left the drapes half closed, as well. There were a few streaks of light filtering in, rays upon which dust motes danced in a slow, magical swirl.

Her hair was soaked, splayed across the pillow. She would have been cold if not for the inferno of heat that seemed to exist between the two of them. She shivered at first, waiting for that heat to radiate through her limbs.

She was still seeing the fused silver of his eyes, so intent upon her own, when he moved against her, the dampness of his body covering her, the pressure of his lips against her throat. The fullness of his body covered hers; the stroking of his hands warmed her.

The focus of his mouth shifted from her pulse to her right breast. Caressing, tugging, rubbing. His knee intruded between her thighs. His hand followed suit. Fingers stroked, caressed, probed.

She shivered no more.

Her fingers bit into his shoulders; her body burst into heat. She shifted, trying to avoid the exquisite pleasure of his touch, then shifted again, eager for more of it. Climbing, rising, feeling the hot spiral that burned at the center of her sex, feeding her limbs, being fed in turn. She closed her eyes as thought momentarily intruded.

No, no, no...

Yes, yes, oh, God, yes...

His lips fed on her left breast. His free hand plunged into her hair, and then his mouth was covering hers, tongue invading so hotly, completely, wetly. In, out, around, decadently, like the motion between her thighs. Cries rose within her throat; she could bear no more, yet she was desperate for more.

Suddenly he drew away, staring at her as he ran his palms down her thighs, then lower. She met his gaze and tried to reach out, to caress him, to hold him intimately, to torment as he had done. To arouse him.

He pressed her back.

Rose over her.

Came into her....

Absorbing the pleasure of him, she briefly remembered words Yancy had said to her once, Yancy spilling out her own desperate emotions, laughter, love, pain....

Sometimes men wanted to be touched.

Sometimes they wanted to get right to it.

Oh, God.

He was getting right to it.

Her arms encircled him; her limbs embraced him. She clung to him, fingers digging, releasing, digging once more, as her breath was swept away again and again. Their bodies dried from the heat emanating from within them, sheened over again from that same heat. She felt him. In her. Deeper. Deeper. More a part of her than ever. Touching, rubbing, stroking. Harder, filling her, arousing her. In, out, she couldn't think, could barely feel, had to, had to...

Suddenly he was gone completely. Her eyes had been closed, but now they opened, met his. Now his lips touched hers again. She made some sound of protest, but it didn't matter. He was stroking her again, kissing her again. Her lips, breast, throat. Her abdomen, the curve of her hip, the soft skin of her inner thigh, higher, circling, never really touching, never touching...

Sam shrieked, twisting, writhing, struggling, constricting, soaring to a pinnacle with passions she thought could crest no higher. Yet he was atop her again, and the fire she felt within was stoked again, maddened, hardened, driven to a wilder, more urgent, desperate level. She was keenly aware of the force of his body, scarcely aware of anything else, the sheets, the dust motes on the air. She knew only the slickness of her flesh, of his, their bodies moving, ever moving, against each other. She could hear the wind, but it wasn't the wind, it was her own breath, the husky, erotic whispers that complemented the scent, taste, the feel of their loving as he urged onward. At last a fountain of light and shadow seemed to erupt, and she heard the keening of the cries that exploded from her lips as the climax seized her.

He slid to her side, gasping for breath. She instantly and instinctively curled against him, her head on his chest so she could listen to the thunder of his heart. This was where she had wanted to be, this was what she had wanted to feel, since she had seen him, heard his voice, touched him. He'd gone out of her life, and sheltered as she might have been, she'd known that what they'd shared had been vivid, that someone to love so fiercely, someone who lived so determinedly and passionately, came along but seldom.

For long moments Sam simply breathed, inhaling deeply, trying to still the wild, erratic beating of her heart. She could still feel his body warmth like a blanket that swept over her in comforting waves.

They'd had sex, she tried to tell herself. Something as physical and natural as the simple breathing she was now trying so hard to achieve. Nothing miraculous, nothing unusual, nothing that wasn't shared millions of times a day across the world. She had no right to look to the past, to make more of this relationship than what existed. She'd done that before, never realizing what a fool she was being. She couldn't blame him for the way things had ended, not completely.

It had never been right between them.

No, it hadn't been right. But it had been nearly perfect.

She didn't want to think about the past right now. About the emotions she'd felt. The things she had done. The life she had been living.

But, oh, dear God, when it was nearly perfect, it was wonderful. Every part of it. The sweetness of wanting, of reaching. Flying higher and higher, savoring sensations, wanting them to go on forever, desperate to reach the climax.

Then the aftermath. The *breathing*. The intimacy. The wonderful closeness that could only be shared in the intimacy following lovemaking. Words could be so awkward, but also personal, reflecting the very uniqueness of being together, that special intimacy.

She felt his fingers on her chin, lifting her face to his. She offered him a slow smile, waiting to hear tender words that would envelop her more fully in the blanket of intimacy that was wrapped around them.

His eyes were sharp, his features taut, his jaw twisted at an angle.

"Tell me about you and Hank Jennings," he demanded.

The phone rang.

The newly showered diver picked it up quickly, looking furtively over one shoulder.

"Yes?"

"We've got real trouble."

"And that is?"

"There's someone on the island who's missing from elsewhere. Get that? Someone is missing from where he's supposed to be. Escaped to the island."

"Then someone is surely dead."

"Bones and body parts make someone dead. Not missing. Missing is trouble."

"All right, all right—"

"I want dead. Understand?"

"Yes."

"A fucking head on a platter, you understand?"

"Yes, yes."

"A head on a platter."

"Yes." Exasperated now.

"Soon. Damned soon."

The diver hung up, shaking. It should never have come to this.

"What?" Sam demanded.

"What was your relationship? He came to study the *Beldona*. You apparently told him everything you knew. You went diving with him constantly."

"Hardly constantly," Sam said, her eyes narrowed.

"What was your relationship?" he insisted.

Sam tried to draw away from him, her temper so fierce that she seemed to be on fire again, her entire body shaking.

But his hold on her seemed fueled by a sudden rise in his own temper. His fingers gripped her arms, his leg, thrown over her lower body, seemed like an iron bar, blocking her.

"Why are you bothering to ask me? It seems to me as if you've already decided what my relationship with him was. Let's see. You think I had a baby with the man, but God forbid I should admit it. So I gave the baby to Yancy and insisted that she raise him. That's it. Hank came to the island, and I thought, wow, I never get a chance to have a relationship, and this guy has come to stay a while. Is that what you think? What the hell difference does it make to you? What right do you even have to ask?''

''I need to know!''

''Well, you know what? That's too damned bad, because I'm not telling you anything. Now, move. Just move. Get your leg off me.'' She threw her hands between them, pressing, straining against his chest. He caught her wrists and rolled atop her to stop the rising impetus of her attack.

Her eyes met his. She wanted to kill him.

She wanted him again.

The sun was murder. Just murder.

Jerry North loved it, but she knew too well what it did to the skin. She'd showered, and now she stroked lotion over the length of her body.

She was in pain.

Not in the flesh, but in the spirit.

And, of course, she knew of no way to ease that pain.

She had made her own choices in life. She couldn't complain of rough beginnings, of having been an abused child. She couldn't blame her actions, her choices, on anyone but herself. She could only blame them on being young. Foolish. On not seeing the forest for the trees. And then...

Well, then it always seemed that one mistake led to another. That once a bad path was chosen, it led farther and farther into ruts and bogs, darkness...even terror.

And now...

Now she could lie down and cry for a week straight. Now she almost longed to die from the pain that filled her, the pain of what she had done and, worse, the pain of what could have been.

She wasn't evil. She knew that. But she had lived in the miasma of evil, and she had not remained unscathed. For her now, there was nothing left but the mechanics of going through day-to-day life. Washing, bathing, dressing. Eating, breathing. Responding.

Watching, and living in the hope that she could, having learned from her mistakes, perhaps keep the blood of evil from touching others.

Still wrapped in her towel, she sat at the foot of the bed, mechanically applying coral polish to her toes.

She realized suddenly that Liam had come into the room, that he was standing in front of her, his hands on his hips, staring at her.

"You're going to dive."

She didn't reply.

"God damn you, bitch, you're going to dive!"

Jerry shrugged.

Then she gasped, stunned from her self-absorption as the back of his hand came flying against her jaw, the force stinging and powerful enough to send her flat against the bed, staring up at him.

Forgotten, the bottle of polish rolled to the floor.

Liam leaned over her, jaw locked, eyes cold. "You are going to dive. And you are going to get me to that ship."

She tried to crawl away from him, but he caught her by the ankles, flipping her violently onto her back again. He smiled. Gripped her ankles harder to drag her closer to him. She didn't know if he meant to strike her again or force himself on her.

She didn't know if she saw much of a difference between the two choices at that moment.

Either way, he would hurt her.

And either way, he would be careful not to leave a bruise.

She lay sleeping.

Propped up on one elbow, Adam watched Sam, smiling bittersweetly. She had to be completely on edge, but Sam was tough, cool, independent. Life had to be taking its toll, but she just kept moving right through it.

But now her exhaustion was evident. Not that they hadn't expended a fair amount of energy between fighting and making love. It was just that the level of tension between them always seemed to remain so high.

Words were exchanged so heatedly. Okay, so maybe he was an ass. Maybe a great bout of sex shouldn't be followed up by a question about a previous lover. It was just weighing so damned heavily on his heart and mind. He was wondering on the one very painful hand just what had befallen Hank, and then on the other hand wondering what had gone on between Hank and Sam. And then there was the question of the baby.

No question. That child was Hank's. There should have been a question, he knew. Most babies just looked like little old men. Sometimes they were bald, sometimes they had hair, but they always had big eyes and round, creased faces. They didn't look like anybody.

This baby was a dead ringer for Hank.

His heart seemed to squeeze. Someone had to be able to tell him. Someone had to know. *He* had to know. He itched to hold the baby. He wondered if he would break down if he did. He couldn't let himself break down. Why ruin a perfectly good image?

So, Sam, what the hell went on? he longed to demand. He wanted to shake the truth out of her. To wake her up and force her to tell him.

He smiled at the thought. If she wasn't ready to tell him, she *wouldn't* tell him.

He moved a hand gently over her bare arm. She didn't move. She was sleeping so deeply. A slight tremor shot through the length of his frame. Damn, it had been good. She reeked of sensuality. He would never forget the first time he'd seen her. He'd arrived on the island in much the same fashion as he had this time, completely undercover. She'd been in a yellow bathing suit that day, and she'd climbed atop the mainmast of a friend's sailboat. A barefoot, hoyden-ish daredevil, diving into the depths below from the mast. She'd been a picture of grace and beauty, so natural, so fluid. Diving into the water, rising from it. Seeing him. Flirting. She'd been an outrageous flirt. And he'd been good, so damned good at first. He'd tried to explain things to her. But it hadn't mattered.

He'd tried to keep his distance from her, but the attempt had been no good at all. He'd fallen in love. Any emotion he'd felt for another woman paled at what she awoke within him. Still, he'd meant to do everything the right way. Once he'd been in love, he'd planned on telling Becky the truth. But then Becky had shown up on the island, and Sam had thrown him out before he'd had a chance to explain anything to anyone.

He wasn't in the clear. Older and wiser now, he knew he'd handled things wrong, no matter what his intentions had been.

Oh, well. At least he and Becky had made a clean break. He'd thrown himself into work. Becky had married a banker, and now she lived in Palm Beach and had two cute kids. The right life for Becky.

He shook his head, smiling, remembering the past. *I'm sort of involved,* he'd tried to tell her. There had been horror on her face. *Oh, my God, you're married?* That had been easy to deal with. His answer had been, *No, but...*

Somehow, he hadn't gotten to the "but" part of it. He had wound up naked with her on the sand, feeling the sun striking them both, warming them against the coolness of the water sweeping over their limbs.

It had been easy to forget what he should have been saying.

No excuses on his part.

No matter how much sensuality radiated from the woman at his side.

He smiled suddenly, glad of the honesty they had shared today. He'd been itching to touch her. Burning to feel her, taste her. He'd fought off his own climax so he could have more and more of her. He could see her in the darkness, every part of her, could see her with his eyes closed, recall her scent, her taste. He knew the texture of her flesh, the size and shape of her breasts, the color of her nipples, the feel of the red thatch at the top of her thighs. Knew the misty look of her eyes, the curve of her lips, the taste of her mouth.

He knew those things in his dreams, waking, sleeping. At the strangest times in his life, he would recall something about her, the slope of a shoulder, the beautiful curve of her back, the pureness of her flesh. In the midst of a business dinner, beneath the currents of a river, he'd recalled Sam.

And now...

Now, for the moment, she had given up the fight. After the last explosive session of lovemaking between them, he'd had the God-given sense to keep his mouth shut. So she'd curled up beside him.

And slept.

Her hair was drying. Deep, dark tendrils of fire, it swept over the pastel-hued sheets. Her body was gloriously tan against that pale background, as well, except for the strips of more intimate flesh that hadn't been bared to the sun. She was naturally toned and perfect, an athlete with the most feminine curves. He smiled, remembering what she'd once said about breasts.

"Yours are perfect, darling," he whispered, kissing the classical sculpture of her cheek lightly. "Perfect. Not too much, not too little. Perfect."

He was tempted to test that perfection again with the cup of his hand, but he rather liked the idea that she was sleeping. He needed to make a phone call.

He rose, pulled the covers over her and found his swim trunks. They were damp. Oh, well. He had no choice. He slipped into them, wincing as the cold hit personal places that had so recently been so warm.

He padded out to the kitchen and put coffee on, hoping that would ease some of the clammy feeling assailing him. When the coffee perked, he poured himself a cup and sat down at the desk in Sam's small sunken office area.

He reached into the small inner front pocket of his bathing trunks and pulled out the encrusted article he had found caught in the step just at the cliffside nearly sixty feet below the surface of the water.

Sea growth was so attached to it that it was almost impossible to realize what the article was. He rubbed at the green and earth-toned growth. Gold appeared. He turned the article over in his hands. Studied it. Felt a plummeting of his heart. Pain. Squeezing.

He pocketed the article and sat thoughtfully for several seconds.

He picked up her private line. Unless the phones were tapped, he was safe.

It took him about sixty seconds to put his call through. He reached Sergeant James Estefan of the Mainland Metro Station dive squad at his desk.

"It would be you—I'm just about to go home," James said.

Adam could picture him. James was thirty-three, blue-eyed, dark-haired. Dark, eternally tousle-haired.

James spent half his days in the water and the other half running his fingers through his drying hair. He was a good man and a good cop, an intuitive one.

"I've got your home number anyway," Adam told him. "What have you got for me?"

"Well, I checked the death records, like you asked, and you were right on the money."

"Yeah?" Adam leaned forward.

"A Marcus Shapiro was washed up around Daytona Beach exactly one week after the reported disappearance of Justin Carlyle."

"Shapiro." Tension seized Adam. "He was one of the main divers with SeaLink, right?"

"Had been," James corrected.

Adam frowned. "So who was he working for when he was found dead?"

"Private concerns."

"Oh, shit," Adam muttered.

"Annoying, ain't it? By the way, have you shared your own private concerns with your hostess yet?"

"No. Help me here, give me more. What was Shapiro's cause of death? Drowning?"

"Stabbed to death."

"Stabbed!"

"Right."

"Carlyle's disappearance and Shapiro's death may have no connection whatsoever."

"True. Maybe not even likely. You asked me to find whatever I could. I found Shapiro's corpse."

"Do you know anything about what Shapiro was doing?"

"No. His wife had reported him missing. She'd known he planned on going out diving, but she hadn't known with whom or for whom. He could have been working for Robert Santino. Santino made no bones about the fact that he was sending divers out to scrounge around for the *Beldona*."

"Anything else? Have you found backgrounds on any of the people I asked you to check up on?"

"I have."

"Well, damn it, James—"

"You know, if this gets solved, I want one hell of a nice vacation out there on that island of yours."

"Done." Adam looked toward Sam's bedroom and shrugged. "Sure. Now, talk to me."

"You've got two people on the island who've changed their names a time or two."

"Who?"

"Well, Mr. Joseph Emerson, for one."

"Joseph Emerson? The honeymooner? Come on, James. Spit it out for me."

"All right. Emerson was born Shapiro."

"You don't mean—"

"I do. His father's body was the one washed up on the Daytona shore."

"Go on," Adam said.

"This one may hurt someone more than a bit," James warned.

"Well?" Adam demanded.

"Might be better if I don't tell you."

"James, you'd damned well better tell me now," Adam insisted. Then he listened. "What?"

James repeated what he had learned. Slowly.

And Adam sat back, stunned, staring toward the bedroom.

"Adam, you there?"

"Yeah. Yeah, I'm here. I, uh, thanks, James. You've gone above and beyond. I'll keep in touch."

He hung up and walked into the kitchen. He stared at his freshly brewed coffee. Then he dug around in the cabinets until he found a bottle of booze. Rum. He hated rum.

He swigged it right down.

Oh, God.

He looked toward the bedroom again. Leaned against the counter. Groaned.

He was going to have to hold out on her about this one. Until...

Until...

Oh, hell.

Sam awoke, vaguely aware of voices in some other room.

She started to jump out of bed in a disoriented panic, then remembered why she was in bed and that she had fallen asleep.

Asleep!

She looked around for her clothing, then remembered that she had dropped her bathing suit in the hall. Shaking her head in disgust at what had surely been a complete mental breakdown, she reached into her closet for a robe. By the time she had belted it on, she had traced the voices to the kitchen. She hurried down the hallway, only to discover that Jem was in her cottage, along with Adam. She must have slept a good while, because both men were showered, shaved and dressed in casual dinner attire.

They had drinks in their hands. And they both stared at her strangely as she joined them.

"Is everything all right?"

"Yeah," Adam said. "Well, other than the fact that something's going on. Actually, nothing's right, but then, you know that already."

She glanced at her watch. "Seven!" she exclaimed. She looked at them both accusingly.

"I just got back here myself," Adam said. "I had to change," he explained awkwardly.

"Dinner will be on. Yancy should have come for me. I can't just ignore this entire business."

"It's not going to make any difference if you miss the cocktail hour and show up late for one evening meal," Jem assured her.

"I've still got to shower," she began, looking at Adam. She felt color filling her cheeks. "And dress."

"We'll wait," Adam said.

She nodded. "I don't believe I fell asleep like that. I don't believe that..." Her voice trailed away. "I...excuse me."

Sam showered in the hottest water she could find, then dressed quickly in a calf-length, teal silk off-the-shoulder dress.

She didn't allow herself to think the entire while.

When she walked into the living room, she still felt that Adam was watching her peculiarly.

The strange thing was that he looked away when he caught her staring at him in return.

Was he feeling guilty again? she wondered. No, he'd never behaved so strangely before. Not now, not in the past.

"Are you sure nothing else has happened?" she demanded, walking toward the door and waiting for the men to follow.

"Nothing," Jem said.

"At all," Adam added.

They were lying.

Well, it didn't matter. They weren't going to tell her anything.

"Let's go to dinner then, shall we?" Dinner. A meal. Everything felt different. She'd been with Adam again. *She* was different.

No control, she mocked herself.

Yet...

Had the past been her own fault? Could things be different now that she was older and wiser?

Sure, she told herself. She could just go for the good sex now.

Like hell. She cared about him, she was entwined with him. She wanted more than what she'd had.

And her business, her island and her life were falling apart.

"Dinner, guys," she persisted, since they seemed to be moving slowly. "That meal that everyone else will be eating or getting ready to eat by the time we get there. I've already missed cocktail hour. You two have had yours while you were waiting, I see."

She spun around, leaving the two of them. The hell with them if they weren't ready to come. This place was her business. Her livelihood. Jem's, too.

They were right behind her, then beside her, Jem to her left, Adam to her right.

Handsome guys, she thought. Both so tall, well-built, immaculately dressed, Jem ebony dark, Adam so bronze, with his clear gray eyes. Flanked to protect her.

She was lucky.

Jem would stay. Her friend for a lifetime.

While Adam...

He would always be a main force in her heart and mind, whether he stayed or sailed away tomorrow. She couldn't change him, but one way or another, he would be with her for a lifetime. She felt a tightness beginning to burn within her chest.

Stay, Adam. This time, stay.

She had to remember, *she had sent him away herself.*

Adam cleared his throat, suddenly stopping, pulling back on her arm so that she stopped in front of him. Jem stood silently, waiting for him to speak. "I told Jem that Yancy thought someone had been in the house. He's going to take the room next to hers until..."

"Until?" Sam stared at him.

Adam shrugged. "Until we know who was in the house with her."

"Then I'll be alone?" she queried, knowing his answer.

"No."

"Because you're going to stay in my cottage?" Sam asked.

"Yes."

"But you haven't stayed there before?" she asked. "Jem hasn't just been letting you in? Or did you arrive early this morning so you could come sit by my bedside? Is that it?"

Jem choked.

Adam didn't reply, just stared at her evenly. "Do you have an objection to my being there this evening?"

"Would it matter if I did?"

He looked at her, smiling slightly. "In a way."

"Yes?"

"It would affect where I actually slept," he said, his voice low.

No secrets here. Jem was too close. Jem knew. Jem *had* known.

Jem had probably been expecting this ever since Adam O'Connor had set foot on the island.

The hell with them both.

She managed to meet Adam's eyes for several seconds, staring hard. But then her eyes dropped. She looked ahead and kept walking. "I don't have an objection to you staying so that Jem can keep guard on Yancy."

Jem made a choking sound.

Or outright laughed.

Sam wasn't at all sure which.

Adam stepped closer to her. "Would you have an objection if Jem wasn't going to guard Yancy?" he asked politely.

"Only regarding where you sleep," she replied sweetly, and hurried by him, anxious to reach the main house.

Or to have the last word—at least this once.

11

Dinner seemed so normal.

By the time they reached the main house, Yancy was lighting the flame under one of the buffet dishes. "Fiesta night," she said, making no note of the fact that they had arrived so late. "Fajitas, burritos, quesadillas. Just a touch of Cajun to the salsa. It's all absolutely delicious. Dig in."

"Looks wonderful," Sam commented. Adam and Jem were already making up plates of food. When she finished with her own, she discovered that the seat next to Jim Santino was open. He smiled when she joined him, tossing his hair back.

She smiled in return. Once upon a time, Jim had seemed cute. Sweet. Now she felt her skin crawling—just a little bit. Did she believe that the sins of the fathers were visited upon the sons? No.

But then again, she didn't completely trust him anymore, either.

"You look lovely, Sam," he said.

"Thanks."

"Different, somehow."

"Oh?"

"Flushed, vibrant," Jim said.

"Well-served," Sukee drawled from across the table.

Sam's eyes flew to the other woman, who smiled with all the cunning grace of a feline. Sam willed herself not to flush. Sukee had just been waiting for her to give herself away.

And now, everyone was staring at Sukee—and at her.

Jerry North stared at Sam with thoughtful, light blue eyes. She lowered them when Sam glanced her way.

It might have gone on forever, but Sam found herself with reason to be grateful to Jim Santino. He stood up, excusing himself. "You're a lucky man, Mr. O'Connor. Very lucky. Sam, the food is delicious tonight. Everything on this island just gets better and better. Can I bring anyone anything?"

"Why is Mr. O'Connor a lucky man, Mom?" Brad asked Judy Walker.

"Lucky to be here," Adam said matter-of-factly. "Is that a water pitcher? Could someone pass it to me, please?"

Jim delivered the water pitcher as he started to the buffet table. "Amazing, though," Jim said, smiling as he filled his plate from the buffet. He started to the table. "I think you've both been holding out on us. Tell me, O'Connor. You already knew Miss Carlyle when you got here, didn't you? From some kind of previous life?"

Adam set down his water.

"I can answer that," Avery Smith said quietly. "Yes, Mr. Santino. They'd met before. Mr. O'Connor used to be a policeman. He was here undercover. I imagine that's why neither one of them acknowledged the previous relationship. Miss Carlyle is the most discreet hostess. She'd keep her guests' secrets right to her dying day, if necessary. Right, Miss Carlyle?"

Sam stared at Avery Smith, alias James Jay Astin. Was he threatening her? Warning her to keep quiet about his identity?

"I've always imagined that if people want others to know something about them, they'll share it themselves in their own good time," she said pleasantly.

Smith smiled. At one time he must have been a very handsome man. He still had quite a look about him. Completely distinguished. Confident.

Evil?

"You know what?" Brad said, ignoring the grownups and addressing Sam. "I started reading about sharks today. Sam, they can be bad, really bad."

Sam frowned, hesitating. "Brad, I never said that sharks never harmed people. What I said was that they hardly ever harm divers. And I don't think they're evil—they're just eternally hungry, and sometimes they bite the wrong food."

"There was this really awful thing that happened during World War Two," Brad said. "A ship sank—"

"The *Indianapolis*," Adam volunteered.

"You know the story!" Brad said, pleased.

"The ship had delivered one of the components of the atom bomb to Tianian Island, in the Marianas, when it was spotted by a Japanese submarine. The *Indianapolis* was torpedoed right after midnight, and it sank within twelve minutes. I'm not sure how many men had originally been on board—"

"One thousand one hundred and ninety-nine," Smith supplied. "Eight hundred and fifty escaped into the sea—the others were killed in the explosions or trapped inside the ship as it sank."

"What happened to the men in the water?" Sukee asked.

Adam shrugged, his eyes meeting Sam's. "During the first night, perhaps another hundred men drowned or perished from their injuries. The next morning they began to worry about sharks. They saw a little four-footer who had adopted them, or so it seemed. The men were mostly wearing life jackets and clinging to what they call floater nets. They knew they'd be best off to stay in large groups, so they did. They came up with a nickname for the shark that kept hovering around them. They called him Whitey. But Whitey was just a hint of the trouble to come. The men were in the water for four days and five nights, praying for rescue. Then the sharks really began to come. They picked off the men who had strayed from their groups. They went for the sick and the injured. There were all different kinds. Makos, whites, tigers—all attacking from below. When they were finally rescued, there were only three hundred and sixteen men remaining alive.''

"Oh, man, you've got to read about it!" Brad said. "One guy thought his friend was sleeping and went to wake him up, only to find that the whole bottom half of the guy's body was gone. And they said that the more blood that was in the water, the more sharks that came—"

He was interrupted as Jerry North suddenly knocked over a dish of salsa.

The red sauce spread quickly across the table.

"Really, Brad, you're a great storyteller," Jerry murmured, "but perhaps this isn't the best time."

"Brad!" his father said.

"Brad, enough, we're at dinner," his mother began.

"Ooh," Darlene said, staring at the red salsa that had stained the table. "Ooh," she said again.

And promptly threw up.

* * *

The Walkers couldn't apologize enough.

The Emersons couldn't leave quickly enough.

The entire concept of dessert was lost. Only Jacques, bemoaning the fate of his exceptional flan, was desolate at the sad demise of the evening meal.

The dining room was cleaned up. Sam, Jem, Adam, Yancy, Jim, Sukee, Liam and Jerry had coffee together, but conversation lagged. Sukee seemed eager to disappear. Jim naturally offered to walk her to her cottage. Jerry looked exhausted. Exceptionally tired, Sam thought.

"I guess we'll head back, too," Liam said. "Jerry's definitely diving tomorrow. Right, sweetheart?"

Jerry looked at Sam. "I—"

"Right, sweetheart?"

"Yeah."

"No one can make you dive, Jerry," Sam began.

"She's just a little uneasy," Liam said smoothly.

"We'll all watch out for you," Sam promised.

Liam set an arm around Jerry. "She'll have me for a buddy. Just like a Siamese twin."

"Well, if you need help, that's what I'm here for," Sam insisted.

"Thanks, sweetie. You're a doll." Impulsively, Jerry kissed her cheek. Then she seemed embarrassed. "Good night," she said, hurrying on to the porch. Liam shrugged, then followed her.

Sam noted that Adam watched Jerry go with a very peculiar expression on his face. He caught her staring at him and shrugged. "I hope she'll be okay."

Sam shrugged, as well. "I guess we'll get going," she said.

"Good night," Yancy told them.

Sam started out. Adam followed and set a hand on her shoulder. She didn't protest; she didn't touch him in return. She walked with him to the cottage, slipping her key into the lock. He followed her into the shadowy living room.

"Where did you want to sleep?" she asked him awkwardly. She didn't know quite what the afternoon had meant to him.

Or to herself.

He didn't reply. He left her standing there as he searched the cottage. He came back to where she stood, waiting in the filter of moonlight.

"Lock the door," he told her.

She did so.

He walked up to her then. She looked at him in the shadows.

He should speak.

She should speak.

He spun her around and unzipped her dress. The silky fabric floated down the length of her body.

And then his hands were on her naked flesh.

And she knew exactly where he was going to sleep.

* * *

This time Yancy woke up entirely on her own. The baby hadn't cried; and at first she wasn't aware of any reason she should have awakened.

Then she listened.

And she heard it.

Movement down below.

Coming from Justin Carlyle's office. Someone going through the papers, going through the books? Was that it? Was someone convinced that there was something to be found in those papers, something that had eluded those who had searched already?

Someone who came by night, determined not to be seen.

Someone who came furtively.

Someone dangerous. Who had killed already? Who would kill again?

Yancy crawled out of bed. The breeze was balmy and warm, lifting the soft cotton of her sheer gown around her. She wondered if she appeared like some demented creature of the night, a slim honey-colored waif, floating through the night in fear.

Alone.

Not alone.

Jem was near tonight.

And the baby...

The baby.

She checked on Brian. He slept like an angel, his breathing perfectly even, his little rump sticking up in the air. Nervously, she hugged her arms around her shoulders and walked to her door. It was locked; there was a chair in front of it. And Jem was sleeping in the room right beside hers.

Didn't Jem hear what was going on in the office?

Maybe not, because Yancy couldn't hear movement any longer. She stood next to the door, her ear against it, listening.

Nothing.

Something.

Yes, she heard something, but it didn't seem to be coming from downstairs.

She swung around. The night breeze rustled, causing the drapes to float inward. The window. The damned window. There was no porch beyond it, but there were a number of trellises around the house, along with drain pipes.

The breeze, nothing more. The breeze rustling. There was no one out there. She could see no one in the moonlight.

She turned.

She could see . . .

A shadow.

A silhouette in the moonlight.

So close that she could feel the heat. . . .

She inhaled to scream, so terrified that she choked and gasped. Jem was close, next door to her.

Too late. The shadow moved like mercury. She was dragged close, into the heat. A hand clamped over her mouth. Words were whispered.

"Hush. Hush! Don't scream. Don't say a word. Not one word. You don't know what you're risking."

Waking beside Adam was a nice way to come back to the world of light, Sam decided.

Very nice.

Where she usually had the shrill sound of an alarm ringing in her ears, this morning she had the exquisite feel of something wet, light, very hot, tantalizing her nape.

The touch of his lips.

Very gentle. So gentle they aroused before they awoke.

Then there was that slow stroking down the length of her back, brushing her spine. Down, down...up again. So evocative.

Once again, gentle. Arousing before awakening.

Then the feel of his body, hard against hers. Those lips again. Whispering hot eroticisms against her ear-lobe, telling her each little thing he was going to do before he did it.

His lips against her spine.

His hands caressing her buttocks, locking onto her hips.

Again the fullness of him, flush against her.

Within her.

And then she was completely awake.

Completely aroused.

The alarm went off. Amazingly, the sound seemed to take its cue from the very moment in which everything inside her seemed to explode. For the space of several seconds, it might have been part of the raw, violent pleasure seizing her, shaking her, searing her.

Then, of course, she knew it was the alarm.

It was good sex, near perfect—not, however, miraculous. Yet even as she realized what the sound was, Sam lay back, her body slick and glistening, cooling, eyes half closed, her lips curled into a half smile, as well. It was Adam who reached over her, swearing, found the clock and nearly broke it before hitting the right button to turn off the alarm.

"Do you ever take a break?" he muttered. "Sleep late?"

"Rainy days," she reminded him.

He shook his head. "I mean a real break. A vacation."

"People come here to vacation. I live in paradise. An island Eden."

"You *work* in paradise," he told her. "And that's quite different." He was propped on one elbow, watching her.

She tried not to let him realize that she was watching him in return. Appreciating the length of his naked body. Darkened by the sun—except in strategic areas. Long, muscled, tight, slick. Handsome chest thickly furred with rich, dark hair. Tapered waist. Strong legs. Sexy legs. And hips. And other attributes.

"You need a break," he continued. "A real break. A place where you don't have to get up to make sure that other people are enjoying their croissants."

She smiled and shrugged. "I love the island. But maybe you're right. One day soon I'll take a break. After . . . this."

He nodded, then frowned slightly. "Where was the baby born?"

"Miami," she said.

"Ah."

"Ah, what?"

"So he *is* your baby?"

She stared at him, refusing to allow him to unsettle her. "Did I say that?"

"You knew where he was born."

"Of course. I took Yancy to the hospital."

"Or Yancy took you."

"Adam, you really should go to hell."

"You really should tell me about Hank."

"Then you should tell me what you found in the water yesterday."

He arched a brow at her, then shrugged with a dry grin. "Touché, Miss Carlyle."

"Just what is it you want to know about Hank Jennings?"

"Your relationship with him."

She smiled. Thinking of Hank always made her smile, even if it was a sad smile. "I loved him," she said simply.

"But the baby is Yancy's?"

"What makes you think that baby belongs to Hank Jennings?" she demanded.

"Because he loo—because from what I understand, Hank was the most likely candidate on the island."

"Why did you just change what you were about to say?"

"I didn't."

"You did."

"Damn it, I don't even know what I was going to say anymore."

"You do, but you're not going to tell me. Fine. My turn. What did you find in the water?" she demanded.

"You didn't tell me anything, why should I tell you?"

"You did find something."

"Maybe."

"Tell me," Sam insisted.

"I'm not telling you anything until you come clean with me," Adam informed her curtly.

She didn't like his attitude. "Why should I tell you anything until you come clean with me?"

"You owe me an explanation."

"*I* owe *you* an explanation!" she exclaimed. "Wait a minute here—I own this island. You show up here, and *I* get attacked."

"I did save your life, remember?"

Sam exploded with an expletive, telling him what he should do with himself, and rose from her side of the bed. She walked into the shower, turning the water on hard and hot.

A second later he had stepped in behind her. Groping for the soap. Groping for... her.

"I thought you didn't like the shower?"

"Not for the first time after so many years."

"Ah."

He lifted her, drawing her legs around him, bracing her against the tile. The tile was cool. The water was stingingly hot. The steam rose around them. Sam felt as if she was sinking into it as they made love within the steam and heat of the water. Finally the water cooled. She was still in his arms, glad of his strength; she couldn't have stood on her own. She didn't speak, neither did he. The water continued to pour around them.

Only now it was turning cold.

"You have to trust me," he said to her at last as she slid down his body, finding her feet, feeling the chill of the water.

"*You* have to trust *me*," she insisted, staring at him. "There's a lot you're not telling me."

To her surprise, he looked away, not denying what she said.

She felt a shivering inside her.

He knew something.

Something she wasn't going to like.

Yancy wasn't at breakfast. Lillie was filling in for her in the dining room.

"Is anything wrong?" Sam asked Lillie. It wasn't like Yancy to have anyone substitute for her.

"No, the baby had a restless night. Yancy says she's exhausted."

"I'll just check on her," Sam said. She left her coffee by the buffet table and hurried up the stairs to Yancy's room. Jem was just coming out of his own.

"Everything okay?" she asked him, not at all sure why she had such an uneasy feeling.

"As far as I know," Jem said. "We're still diving the Steps, huh?"

"I guess."

"You're the boss here. You can change the itinerary if you want."

"If everyone is obsessed with the Steps, then we'll go there. My dad was obsessed with them—you know that's why I'm not crazy about diving there. But I haven't got the right to keep others from it because of my own hang-ups."

Jem grinned. "That sounds like a bunch of psychological claptrap to me. You want to go, we go— that's where the truth of it lies. You almost ready to head down to the boat?"

"I'm just checking on Yancy."

"Yeah, she seems wiped out today."

"You talked to her?"

"Yeah. She looked like hell. Well, you check up on her, and I'll see you down at the boat. By the way, we've got to keep an eye on the weather in the next few days."

"A storm?" Sam asked, pausing.

"Yeah. That depression that formed off the east coast of Africa last week has been steadily strengthening. It rose to tropical storm velocity last night, and they're expecting it to reach hurricane proportions by midnight tonight. It's still a fair distance away, and you know how these things go. It probably won't even hit here."

"Yeah," Sam muttered. "That's what we were all saying about Hurricane Andrew right before it wiped out half a dozen cities. You're right, we've got to keep an eye on it."

"Yeah. Thank God *one* of us still has a little time left to watch the news now and then."

"Don't you dare torment me about Adam O'Connor, Jem Fisher. You brought that wretch right into my house."

"And I suppose I twisted your arm into sleeping with him?"

"Jem!"

He chuckled softly. "Hey, the poor fellow didn't have a chance the last time he was here. He would have had to be dead to resist you, the way you went after him."

"Jem Fisher, that's terrible."

"Samantha Carlyle, that's the truth!"

"Will you just go—go eat a doughnut or something!"

"We can use him here now," Jem said quietly. Then he smiled and started down the stairs.

Sam looked after him thoughtfully for a moment. He was right. Maybe she did need Adam now.

And maybe he had been right in other ways. Maybe a lot of what had happened had been her fault.

She turned, still thoughtful, and tapped at Yancy's door. There was no answer. She tried the knob. It was open.

She tiptoed into the room.

Brian was in his crib, sleeping away. He looked so sweet, in fact, that Sam experienced one of those little surges of panic that he might not be breathing. She gently set a hand on his back, then smiled. He was breathing quite nicely.

She turned and tiptoed to Yancy's bed. Yancy, too, was asleep. Deeply asleep. The covers were practically over her head.

"Yancy?" Sam whispered.

"Umm."

"I don't mean to wake you, but do you need anything? Are you all right?"

"Hmm... tired."

"Okay, get some sleep. I'll see you later."

Sam quietly left the room, closing the door firmly behind her.

When Sam had gone, Yancy sat up. Emotion began to shake her. Sobs, laughter. Laughter, sobs.

Oh, God....

Sam....

Soon, Sam, soon....

Adam watched Sam as they motored out to the dive site at the Steps. It was a beautiful day. There might be a storm coming, perhaps presaged by the very calm that seemed to sit upon the water, but it made for great conditions today.

Sam didn't get much of a chance to reflect upon their trip. She was seated in the back of the *Sloop Bee*, an arm casually around Darlene's shoulders as she tried very hard to explain that though it wasn't impossible for a great white to be swimming in their warm tropical waters, it *was* unlikely. She was also trying to explain how the sharks who attacked people usually did so because they were attracted by blood or perhaps, on occasion, by the swimming, kicking motion of legs that dangled into the water. Divers were another case. They were beneath the surface, face to face with the sea's great predators.

Darlene listened, wide-eyed.

It was fun to watch Sam with the little girl. Sam was a natural, Adam thought.

"There are dangers everywhere, Darlene."

"Right," Brad said. "I mean, houses fall on people. Things fall out of buildings. You can walk down a street and a big truck can hit you, right?"

Adam arched a brow at Brad, then decided that making the water appealing again for Darlene might be better than trying to convince her that she was going to meet a grisly end on solid ground.

"You know, when you become a more advanced diver, Darlene, there are more wrecks to see. There's an old English ship, a man-of-war, that went down in about one hundred and twenty-five feet of water another hour's ride out from the Steps."

"A man-of-war?" Brad said.

"She was called *Our Lady of Mercy.* She was a ship in the English Navy. She went down in 1813—after a battle with the American ship *Tallymar*. The English ship was more powerful, but the *Tallymar*'s guns caught her just right, and down she went. Treasure hunters over the years since have dredged up most of what was of value on her, but she's a great wreck to dive. You can almost imagine what she was like when she was under sail. Her figurehead is in a museum in Salem, Massachusetts, but one of the cruise ship companies put a copy of it back on her. Say, do you know why they call English sailors, and sometimes just Englishmen, limeys?''

"I didn't know that they did call them limeys," Darlene said mournfully.

Adam grinned. "Ships' doctors back then didn't understand about vitamin C, but they did realize that men got scurvy when they were kept from fresh fruit and vegetables too long. Limes lasted, and they were easy to purchase in any tropical port. English sailors were frequently given limes, so they became limeys."

"Yeah, and the officers used to drink like fish, young man!" Liam Hinnerman added. "Water got bad on the ships quickly, turned green with slime. Didn't matter to the bigwigs in charge if the ordinary seamen drank scum. Those officers, they kept all the liquor around that they could."

"Sounds smart to me," Sukee commented.

"Ah, it was a rough life," Hinnerman continued. He had a look in his eye that said he was going to tell

Brad about something bloody. "A British sailor often went to sea for a few square meals, but his meals were filled with weevils and maggots. Know one of the ways they got rid of the maggots that had gotten into their biscuits? They put a dead fish on top of the biscuits. The maggots crawled right for it. They kept putting in dead fish until all the maggots were gone."

Sam looked at Adam and grimaced.

Darlene was looking a little green again, but Brad was fascinated.

"Being a sailor was hard," Adam told Darlene. "They could punish men harshly for fairly minor infractions of the rules. One of the things they did was called 'flogging around the fleet.' The poor fellow was tied standing in one of the small boats, his back bared, and the boatswain's mates from his fleet lashed him twenty-four times each. If there were a lot of ships, he could wind up with more than three hundred lashes."

"He would die!" Darlene protested.

"He often did," Adam told her. "If he survived, it was said that he had been given a 'checkered shirt,' because the lashes on his back crisscrossed in red ribbons and looked like a checked shirt."

"I'm glad I didn't live back then."

"Yeah," her mother teased, tousling her hair. "Now moms and dads have a bad time giving a kid a spanking! Not that children should be abused...."

"But a good spanking now and then seems in order to me," Liam Hinnerman said, eyes glittering.

"Want to hear a funny one?" Adam asked Darlene.

"The seamen weren't allowed to smoke—the fire hazard was too dangerous. They chewed tobacco instead. They were supposed to spit their tobacco into something called a spit kid. When they spat on the deck instead, their punishment was to have the spit kid tied around their necks. Then their shipmates were allowed to use them for a tobacco-spitting target."

"Ugh. That's gross!" Darlene said. But she grinned suddenly. "Brad would make a good target."

"Maybe."

Sam stood suddenly. She looked tense. "Suit up time," she said. "We've got lots of company today."

They did have company, Adam saw. At least half a dozen dive boats were anchored around the site, their flags waving. Beautiful weather, Adam thought.

The calm before the storm.

"Everybody buddied up?" Sam asked. Jem had cut the motor on the *Sloop Bee,* and was dropping the anchor.

"Joey and me forever!" Sue Emerson said happily.

"We expected nothing less," Sukee murmured.

"I've got my honey today," Liam said, lifting Jerry's hand. Poor Jerry. She was very pale. Well, maybe she had a right to be. Adam made a mental note to keep a good eye on the pair.

"Thank God!" Jim Santino said, flipping back his hair. "I get a woman today! Sam—"

"I've got Darlene," Sam said.

"There's me," Sukee offered dryly.

"So there is!" Jim murmured.

"Mr. O'Connor?" Brad said.

"Fine. You got me, kid." Good. That made it a foursome—Darlene and Brad, Sam and himself.

He had to find a few minutes to get off on his own. And come tomorrow, he was going to have to get out here alone somehow.

Well, not alone.

With Sam.

"If we're all buddied up, let's take the dive. We have lots of time. Don't forget, though—you especially, my talented new students," Sam told the kids, smiling, "to always keep an eye on your air and your time. Right?"

"Right. But I'm with you," Darlene said.

"Still . . ." Sam began.

"Still, if a big shark came along and ate Sam, you'd want to survive on your own, right?" Liam asked her politely.

"No big shark is coming along," Adam said evenly. Liam Hinnerman was the kind of man who deserved a hard right to the jaw.

But this wasn't the time or the place, and Hinnerman could probably also hit back. No matter. One to his kisser would be worth whatever he dished out in return.

"Divers in the water!" Jem called.

Suits on, masks on, fins, vests and cylinders, they entered the water. It was a familiar realm for Adam. A world he loved. Moving slowly, neutralizing the natural squeezes that occurred with the pressure as man moved deeper into the sea. In his work, he'd dived rivers, lakes, creeks, streams and canals, as well as dozens of different places in the ocean. Nothing was so beautiful as the tropical and semitropical sea. The reefs with their teeming, multicolored life, sea fans waving, anemones, tubes and more. Brad pointed to an outcropping of fire coral, bloodred, beautiful, painfully dangerous. They enjoyed its beauty and steered clear of it.

Following Sam and Darlene.

Following the Steps.

Twenty feet down, twenty-five feet. The air from their regulators bubbled around them, making a soft, constant sound within the watery world. Thirty feet, thirty-five feet. Forty feet, forty-five. Fifty. Fifty-five.

Sam had stopped at one of the Steps, studying it. Darlene paused with her. Adam pointed out the step to Brad, and they swam toward it. Adam caught Sam's eyes beneath the glass of her mask. Framed there, a deep beautiful green. Her hair flared out, redder in the water. As red as the fire coral, or so it seemed. He motioned to Brad, drawing her attention to the boy. She frowned, alarmed to realize that he was about to move out on his own.

Alarmed...

Or curious. Determined to know what he was doing.

She couldn't follow. He quickly left her with the children, kicking his fins hard against the water to reach the cliff and the last step embedded there.

The step where he had previously found the gold watch.

Hank's watch.

He kept his eye out for the other divers as he swam, mentally counting off those in his party, trying to make certain they were all involved in their own explorations. Jerry and Liam, Sukee and Jim, the Emersons, the Walkers. They were all present and accounted for, all looking around.

Searching?

He kicked his way deeper, following the cliff face. The drop-off brought the ocean floor from a mere sixty feet to deeper than a hundred. He sank deeper still, studying the ragged edges of coral and rock along the way.

The watery world grew darker as he went ever downward.

He blinked suddenly, certain he had seen a light. It couldn't be a light, logic told him. A reflection, perhaps.

Reflecting from what?

The world was silent, other than his air bubbles and the constant rhythm of his breathing. The light...

Flickered. Somewhere within the coral shelf. He moved along. Slowly, carefully.

The light, hazy in the shadowy darkness, flickered and blinked. He moved closer. Closer.

Bubbles. There were bubbles other than his own. Ahead of him. His muscles tensed. Someone was diving within the catacomb of coral. He moved closer, closer. He slipped through a break in the reef.

There was a diver ahead of him. A diver with his back to him and a light focused on the coral surrounding them. A lone diver, deep in a world of shadow.

Adam reached to his calf for his diving knife, tensed and ready.

The diver sensed Adam's presence and turned with a defensive swirl, his own knife raised.

Adam met the diver's eyes.

He gasped, stunned. Choked.

And the knife slipped from his suddenly frozen fingers and drifted endlessly downward to the shadowy depths below.

12

Where the hell had Adam gone?

Sam remained with the children, having little choice. But she couldn't see Adam.

Minutes ticked by. Five, ten, fifteen. Twenty. She glanced at her computer, checking the time remaining until they had to surface. How deep had he gone? How much air was he using? Was he going to need a long decompression time?

Was he going to come back up?

Sheer panic seemed to seize her heart. She hadn't had the sense to be alarmed at first when her father had disappeared. And she hadn't even panicked when Hank had first come up missing; lightning didn't strike twice.

But it had. And this might be the third time.

She waited miserably in the water, trying to pretend that everything was all right, forcing herself to remember that she was responsible for two innocent children. Crabs scuttled by; shrimp shot past. A friendly grouper brushed against her, startling her.

Darlene tugged her in one direction to see a magnificent ray floating by, majestically cloaked and graceful. Brad found a silver barracuda hulking in the coral. Darlene jerked them away from the barracuda.

More minutes passed.

Sam watched for Adam, trying at the same time to watch for the other divers. Liam and Jerry. Sukee and Jim. The Walkers. The Emersons.

They all seemed to disappear, yet when she looked again, they had reappeared.

This was crazy.

Crazy.

She needed to dive alone with Jem and Adam.

She needed to look for the *Beldona*.

Just when she might truly have begun to panic about Adam's disappearance, he materialized. Brad was pointing to a large blue fish swimming over from behind them. Darlene was suddenly by her side, gripping Sam's arms so tightly that Sam thought the teenager's nails might rip through her suit.

The fish was a shark. A blue, Sam thought. Perhaps five or six feet long, magnified by the water. It cruised closer to them.

She slipped an arm around Darlene, holding her steady. She felt the girl shaking.

The shark, she thought, must smell the girl's fear.

But the animal behaved in a natural fashion, swimming toward them, glassy eyes on them, sleek body cutting the water smoothly.

It took a good look at them.

Veered.

And swam by.

Darlene was still shaking. She burst away from Sam, kicking hard to reach the surface, fifty-five feet over their heads.

Sam shot up, catching Darlene by the legs, pulling her down. She shook her head sternly, indicating that they had to rise slowly. Darlene blinked and seemed to bring herself under control.

That was when Adam appeared, taking Darlene's hand. A second later Brad was with them, and as a foursome, they slowly made a proper ascent.

They were the first to reboard the dive boat. Freed from her heavy gear, Darlene began to gasp again. "Did you see it? It was huge! Ten feet—"

"Honey, that shark was no more than six feet, tops," Adam told her. "The water magnifies what we see."

"A shark. It was a shark. Just like the ones that ate all those men in World War Two."

"Darlene, it was a blue. It took a look at us, and it said, 'People, yuck. Way too much body fat in those suckers!' And it swam by, because the sea is full of delicious fish."

"But it was there, in the water—"

"Water is where sharks live," Adam said.

Sam stood in front of Darlene and asked her sternly, "First rule of scuba?"

Darlene swallowed guiltily. "It was a shark."

"First rule of scuba?"

"Breathe continuously."

"Right. Second rule?"

"Regain control, respond, react."

"Right. It was a shark. And we've talked a lot about sharks, and about seeing sharks in the water. It looked at you, you looked at it—it swam away. Right?"

Darlene swallowed again. "Yeah. We're not diving again today, right?"

"Oh, man, she's really going to be a 'fraidy cat now!" Brad moaned. "Right when things were getting so neat!"

"You leave me alone, Brad Walker!" Darlene threatened.

"What's going on?" Judy Walker asked, climbing aboard, dripping water as Jem helped her off with her equipment. "Oh, no, Lew. Darlene *did* see the shark," she said to her husband, who was climbing the ladder behind her. "You're not going to be afraid now, are you, honey?"

Darlene was stubbornly silent for a minute.

"There's no need to be afraid," Sam said quietly.

"I . . ." Darlene paused, puzzled by the answer she seemed to come up with in her own mind. "No, I'm not afraid." She looked at Sam triumphantly. "We stared it down, right? Isn't that right, Mr. O'Connor?"

"Sure is. Something like that, anyway. If it had come closer, one of us would have bumped it on the nose with a dive light. They don't like being bumped on their noses."

Liam Hinnerman was up by then. "Hey, kid, do you know where we got the word shark?"

Darlene shook her head.

"It came from the German word *schurke*. It was a word for a land creature—man. It means 'greedy parasite.'"

"Hey, that's cool!" Brad laughed.

"Yeah," Darlene agreed.

"And it's not going to stop you from diving, right, sweetheart?" her father said. Lew Walker looked at Sam as he spoke. "Especially when you can go down with Miss Carlyle and see the underwater world through her eyes."

He was looking at her peculiarly, Sam thought.

Schurkes.

Sharks.

She felt for a moment as if she was surrounded by greedy parasites. Who was innocent? Who was not?

She glanced at Adam.

Even Adam had a peculiar look about him. Perhaps the most peculiar look.

Just who was this "private concern" he was working for?

She shivered suddenly, looking around. Liam Hinnerman—hammerhead. Jim Santino—tiger shark. Joey Emerson—white tip. Sukee—mako. Lew Walker—a blue.

And Adam...

If Adam was a shark, he would be a damned great white. Deadly.

And the way he was looking at her now...

She was definitely surrounded by sharks.

Adam remained in an odd mood as they docked and left the *Sloop Bee.*

He remained close by her side, but he seemed completely withdrawn.

"I know what you found," she told him as they entered her cottage.

"What?" he demanded, startled, staring at her, his gray eyes sharp.

"You disappeared for a long time. You must have found the *Beldona,* right? She's just over the cliff. We've been staring straight at her for years, but we've simply never noticed her. Hundreds of divers swim over her and never see her, right."

"No, I didn't find the *Beldona,*" he told her.

"Then..."

"I went exploring the sides of that coral shelf. It plunges down at least another thirty feet, you know."

She nodded. "Yes, but there's nothing to see there, just sand and rock and water. No pretty vegetation. Just...nothing."

"You have nitrox on the island, don't you?"

Sam frowned, studying him. Sport divers never used pure oxygen; at depths past thirty-three feet it became toxic. Generally sport divers used a mixture of compressed air that was twenty percent oxygen and eighty percent nitrogen. The nitrogen, however, could produce a narcotic effect at depths of a hundred feet or more. Nitrox was a combination air that prevented that hallucinatory buildup. Sam never used it for the cylinders the guests used, but she and Jem sometimes used it when they went to greater depths with experienced friends who came to the island.

"Do you have it or not?"

"Of course."

"Good."

"Why?"

"I was thinking of making a few deeper dives."

Sam hesitated. "You did find the ship."

"No, I didn't find the ship."

He said it so strangely.

"Adam, what the hell is going on? Are you lying to me? Did you find something connected to that damn ship?"

"I'm not lying. I didn't find the ship."

"You think you can find her, though."

"I don't know. I'd just like to dive a little deeper, that's all." He stared straight at her. "I think I'll shower."

She arched a brow. "This is my cottage, you're refusing to tell me what's going on, and now you think you'll shower."

"Okay, then, you go ahead and shower."

Baffled and irritated, Sam left him in the hallway.

"I'll make some coffee," he called after her. "When we're all set, let's head over to the main house and your father's office. I want to read through some of those diaries and logbooks again."

She slipped out of her suit and turned on the water in the shower. The fresh warmth rinsing away the salt from her body felt delicious. She dimly heard that Adam had turned on the news. She closed her eyes, leaning back, just feeling the water.

Why was he acting so strangely?

Why was he lying to her?

Just who in hell was he working for?

Her eyes flew open when she felt him step in behind her, sweeping his arms around her, drawing her close against him. The water splashed over her breasts, then over his hands. He rubbed his palms sensually down her rib cage and her belly, fingers splayed. Lower down over her abdomen, the gentle pressure became sweetly erotic. Step away, she told herself. Protest intimacy without honesty.

But then he spoke.

"I wonder if you ever knew just how deeply I was in love with you?" he said.

"Ah. But you were also in love with Becky."

"I was seeing Becky. I was involved with Becky. I told you I was no innocent. You were determined to win whatever you set out to get in those days. What you wanted was me. You didn't ask questions, and when you got answers anyway, you didn't want them."

"You could have—"

"I could have what? I wondered at the time if I was some kind of practice for you. Look at him, full-grown, definitely male. Test your powers. Look, touch, crook a finger. Get what you want. Use him. Then just shoot him when he doesn't turn out to be exactly what you thought."

He was saying these things to her, bitterly, with his hands still on her.

She closed her fingers around his. Wanting to stop their movement. Wanting to stop wanting him.

He held her more tightly against him. "I really was in love, you know. I didn't want to be. I resisted."

"Like hell. I wasn't that good, I didn't know what I was doing."

"You knew exactly what you were doing."

"You know that's a lie—"

"I know I was your first experiment. You had damned good instincts."

"You could have said that you were living with someone."

"We weren't actually living together at the time. We'd had a fight. She'd gone to her sister's."

"It was hard to tell you'd been fighting when she arrived on the island. The first time I saw her, she had her tongue down your throat. And that wasn't an hour after..."

"An hour after," he mused, his voice very strange. "An hour after. Everything so perfect, and then... Well, perfect can change quickly, can't it?"

"What are you talking about?"

"Nothing."

"If you'd wanted to explain something to her, don't you think it would have been a lot easier if your mouth hadn't been quite so full with her tongue?"

"Right. She comes out here because she's worried about me, she heard about the case and I haven't appeared back home. Before she sets foot on dry land, I'm supposed to shout at her to get away, someone else has entered my life? I knew I was going to hurt her one

way or the other. I wanted to be a little gentle about
it.''

"A passionate kiss is always gentle."

"I wasn't kissing her. She was kissing me."

"But resistance isn't your strong point?"

She thought she'd angered him. He was silent for
several seconds. "Sam, other than rather brutally dis-
engaging myself, I couldn't do much at the time. I was
hoping to talk to her. And I didn't realize you were
there."

"Obviously."

He released her suddenly and stepped out of the
shower. The water continued to run over Samantha as
she still stood there, at a loss. She hadn't meant to
push so hard—yes, perhaps she had. She wanted an
admission from him. She wanted to hear him say that
he had been completely wrong. She was free from
guilt.

She hadn't wanted him to walk away just now, she
realized. She'd wanted him to keep trying his best to
earn her forgiveness.

She turned off the shower and wrapped herself in a
large towel, then padded to the kitchen. He'd made
coffee; it sat ready, letting off a pleasant aroma. But
he wasn't in the kitchen.

She walked down the hallway, pausing at her bedroom door. Adam was stretched out on her bed, a

white bath towel wrapped around his hips. He was staring at the ceiling. Thinking? Waiting? Both?

She walked slowly to the bed, arms crossed over her chest as she stared at him. His fingers were laced behind his head. He met her eyes.

"Has it ever occurred to you that maybe we were both just a little bit wrong?" he asked gravely.

She started to shake her head; then he was suddenly on his feet, moving like a panther, catching her by the waist and flinging her down on the bed where he straddled her. "No lies. Let's go back. You were ripe. You—"

"Ripe!" she protested. "Now that should sweep me right off my feet. You're making me sound like a banana."

"Ripe. Like a piece of fruit. Just ready to be plucked."

"It sounds awful."

"It's the exact word. Lots of women your age were already married, with children. The island offered slim pickings for a woman looking for a little experience."

"And you were the best of those slim pickings?" she demanded.

He nodded.

"Get off me!"

"Admit it."

She shook her head.

"You were ripe. You needed a man in your life. From the minute you saw me, you wanted sex."

"I did not, I—"

"You wanted to be fu—"

"Don't you dare say that!"

"Okay, but it won't matter. It won't change the truth."

"I didn't just decide that I was old enough and about to rot and that I needed sex. I wanted—I wanted—" She broke off.

"What, damn you? Say it!"

"I wanted *you,*" she whispered painfully.

He groaned suddenly. A deep groan that reverberated in his chest, tensed and tautened the length of him. He lay against her, enveloping her in his arms, holding her against him with both the greatest strength and the greatest tenderness. His lips brushed her forehead, found the pulse at her throat, pressed against the pounding there that grew ever more fierce with each millisecond slipping by. Again his lips brushed her forehead, and his whispers fanned her cheeks, her face, her earlobe. "I wanted you. I knew I was wrong, in a way, but by the time we actually made love, I wanted you so much that I would have risked the eternal fires of hell for one hour with you. Naked, of course. But I would have been willing to burn forever for my sins, for that damned hour. Except, of course, love is never so simple. I got more than an hour, and I didn't go to hell—not yet, anyway. But I didn't know how to tell you then that I was already involved with someone, that I needed a chance to explain to the woman I'd been living with that it was over, because I had fallen in love. Then she was suddenly here.''

''With her tongue down your throat,'' Sam interjected softly, tears stinging her eyes. Silly. They'd both been wrong. So wrong.

''You could have given me a chance.''

''I could have,'' she said.

''But you didn't.''

She smiled slowly, ruefully. ''I was too proud. And I felt like too big a fool. I'd never known anything like you. Never.''

''Maybe we were both a little wrong.''

''Maybe a lot wrong.''

''Both of us.''

''You were wrong, too?''

''Oh, God, yes. Wrong not to insist on you knowing there had been someone. Wrong not to tell Becky about you the second I saw her, even if it did hurt her. Most of all, I was wrong to leave, wrong not to fight for you. Wrong to let something as pathetic as pride make me walk away from you, when I should have realized what you saw and what you thought. I was just as mad at myself. I've paid for what I did since. More than you can know.''

"You've really missed me, remembered me, all this time?"

"I've really missed you."

"There have been other women."

"Yes. But not like you. There have been other men on the island."

"You're referring to Hank Jennings again?"

He made a strange sound at the back of his throat. Irritated, fierce.

"Why the hell are we still talking about the past?" he demanded with sudden anger. "This is now. And, Miss Carlyle, I do want you now."

His mouth moved down on to hers then. Hard. Almost brutal. Tongue filling the void, stroking her teeth, her lips and her tongue, hungrily, kissing again and again, openmouthed, deeper, deeper, ever more insinuating. The towels tangled between them. He wasn't exactly straddling her anymore, he was atop her, limbs burning against her, sex hot, hard, vibrant, against her abdomen, her thighs, stroking against her flesh with his every movement as he kissed her again...again. Her arms encircled him, tried to hold him. She kissed him passionately in return. Missed his mouth. Found his throat, his shoulders. She dug her fingers into his back, stroked the length of it with her nails, trailed her fingers along his spine, rounded his buttocks. But he was moving against her, and he was more powerful, one hand on her breast, kneading it, cupping it, holding it up to the tantalizing torment of his mouth, his lips closing around it, tongue edging against the nipple, laving the areola, teeth grazing. She strained against him, her fingers curling into the dark thickness of his hair. His tongue trailed the length of her side as his hand slipped beneath her thigh. His fingers stroked the length of it over and over, while the searingly subtle stroke of his tongue bathed her abdomen, delved into her navel. She began to burn, aching for him to touch her more deeply. Hunger gnawed at her, urging her to arch and writhe against him, to whisper his name, to whisper the truth.

"Adam, you were right. I did everything I could to get you. I didn't want to know about any other woman. I didn't want you to have a past. I wanted *you.*"

Fool, Adam taunted himself. *Fool!*

They were talking about honesty, about feelings, now.

Wanted. The key word. Wanted, yes. He'd wanted her then. He wanted her now. He spoke honestly of the past while the present remained a lie. No, not a lie, exactly. An omission of the truth. And when she knew...

But that was the point, wasn't it? Have her, hold her, love her. Sink into the cauldron of desire, of hunger, of wanting. Hold as tight and fast to the intimacy, to the tenderness, to the passion, hold tight and fight the honesty that would have to come.

Down to the basics of it.

God, yes, he wanted her.

And she might not want him later.

He rose above her, finding her lips, kissing her, whispering just above them.

"Wanted? Did you say that you *wanted* me? Past tense? Tell me about the present."

He watched her lips. Watched their fullness, the sensuality, watched the smile that curved them. "Wanted...want," she promised breathlessly.

"Want?"

"Want."

Odd, the things a man remembered about a woman. There was laughter, yes. A smile, a look, a touch. Her scent had lived with him. Unique. Both subtle and distinctive. She used a very softly scented soap, and it was a part of the mixture. She smelled of the freshness of a sea breeze. Somehow she was sweet, somehow musky, always evocative. He loved to bury himself against her, against that scent, against her flesh. Taste her, feel her, breathe her. Know her. Touch, stroke, intimately invade. Feel her response, the quickening of her breath, the undulation of her body, beginning within, touching him, rousing him. There were moments in life to hold fast, to savor....

Lips, breasts. The red thatch, as sensual as the woman. What lay within it. Touch, play, feel the warmth, caress. Find each tiny spot of absolute sensitivity. Watch her face. Feel her move. Caress anew with fingers, lips, tongue ... feel the fever grow until it was unbearable, until there was nothing left but to sink within her, deeper. Nothing left but to drown within her, to feel the all-encompassing warmth, the agony and the ecstasy, the hunger that escalated, the urgency, the bursting, imploding, exploding, sleek, wet, searing, inhaling, exhaling, the tension, straining ... and all the while, her.

The scent, the feel, the touch. The length of her limbs, the silk of her flesh, dampened, glistening with sweat. The sound of her whispers, gasps, moans.

He braced himself as the sudden bursting thrust of his climax seized him, slamming deeply inside of her. Once, again, again. A soft, gentle warmth spilled over him after the violence as the warmth of his own seed filled her.

And Samantha ...

He held her against him, realizing that he hadn't closed his eyes for a full second throughout. He'd watched her face. Watched the dark flame of her hair, fanning out, tangling on the pillow.

He'd watched her eyes as they glazed, narrowed, closed. Watched her mouth, her breathing, her breasts. The sheen upon her body.

He fell to her side at last, staring at the ceiling. Then he pulled her against him, kissing the top of her head, feeling the soft brush of her hair against his chin.

She raised her head, meeting his eyes. "Who are you working for, Adam?" she demanded.

He tensed, trying to keep her from realizing that he had done so.

"Well, hell, I must be losing my touch. Great sex, but no whispers or sighs or even a warm silence. Just a 'Who are you working for, Adam?'"

"If I recall correctly, once I was naked and vulnerable and drifting in a nice little niche of pleasure, you were quick to ask me if I'd shared my sex life with another man."

"I was never so blunt."

"Damned close. So who are you working for?" Sam demanded.

"Always a question from you. You think I should answer you, but you never give me any answers. I don't recall you ever answering me about your relationship with Hank Jennings. Am I here in his place?"

She smiled wryly. "Whoa. Testy question."

"What's the answer?"

"I loved Hank."

He started to roll away from her.

"Like a brother."

He paused, his back to her. "What did you say?" he demanded huskily.

"I considered Hank to be one of the finest men I had ever met. He was caring, concerned, intelligent. Loyal, gentle, kind. Who are you working for, Adam?"

"You loved him like a brother. Now, I hope that means you didn't sleep with him."

"Who are you working for, Adam?"

"You're answering a question with another question again, Sam."

"I know. What did you find in the water the other day?"

"You are annoyingly persistent."

"It's my island, remember?"

"Your bedroom," he said agreeably.

"Adam..."

She suddenly found herself drawn into his arms. His eyes, glittering silver with intensity, searched hers. "I promise I'll tell you soon."

"That's not an answer."

"But you don't give me any answers, either."

"Maybe we don't trust each other enough yet."

"I do trust you, I just... Do me a favor."

"What?" Sam asked cautiously.

"Pretend that the world is perfect. Just for a few more minutes."

"Why?"

"Because I love you, Samantha."

"What?" she whispered.

"I love you. I know the world isn't perfect. It's gone straight to hell around here, and we don't know what's going on. I think that secrets may start opening up like a summer shower, and I want to hold on to something very special between us right now. Something unique, something you don't get many opportunities to touch, to feel, in a lifetime. Years ago I fell in love with a wild red-haired siren with a temper to match. I had too much pride to insist that you listen to me, that you love me back. I broke it off with Becky when I left here and I admit, I kept trying to fall in love with other people after that. Even when I came here, I told myself that I wasn't going to want you, wasn't going to touch you. I was determined to keep my dick in my dive suit, my mind on my own business. The concept of not touching you went out the window the minute I saw you. Time and distance can change everything. I shouldn't even have known you anymore. But I touched you, and I love you. And it seems we've still got a long hard road ahead of us, so right now, I'd appreciate it very much if you would love the hell out of me for just a few more minutes."

For long seconds Sam just stared at him. In a thousand years, she never would have expected such a declaration.

"Sam?"

She didn't answer him. Instead she pulled his head down and kissed him.

And kissed him.

And forgot all about cocktail hour completely.

It was time to see Sam. No help for it. He had to pay a visit to Sam.

He could take no more chances.

He'd learned a few lessons.

He carried a Smith & Wesson thirty-two calibre thrust in the shoulder holster beneath his dark jacket.

An unfortunate necessity, he thought grimly.

Just as the shadows and the night were necessary.

He waited for darkness to fall, then walked quickly and silently across the island. He stuck to the shadows and the bushes as he approached her cottage, and he kept a determined eye out.

He saw no one.

One dilemma still remained. He had to get to her without frightening her. He had to find a way to get close to her before she could scream.

Silence. He had to keep moving in silence. Dead silence. Around the cottage, listening carefully, watching. He could easily see into the front of the cottage. The drapes hadn't been drawn over the living room windows. It was empty, as the kitchen beyond seemed to be, as well.

For a moment he thought that she might have left the cottage for the main house. Not yet, he decided.

He would have seen her, heard her. Their paths would have crossed. No. She was there. He was certain of it.

He tried the front door, twisting the knob slowly, carefully.

Silently.

It was securely locked.

Fine. He would have to try another way. He kept moving. Around to her bedroom. He heard movement. Voices.

Voices....

The drapes were drawn here, but there was a slim space at the far right side of the windows where light was escaping into the night. He ducked down, one with the shadows, trying to see what she was doing.

And with whom.

He saw her back. Long, sleek, beautiful. Naked. Saw the fall of her hair, deep, rich, fire red, flowing down her back, swaying....

He saw the movement of her hips. Saw the man beneath her.

She was...

Making love.

With Adam.

Adam O'Connor.

He leaned against the wall of her cottage, gritting his teeth.

13

Liam was out on the porch, drinking.

He'd been drinking since they'd come in from the dive earlier.

At least, Jerry thought that he had. She hadn't actually seen him. He hadn't bothered her, and she had been grateful.

She had certainly been determined to keep her distance from him. She'd spent the time doing the usual things. Showering. Rubbing lotion into her skin. Putting polish on her nails. Trying not to think.

She prayed instead. Prayed that Liam would stay on the porch until it was time to go to the main house. Praying that she could just walk away.

Funny. Once she had thought she could actually do just that. But she couldn't.

And she knew it now.

She was brushing her hair when he came in at last. Still in his trunks, smelling like sea and salt and whiskey. She tried not to wrinkle her nose when he walked by. She thought he was heading for the bathroom.

He walked to her instead.

"Bitch," he muttered.

She took a step back, looking downward, still moving the brush through her hair.

"I went diving," she reminded him. "I dove the damn Steps."

She cried out when he suddenly backhanded her so hard that she was flung across the room. She hit the wall and slid down the length of it, shaking.

He knew how to hit. It was a talent, actually.

Her lip was cut, bleeding. A little trickle fell down her chin. She quickly caught it with her finger, staring at Liam. He walked to her, standing over her. He pulled her up by the hair.

"You're going diving again. This time, you're finding the way in."

"Let go of me, you bastard."

He hit her again.

She started to laugh. "You don't dare hit me too hard. You could find yourself thrown right off this island."

"I don't think so. What right would Miss Carlyle have to interfere with a domestic dispute? Would you really ever want her to know?"

Jerry stared at him, hating him, wondering how she had ever thought she could use him toward her own ends. Foolish. She'd made so many mistakes in her life. So damned many.

Suddenly both his hands were in her hair, pulling painfully. "You will dive again. You will dive, or you will get hurt. And when I'm through hurting you . . ."

It was Liam's turn to smile. "When I'm through hurting you, I'll hurt her, as well. Badly. Anything that happened to her before will just be child's play, understand?"

Jerry stared at him.

He hit her one last time for good measure.

"Understand?"

"I understand."

"Now, next time we dive, what are you going to do?"

"Find the *Beldona*," she said tonelessly.

He slammed her against the wall, then walked away. She sank to the floor.

He was good at hitting people. But he might have left a few bruises this time. She would have to do her makeup again. She was going to have to do her makeup again anyway.

Everything on her was running.

Silent tears were sliding down her cheeks.

Not because he had hurt her. He really couldn't hurt her. Not really. She'd managed to hurt herself enough.

And he probably couldn't hurt Sam. Sam had Adam. Jerry smiled despite her tears. Maybe Sam and Adam would never make it, but Adam wouldn't let anything happen to Sam. Neither would Jem. Sam was going to be okay.

Oh, God. Sam had to be okay.

Especially if Jerry did as she was told.

And still...

The tears kept falling silently down her face. Danger remained for them all, but she wasn't crying because of the danger.

She was crying because of what she had become.

And because she didn't want Sam to know what she might have been....

It was late, Sam thought. Very late. She should have been at the main house a long time ago. She was completely falling apart as a hostess on her own island. Did it matter? Half her guests were obviously involved in some manner of intrigue.

Adam seemed suspicious of them, as well. So were they all guilty? Of what? And if they were guilty of some evil in life, did it mean that they had come to Seafire Isle with evil designs?

This was a vacation destination, and even crooks took vacations.

She stretched, realizing that, curled in Adam's arms, she had dozed. Now, glancing at her watch, she discovered just how late it was. Nearly seven-thirty. With a groan, she moved her hand over the bed, seeking Adam.

But Adam was gone.

He would be nearby, though, she was certain of it. And though it was late, she stretched again, smiling, and for long moments she allowed herself the luxury of enjoying what they had shared.

The intimacy.

The words.

And still . . .

All the trust that should have been there wasn't. He still wanted to know about Hank Jennings.

At first she'd been glad that he wondered.

Now she just wanted an exchange of information. Especially since there really was nothing to tell him about Hank Jennings.

Hank had come to the island as a student. He'd pitched in to help with anything any time his help was needed. He had talked about her father for hours on end.

She had even told him some of the stories she knew about the *Beldona*.

He'd become like a brother to her, always entirely decent, honest, gentle, kind, smart. And he'd fallen in love with Yancy. Yancy had tried hard not to fall in love back—she'd been convinced that interracial marriages didn't work, and it didn't matter that she was biracial herself. "You don't understand, Sam, because you're like Hank—you don't want to understand. One drop of black blood and a woman is black.''

''But who cares, if you and Hank don't?''

''The world cares,'' Yancy had insisted. ''Eventually, I'd hurt him.''

''You wouldn't.''

''I would. I wish I didn't think it was so.''

''I wish you'd believe enough in Hank.''

Hank asked Yancy daily to marry him. Yancy turned him down daily. Hank persisted, insisting to Sam that he would wear Yancy down eventually. The three of them and Jem did everything together. Picnic, swim, dive. Watch tapes on the VCR, listen to music, dance, discuss the world at large, the sea . . .

The *Beldona*.

She hated that ship. He had been so excited listening to her talk about it. She'd given him information and he'd used it.

And then he'd disappeared.

Yancy had had her baby soon after Hank disappeared. They all adored Brian, but Yancy refused to let anyone in Hank's family know about the baby's existence. ''It's better that way. It's the way I want it. He's my baby. I'll love him. You'll love him. Jem will act as his dad. We'll make it this way, and that's that.''

It still hurt that Hank was gone. It hurt because she *had* loved him, though not the way Adam so clearly thought, and because Yancy had been in so much pain, and because Brian didn't have his father.

It hurt because she blamed the ship. *Beldona*. And herself, for telling him about it.

It was getting later and later, she reminded herself.

She rose quickly, finding her towel on the floor, slipping it around her. She looked for Adam and came upon him in the living room. He was showered and dressed. She didn't think that he'd left her alone so he could go get fresh clothing, and the realization that he and Jem had moved him in here so completely without her knowledge was both reassuring and annoying. He was staring at the charts on the wall.

"Adam, it's late. You should have woken me."

He glanced at her, smiling, tall, dark, very handsome in his casual suit. "I thought you needed the sleep."

"I thought you liked to talk to the others at cocktail hour and try to draw out all their secrets."

He shrugged. "We have to dive alone. That's our only hope."

"Our hope of what?"

"Finding the *Beldona*."

He was staring pointedly at the chart of the island.

"What if I don't want to find the *Beldona*?" she asked him quietly.

He looked from the chart to her. "I figured you didn't want to find the ship," he said softly. "Because if you *had* wanted to find it, you would have."

She shook her head. "That isn't true. But it doesn't matter. She's a wretched ship. She destroys lives."

He shook his head firmly. "That ship is an inanimate object. It destroys nothing. Men destroyed your father's life. And the *Beldona* may provide the clue to finding out what happened. Besides, even more is at stake now. Remember? Hank Jennings disappeared, too. You were attacked. Unless you want me on your tail night and day for the rest of your life, we've got to find out what happened."

She thought about that, lowering her lashes. It wasn't actually so bad to have him on her tail.

Telling her that he had been in love with her. That he still loved her. That he wanted her.

Making love to her. Holding her....

But she could feel it just the same—tension was growing on Seafire Isle. Like the pressure that came with a storm. She was in danger. He couldn't guard her every moment of his life, but she wasn't equipped to fight off whatever the threat might be by herself. She was strong, she was independent, she could fight—but she was also smart enough to realize that she could be caught unaware.

Drugged.

Taken.

And then what?

She didn't know.

Emotional involvement aside, she needed Adam right now, and Adam needed her.

But Adam was holding out on her. She knew it, and she didn't understand it. She couldn't give herself totally to him when she knew he was still keeping secrets from her.

He could be so damned relentless. Like the others, it seemed he believed that she could find the ship. He saw more clearly than the others, though; he knew she didn't want to find the ship.

She didn't want to find her father's remains.

Adam was staring at the charts again. "What are you looking for?" she asked him.

He shook his head. "I don't know. Something, some little clue that we're all missing." He spun around and stared at her. "Sam, you must know something," he insisted.

"I have to shower and dress," she told him, going quickly back down the hallway.

In the shower, she felt the water rushing over her. Her head seemed to pound in time with the beat of the water. She leaned against the tile while the water continued to fall.

Okay, so it was true that she had denied knowing anything about the *Beldona* because she didn't want to find the ship.

She didn't want to find her father's body.

And Hank's.

Then again, it was also true that she really *didn't* know anything. Okay, perhaps that wasn't quite true. She knew all the theories regarding the ship. She knew the *Beldona*'s history. The ship had gone down just after her English captain and crew had seized the Spanish ship *Yolanda*. Captain Reynolds of the *Beldona* had made prisoners of the Spaniard's captain, his lieutenants—and the woman Reynolds had loved, a passenger on the *Yolanda*. So what did this give her?

Sam finished showering. She slipped into a short slinky silver-knit halter dress, then went out to the living room. Adam was still staring at the chart on the wall.

"I think I know why Robert Santino might have sent his son out to look for the *Beldona*," she said.

Adam turned to stare at her. She walked into the room. "Captain Reynolds of the *Beldona* had fallen in love with Theresa-Maria Rodriguez, daughter of Don José Martinez-Rodriguez, a high official of the Spanish court. Theresa-Maria's mother was an Englishwoman, and the young lady had lived in London for quite some time, long enough for her and Reynolds to form a passionate bond. Her father, however, was determined that she have nothing to do with an Englishman. He pulled her out of England and betrothed her to Don Carlos Esperanza, the—"

"The captain of the *Yolanda*," Adam said. "Which made it an even greater triumph for Captain Reynolds when he seized the *Yolanda*. Unfortunately for him, of course, his own ship went down, as well."

Sam hesitated for a second. "There was a theft of certain Spanish jewels at just around the same time," she said. "I'd never heard of the theft in conjunction with the *Beldona* before, but my father was convinced that Don Carlos Esperanza had stolen the jewels. He was a man of standing in the community, and well to do, but not as rich as royalty, and it was often said that the young lady's attraction to Captain Reynolds had a great deal to do with the fact that Captain Reynolds was as rich as Croesus. My father believed that, to convince the sweet and lovely young Theresa-Maria to fall in love with him, Don Carlos Esperanza stole the two missing Crown rubies. They were a matched set of rings, with enormous stones, nicknamed the Eyes of Fire."

"Such jewels would definitely be enough to interest Robert Santino in finding the *Beldona*."

Sam sat down across from him. "It's obvious that Santino wants to find the ship. And maybe he's sent his son here as a spy or whatever. But anyone can look for the ship. There's nothing illegal in that."

"There *is* something illegal about it if one party murders another party of that search."

She raised a hand. "Let me try to get a solid grasp on everything you know—and suspect. Avery Smith is really James Jay Astin, we've established that. SeaLink is naturally interested in the discovery of the *Beldona*. They're a marine company, and they have the financial backing and the wherewithal to bring up the treasure, should it be found. However, we have to assume that someone else is working for SeaLink— doing the actual diving with us, since we have the charming company of Mr. Smith for dinner but have yet to see him on the dive boat. Okay, back to the jewels. We have Jim Santino, son of organized crime boss Robert Santino—a man who might kill without blinking to acquire certain Spanish treasures. So it should be simple. One of them had probably been involved in the search for a long time, and when my father found the ship, he was killed."

"You think your father found the ship?" Adam said.

Sam nodded.

"Then what happened?"

"What do you mean?"

"If he found the ship and was killed for finding it, why is the ship still missing?"

"I don't know. It doesn't make any sense, does it?"

"If someone killed him once he found the ship so they could seize the treasure for themselves, wouldn't the treasure and the ship have surfaced by now?" Adam mused.

"And why is Hank still missing?" she added.

Adam cleared his throat awkwardly and stood. "I've just found out about another guest on your island."

"Who?" Sam asked.

"I'd asked a friend of mine who's with the Metro cops in Dade County to do some searching for me. There was a diver with suspected crime connections who washed ashore about a week after your father's disappearance was reported."

Sam arched a brow. "Washed up—dead?"

"Yes."

"Adam, if he was dead then and he's on the island now, something strange is definitely going on."

"Not the dead man," Adam said, exasperated.

"Then . . . ?"

"His name was Marcus Shapiro."

"There are no Shapiros here."

"Your honeymooner is his son."

"My honeymooner—Joey Emerson?"

Adam nodded.

"You think that Joey Emerson is here for a reason other than his honeymoon?"

"Well, I know that Emerson isn't the name he was given when he was born."

"But he looks so . . ."

"Harmless?"

"Doting," Sam said.

"Pussy whipped." Adam laughed.

She cast him a glance of irritation. "Like Brad Walker would say, Joey and Sue are all mush."

"They may really be honeymooners."

"Right. So, this Marcus guy washed up on the Florida coast. Was he connected to the island in any way?"

"Not that I know about. He might have worked for Robert Santino now and then."

"So Joey may just be a nice young man on his honeymoon who changed his name because his dad had mob connections."

"Maybe."

"You're suspicious of everyone."

"Sam, someone on this island tried to kidnap you," he said in exasperation.

"There is the possibility that whoever attacked me isn't a guest. Other boats do come here. Lots of people stop by for our lunch and dinner buffets, even breakfast. Sometimes they stop just for directions."

"There is a slight possibility that our attacker came from somewhere else."

"But you don't believe that."

"Not for a moment."

"So what *do* you think?"

"I don't know."

She threw up her hands. "Who are you working for?" she asked again.

"I told you that I'd tell you soon. Very soon. For now, don't you think we'd maybe better get on over for cocktail hour?"

"I think cocktail hour is over."

"I'm famished, aren't you?"

"Yes, I suppose," she murmured.

"Weren't you the one in a hurry before?"

"Before I thought that you weren't telling me something important."

He flashed her a smile. "You're not telling me everything, either."

"I'm trying to."

"So am I," he said softly. "Let's go over, shall we?"

Sam stared at him, then nodded slowly. "Yes, let's go over."

It was Chinese night. Jacques had put together three different kinds of lo mein, vegetable, beef and pork. The fried rice came in "house special" and vegetarian. There were deliciously seasoned little ribs, shrimp or vegetarian egg rolls, hot and sour soup, mushu pork and beef, chicken chow mein, and more.

The mood in the dining room seemed strangely festive.

Sam was glad to see that Yancy had come down, and that the baby was with her as well. Sukee had decided to play with Brian, who was in his high chair, contentedly gumming a teething cookie and watching the conversation around him.

"Yancy, you okay?" Sam asked her, getting a word in while replenishing one of the chafing dishes.

Yancy jumped, startled. She looked pale.

"I'm, uh, fine. Why wouldn't I be?"

"I thought you didn't feel well this morning."

"I was tired this morning, that's all."

Tired, and jumpy, Sam thought. Either that, or she was becoming paranoid herself, seeing things in others that just weren't there.

"Jem's cousin Matthew came in on the mail boat. He and Jem took their dinner over to Jem's cottage," Yancy said, changing the subject.

Sam frowned. "I don't want you left alone," she began in a whisper.

"I won't be alone," Yancy said.

"They'll be back after dinner?"

"I need to talk to you then, anyway. Privately."

"I'll never ditch Adam."

"I meant privately *with* Adam."

"Oh. Okay."

Sam left and took a seat beside Darlene, smiling in return at the pleased grin the girl offered her.

"Did you have fun today?" Sam asked her.

Darlene nodded strenuously. "I had a wonderful time. I love to dive so much—I'm just afraid of some of the things in the water. I can't help it. I'd never be able to dive alone."

Sam reached over to help herself to some of the sake sitting on the table in a little white porcelain ewer. "You're never supposed to go diving alone."

"Your father did," Avery Smith said suddenly, quietly.

Sam looked at him across the table. She couldn't read his expression. She wondered if the words had been said with sorrow or malice.

"Yes, my father did," she said softly. She looked at Darlene. "My father was probably one of the best divers who ever lived. He knew the sea, respected all the creatures in it and was confident of his own abilities. He taught me never to go diving alone. But then he did it himself. And something happened to him. So no matter how good you are, or how brave, you should never go down alone."

"Never!" came an emphatic exclamation from the end of the table.

Joey Emerson.

Née Shapiro.

His gaze was level. He smiled at Darlene, then offered Sam a rather awkward grin. "My dad died diving alone, too. It's very dangerous. So it's good that you have a healthy respect for the water."

"Your father died while diving?" Adam said, sounding casual as he pulled up the chair next to baby

Brian. A piece of teething cookie landed on Adam's lo mein.

Brad shuddered.

Adam picked up the piece of cookie, staring nonplussed at Brad while he spoke to Joey. "I'm sorry to hear that about your father. What happened to him?"

Joey Emerson stared across the table at Sam. "It was just like Justin Carlyle. No one knows what happened."

"Maybe neither one of them is dead!" Darlene said excitedly. She looked at Sam. "Maybe we could find that ship—that *Beldona* your father was looking for. My folks would be so excited. They're just dying to find it."

"Darlene!" her father snapped, a definite edge to his voice. His wife kicked him beneath the table—Sam saw the motion, then heard Lew Walker grunt. "Buried treasure and all. You know. It would be great to find the ship."

"Right!" Darlene said happily. "We might find the ship, then find out that there's some kind of air line going into it. We'd find your dad, Sam, and maybe we'd find your father, too, Mr. Emerson."

Joey Emerson née Shapiro grimaced. "That would be real nice, kid," he said softly. "Except that they found my dad. He washed up on shore."

"Oh," Darlene said. "I'm sorry."

Sukee wagged a finger at her. "So there's a lesson in that, young lady. No diving alone."

"Right," Darlene said.

Brad stared at Sam. "So why did your dad do it, Sam?"

She shook her head. "I don't know. But don't you go getting any ideas, huh?"

"He won't," Judy Walker said sternly. "Actually, Sam, both my kids have gotten so fond of diving with you that they're not going to want to go with anyone else."

"Even Jerry had a wonderful time diving with you, Sam," Liam Hinnerman said, setting his arm around Jerry's shoulder.

Jerry offered Sam a weak smile. She looked lovely, as usual. Small, blond and delicate in a long-sleeved black knit. Pale, though. She didn't seem to have acquired any sun while they were out, and not a trace of windburn. She was wearing more makeup than usual, though, Sam decided.

And she looked miserably nervous.

"Jerry, did you like the dive?" Sam asked.

"It was fine, thank you," Jerry said politely.

"She can't wait to dive the Steps again," Liam said.

That was a lie. Jerry would like to do anything but dive the Steps again, Sam decided.

Yancy came around the buffet table with a wash-cloth, determined to clean Brian's face, though the baby wanted no part of it.

"That storm's brewing harder and faster," Yancy warned. "If anyone wants to do any more diving, I think tomorrow has got to be it for a few days."

"The Steps!" Liam said.

"Oh, come on, now, we've done those," Sam protested.

"But it was wonderful!" Jim Santino exclaimed from the end of the table. He flashed a smile at Sam, but she realized he was studying Joey Emerson.

Shapiro.

"Even Jerry loves to dive the Steps," Liam insisted. "Tell Sam, honey. Tell her that you're dying to dive the Steps again. Just dying to."

Jerry looked at her. Still so pale. "I'm just dying to dive the Steps," she said flatly.

"Please, Sam, please!" Darlene said.

"This is really getting repetitious," Sam said.

"But if it's what everyone wants," Adam said, "why not do it?"

"We'll keep an eye on the storm," Sam said, determined to maintain some kind of control.

"Well, of course," Sukee said. "It would be just as dangerous to dive in bad weather as it would be to dive alone, right, Sam?"

"Yeah, it would be."

Jim Santino stood and stretched. "One more excursion to the Steps! Well, folks, I'm for bed. If the weather is going to get us later, I'm going to dive bright-eyed and bushy-tailed tomorrow. Good night, all."

"Walk me, Jim?" Sukee asked sweetly.

"Sure thing."

"The kids should be in bed, too," Lew Walker said firmly.

"Dad...." Brad protested.

"It may be our last diving day," Judy said quickly, and the Walkers said their good-nights.

The Emersons followed suit.

Sam thought that Joey Emerson watched Jim Santino as he followed the other man out.

"Well, then, I shall retire myself," Avery Smith said.

"Guess we're all ready for bed, eh, sweetie?" Hinnerman asked Jerry, rubbing his fingers down her neck. Jerry seemed to grow even more pale.

"Is something wrong, Jerry?" Sam asked worriedly.

"Is there, sweetheart?" Liam asked.

"No," Jerry said, shaking her head. "Everything is wonderful. Good night, Sam, Mr. O'Connor, Yancy. Do tell Jacques that dinner was wonderful."

Sam had risen to say good-night. As Jerry North walked past her, Sam realized why she appeared so pale.

She was wearing too much makeup.

Trying to hide a growing bruise beneath her eye.

Sam followed the two of them out. "Jerry. Jerry!"

They stopped together.

"Are you sure you're all right? If you're not feeling well and don't, er, and don't want to disturb Liam, I can set up one of the rooms in the main house."

"Thank you," Jerry said as she looked at Liam and firmly put an arm around him. "I prefer being with—" she hesitated, then smiled and went on "—my man."

Liam kissed her. "We're just fine, Sam. You go on back in to that man of yours."

Feeling frustrated, Sam went into the house. Was Jerry's smile real? Had Liam been beating her? Some women just kept going back with a man no matter what.

Sam discovered that Adam was waiting for her at the door. Watching her.

"You can't run off alone," he told her.

"I just walked them out."

"You can't run off alone," he repeated curtly. Then he inhaled deeply. "Come in. To the bar."

Frowning, Sam let him lead her to the bar. Yancy was there, looking slightly ill.

"What the hell is going on?" Sam demanded.

Yancy drew a finger to her lips, then made certain that the doors to the porch were tightly closed. She nodded toward the stairs.

Sam turned to look.

She gasped, so stunned she nearly passed out.

A man was coming down the stairs. A young man with soft brown longish hair, blue eyes and an overgrown beard. He was incredibly thin, but other than that, he looked no worse for wear.

He was a man she knew very well. A man who had caused her endless hours of torment.

Because she had thought he was dead.

But he wasn't. He was alive.

Alive and well and walking toward her.

"Sam," he said.

He was alive! She gave a cry and streaked for him, throwing her arms around him.

He hugged her fiercely in return.

Shaking, she suddenly drew away from him. "You're alive. You're *alive*. We've been suffering all this time, and you're here. Alive and well. And you didn't try to contact us."

"Sam, you don't understand," Adam began from behind her.

"No! *You* don't understand!" she cried out. "This is—this is Hank. Hank Jennings. Hank! Damn you."

She hit Hank suddenly. Hit him again and again. Hank didn't defend himself. He let her hit him.

It was Adam who stopped her at last, capturing her arms, pulling her against him.

"You don't understand!" Sam lashed out. Hank was still staring at her, a sick look on his handsome face. "This is the man who supposedly disappeared. Who broke Yancy's heart, who worried me halfway into an early grave. This is Hank—"

"I know," Adam told her.

She pulled away. "How the hell do you know? How do you always know everything all the time? How do you know—"

"Sam, please, if you would just calm down...." Yancy tried.

"How?" Sam demanded. "Damn you, how do you know?"

Adam glanced at Hank. "I know Hank because... he's my brother," he said quietly.

Sam stared from one of them to the other. "What?" she demanded again, certain she hadn't heard correctly.

"He's my brother. Half brother, baby brother."

"But—"

"It's the truth, Sam," Hank said wearily.

Sam took a step forward. This time she took a swing at Adam. He didn't stop the first blow, or the second. Then he caught her wrists, saying, "Sam..."

"I don't know what the hell is going on here, but I am sick of whatever game you horrible people are playing. I hate you, Hank, and I swear to God, I *despise* you, Adam. You're a pair of bloody bastards, and the sharks should have taken you both!" she cried.

She turned and burst through the doors from the bar to the porch, determined to leave with all the swift, sure, no-nonsense speed of light.

"Sam!" she heard Adam roaring.

She didn't care. She started to run. Not toward her cottage; that was the way he would expect her to go.

Instead she ran toward the docks, almost blinded by the tears that sprang into her eyes. What the hell were they trying to do to her?

He'd known! It was obvious, Adam had known all afternoon that Hank was there, and he'd known Hank all along. He hadn't come to the island to help her; he'd come because Hank was his brother. And he'd probably made up everything he'd ever said about loving her because, just like everyone else, the only thing he wanted was the *Beldona*.

Furious, hurt beyond measure, she ran across the lawn.

And that was when the dark figure stepped out from the bushes.

All in black from head to toe.

Black ski mask.

Black turtleneck. Black shoes.

Black cloth. Saturated in chloroform.

''No!'' She had a chance to shriek the single word, but then the cloth was over her face. She tried not to breathe.

But she had been running.

She had to breathe.

She struggled. Fought the arms that held her. Kicked, fought...

But she had to breathe.

Soon her arms ceased to flail. She couldn't kick.

And, like the figure attacking her, the world around her faded, blurred and deepened....

Until it, too, was totally black.

14

"Well, we certainly handled that well, didn't we?" Yancy murmured dryly, looking from Hank to Adam.

Adam stared at his brother. "I should have told her."

"I thought she'd be happy I was alive," Hank said miserably.

Yancy lowered her head, smiling slightly. "You came through my window and nearly gave me a heart attack. We should have realized that Sam was going to have a similar reaction."

"She's just as mad at me as she is at Hank," Adam said.

"Obviously," Yancy agreed. "You two have gotten pretty close again in the past few days. She probably thought you came back because of her. Now she realizes that not only did you and Hank keep your relationship from her, you knew that Hank was here and didn't tell her."

"I didn't hold out on her when we met," Adam said flatly. "I said that I had a half brother. And I had no idea he was alive myself until I nearly had a heart attack when I saw him in the water. Which I'm still trying very hard to understand myself!''

"Damn it, Adam, if I knew more myself, don't you think I'd share the information? I'm the reader, remember? You were always the tough guy, the one who became the cop. I just wanted to explain to Sam what had happened to me. Adam, none of this was my fault. I was kidnapped.''

Adam looked at him inquiringly.

''I found out that Justin went to the Steps the day he disappeared. Along with thinking that the *Beldona* was in that vicinity, he'd started to see activity out there. If he was right, others were heading for the location, and he needed to move quickly. Anyway, I was certain I'd figured out that the ship had to be around the drop-off somewhere, and that's where I was headed.''

"Diving alone,'' Adam said.

''Well, that's rather beside the point right now, isn't it?'' Hank asked. ''Sweet Jesus, older brothers never do let you grow up, do they?'' he said to Yancy with a smile.

"Hank....'' Adam said, steering him back to the conversation.

''I was hit on the head. I woke up in what I thought was a damp basement. It seemed like I was kept in complete darkness forever. I was threatened daily to get me to talk about the ship. Water was kept from me. Food, too. I was stripped, left to lie on a concrete floor. I never saw my attackers. No one ever talked to me, except one man. His tone was always flat, no accent to his voice. He warned me to tell him what I knew about the ship or face torture, even death. Whoever it was eventually decided that I didn't know as much as he had thought originally, but that maybe I could be helpful.

"One day I was given back my clothes and fed, I was even given wine and beer. Things were passed to me through a little swing in the bottom of a barred wooden door. There was always one guard at the door, and he was always replaced at about five in the evening.

"One day, I was given research books and materials, some that I'd never seen before. I was told that I could be a free man as soon as I could guarantee that I could find the ship. I never believed that. I figured I'd be a dead man as soon as I discovered where the ship might be.

"Anyway, a few days ago, it seemed that I became much less interesting. No one came to ask me what I might have learned. When the new guard came to replace the old guard in the afternoon, I heard them whispering to each other outside the door. I couldn't hear everything, but they knew, Adam, that you'd come to Seafire Isle and that it might mess up some plans that were already under way here. Well, anyway, I'm not exactly the hero type. I'd never tried to bash down the door and kill the guards or anything. But I'd made a pet out of a rat, and he'd made a hole in the concrete. I spent months digging at that hole, and hiding it with the one blanket they'd given me. I managed to sneak out that night. I'd been in a warehouse on a river. I might have tried to reach the police, but there were men around the place, and I didn't know who might be a legitimate worker and who might be ready to slit my throat. There happened to be a nice little yacht at the dock in front of the warehouse. I stole it. I let the current take me downriver at first so that I could make a silent getaway. I realized I was on the Miami River, revved up the motor, and hightailed it for the sea. I knew I had to get here, because you were here, and I had to see Yancy and Sam. Besides, I was afraid to trust anyone else.''

Adam felt a shiver rake through him. Hank was alive. He had to remember just to be grateful for that fact. He had always blamed himself for Hank's having come to the island. He'd never told him about his affair with Sam; he'd just told him about the diving.

And the *Beldona*.

Hank's letters to him from the island had been filled with excitement. They'd described the diving, the house—and the dive mistress. The tragedy of Justin's disappearance—and the dive mistress. The assumption that his little brother had fallen in love with Sam had been half of what had sent him flying off to work in South America.

The determination to find either Hank or his killer had brought him to the island.

He stepped forward a little awkwardly, taking his brother in his arms. Adam's dad had been a cop, killed in action. Hank's father had lost a battle with cancer, and their mother had died seven years ago of pneumonia. Each was all the other had.

"I wish Sam had been willing to wait for an explanation," Hank said. "I just couldn't step out in front of everyone. I took a boat out alone today with Yancy's help because I was praying I could find the answer before anything else happened. I was wrong. I need help. I need Sam. But I also need to stay hidden, because I know if I'm discovered here, I'm dead. Someone on this island is working for the same people who made my life hell for a year."

"You're certain no one has seen you except for Yancy, Sam and me?"

Hank gave him an awkward grin. "And my baby. Adam, have you seen my baby? Isn't he beautiful?" Hank slipped an arm around Yancy, pulling her against him. "Even when I was gone, when she thought I was dead, she wanted my baby."

"The baby is great," Adam said huskily. He didn't want to tell his brother what a fool he felt, certain that

Brian had belonged to Hank and *Sam* rather than Hank and Yancy. "I've got to find Sam, got to make her understand. Damn her, I was right about this. I couldn't tell her about Hank when he insisted he had to tell her himself."

"Adam, whether you're right or wrong, what she feels right now is what matters. You've got to find a way to explain this to her," Yancy said.

"Let me go after her," Hank said. "And tell her that I was being held prisoner."

"You can't go after her. You can't be seen, remember? Hank, it's imperative now that you be extremely careful. Fool. You should have come to me before you went diving."

"I tried to go to Sam, and I would have come to you. I came out to talk to you both earlier, but . . ."

"But what?"

"Well, damn it, Adam, you were both busy—with each other." Hank looked down, embarrassed.

"Oh, God!" Adam groaned. So Hank had tried to see Sam earlier. Instead, he'd seen . . .

"Hank, don't you think of leaving this house. You don't know who's working for the people who kidnapped you. You have to stay hidden here and try to think of anything at all that might help us, any little detail. Sam will understand once she's had a chance to talk to you."

"Maybe I should go look for her," Yancy said. "Talk to her."

"Oh, God," Adam said suddenly.

"What?" Yancy demanded.

"She's alone!" Adam hissed.

"We're on an island. Where can she go?" Hank asked.

"Oh, God, I'd forgotten!" Yancy breathed.

"Forgotten what?" Hank demanded.

"I told you that she'd been attacked!" Yancy said to Hank. "Adam—"

Adam was already heading out of the house. "Damn, but we are fools! Hide Hank, Yancy, he's in tremendous danger now. Sweet Jesus, she's alone!" He swore, swiftly following in Sam's wake. By the time he reached the porch, he was calling her name. By the time he reached the lawn, he was running, fear igniting inside him like wildfire.

What fools. Someone had surely just been waiting for them to make a mistake!

And they'd made it. Oh, God, they'd made it.

Water...

She could feel it. Not touching her, but around her. Rocking her. Her head was spinning painfully with the kind of spiraling sensation that made her afraid she was going to be sick.

As the whirling mire within her head began to subside, Sam realized that she was on a boat. She was feeling the rise and fall of the surf lifting the vessel, letting it fall again, lifting it once more.

She listened for the sound of a motor.

There was none.

She tried to open her eyes and realized that she was blindfolded.

She tried to move.

Her wrists were bound to something.

Oh, my God, Adam, what a fool I was to forget. Why didn't you talk to me? Why didn't you trust me? Why did I get so angry at seeing Hank when I'm so happy he's alive? Why didn't I realize my danger even when I was ready to wring your neck? Do you really love me, Adam, or were you after something else all along?

Will it ever matter?

She swallowed hard. Adam wasn't here to help her. She would have to save herself.

She inhaled deeply, trying to remain calm, to keep some sense of reason. Trying to picture her position in her mind's eye. She was lying on her back, head slightly propped. Once the spinning subsided a little more, she could even appreciate the fact that her head was on a pillow. Her legs were free, stretched out on a boat bunk. She had the sensation of close confinement and imagined that the boat had to be some kind of sport vessel, somewhere between twenty and forty feet, with perhaps a master's and a guest cabin. The movement that rocked her made her think that she was in the aft of the boat—the guest cabin, perhaps? The bunk was center of the aft section, bolted down.

She struggled to free her wrists. She was bound with some material that wasn't rough, like rope, but that seemed even stronger than rope might be. The more she struggled, the tighter her bounds seemed to get.

"I tie good knots."

The strange, husky whisper startled her. She went dead still, listening.

Breathing. Slow, easy, even breathing. Near her. Very near her.

"Who are you? What do you want?" The words should have been forceful, adamant. Show no fear, she told herself.

But, of course, she was terrified. And the words were neither forceful nor adamant. They were a bare whisper.

"Who the hell are you?" That was better. "Other than a complete ass, because you can't possibly get away with this."

"I can, easily, because that storm is moving in much more quickly than you might imagine. And let's see..."

There was a sibilant hiss to the words. They were drawn out, spoken very low. Deep. They had an edge that seemed to creep right beneath her skin.

"Let's see . . . you fought with your lover, Miss Carlyle. Silly girl. So things aren't always perfect with the ex-cop. But he's a good lover, eh? Strong fellow. You should have stayed with him. He was trying very hard to protect you. But you know what, Miss Carlyle? The good guys don't always win."

"Who are you and what do you want?" she asked stubbornly. Her throat was bone dry. She was afraid to move. She was shivering, and yet she was surely dripping sweat. Her arms were beginning to feel painfully numb. She was beginning to feel a rise of absolute hysteria, desperate to get the blindfold off her eyes.

"I want you to dive, Miss Carlyle."

"Why?"

"To take me to the *Beldona*."

"I don't know where she is."

"I know you can find her."

"I'm telling you, I don't know where she is."

"Well, then, Miss Carlyle, you can find the ship, or you can rest with her. Do you understand?"

Sibilant laughter seemed to touch and surround her.

Fear crept along her spine. Like a crawling maggot. One maggot, two maggots, dozens of them. . . .

"Who in God's name are you?"

"It doesn't matter. What matters is that you dive."

"Dive—like my father?" she said. "Dive and wind up dead just the same? You can kill me now."

No, no, no, she didn't mean that. She didn't mean that at all. In seconds she would start crying, begging for her life. She wanted to live. She wanted to run to the house and the bar. Maybe take another good swing at Hank, and then one at Adam. Then she would stand her ground. Find out just what was going on. Demand to know what had happened, who had known what, where Hank had been ...

What Adam had known.

And why Adam had come. What was real and what was not.

"Kill you," the voice mused.

She felt him come closer. Felt his breath. She started to twist and kick. Hard. She lashed out with her feet and caught some body part.

He swore.

Then something was slipped around her feet and pulled tight. A belt? It was lashed to something at the foot of the bed, and she could no longer move her legs.

"This is going to be a difficult position to dive from," she managed to say sarcastically.

"We're not ready to dive yet. Besides, didn't you suggest that I just go ahead and kill you now?"

"I—"

"But I'm not going to kill you. Yet. You've got to bear in mind, Miss Carlyle, that there are many things that are worse. Much worse than death...."

Husky, warm laughter fanned her cheeks.

Then she felt a touch on her bare thigh, moving upward along it.

"There are much, much worse things...."

Adam burst into Sam's cottage.

"Sam!"

No reply.

He ran through the house quickly, calling her name. "Sam, please, for the love of God, talk to me!"

Silence.

He came running out on the lawn just as Yancy ran up to him worriedly. "She's not here?"

"No."

"We can't just panic."

"We have to panic. I'm going to keep looking. You get Jem and Matthew out, tell them to search everywhere."

Yancy nodded and hurried toward the other cottages. Adam looked at the house, his heart pounding. She was upset, furious with both him and Hank, he told himself. Just because he couldn't find her that minute, it didn't mean something bad had happened.

He started around the main house, feeling the coolness of the wind.

It was rising already, though the storm wasn't actually due for another day. That was what Yancy had said.

But storms were moody. They didn't always do what the weather forecasters said they were supposed to. They could quicken without warning. Their velocity could rise.

The air was cool. Definitely a portent of a storm coming.

"Sam!" He shouted her name. The sound of it was carried on the rising wind. The damp air brushed against his cheeks; the breeze lifted the hair from his brow. "Sam!"

No answer. He started jogging toward the path that led to the docks.

The night was dark. The grounds were illuminated by spotlights, but bushes, trees and the angles of the main house and the cottages cast huge pools of shadow and blackness here and there, Stygian voids like black holes in time and space.

"Sam!" he called again.

Where the hell had she gone? Adam swore to himself. He should have told her earlier, but he hadn't really understood a damned thing himself, except that Hank had been taken and held in a warehouse for nearly a year. Communicating a hundred feet beneath the water when he had been half in shock hadn't been easy, even with a dive slate. Besides, Hank had begged his brother to keep his secret until he'd seen Sam.

And now this.

He was a fool, an ass....

Too late. Where the hell was she?

He heard footsteps, feet running on the grass behind him. He swung around.

Jem and his young cousin, Matt, a slimmer version of Jem, were running toward him, Yancy following a little breathlessly behind.

"Have you seen her?" Adam demanded.

"No," Jem said.

"The only thing we can do is go from cabin to cabin," Adam said.

"Yancy said she was upset," Jem said calmly. "Maybe she just wants to stay away from you, Adam."

"I—" he began, then broke off.

He bent down and picked up a shoe. A slim black heel, nine double A. He could remember her slipping into the shoes just before they had left her cottage earlier. A slim black heel to go with her short silver cocktail dress.

"Oh, God!" Yancy breathed.

"What do we do?" Jem asked.

"We go from cottage to cottage," Adam said.

"Where do we start?"

"Avery Smith," Adam said grimly. "But then, what the hell? Everyone on this island is living some kind of a lie."

"I really don't know about the *Beldona!*" Sam gasped. The fingers that had moved over her flesh went still for a minute. Then patterns were again being drawn on her skin. She felt the knit dress shoved up against her thighs, bunching at her hips. Felt the touch resume, circles being drawn higher and higher.

"What a waste to kill you, Miss Carlyle. You really are quite a phenomenal woman. Tell me why your father was so interested in the *Beldona*."

She moistened her lips. "My father thought that— that some unique Spanish gems had been stolen and were aboard the ship."

"Yes, and . . . ?"

"He thought maybe there was something about the way the ship went down—perhaps a different reason than a storm that caused it to sink that might help in the finding of it."

The fear was mounting in her again.

Maggots. Creeping all over her. Oh, God. His fingers felt like horrible crawling creatures. Just touching her. Not hurting. Just touching. Going up and down her leg. Now . . . oh, God. A finger slipping beneath the elastic of her black satin panties.

"What a waste it will be if I kill you. . . ."

He spoke so close to her. The whisper directly above her lips. The breath fanning her flesh. His face coming closer and closer to her own....

"No, please..."

Oh, God, she sounded so pathetic. Like such a whimpering coward.

There had to be a way to fight. Hands tied, ankles bound, she could scarcely move.

She couldn't see....

There was hope. As long as she was living, there was hope.

But, oh, God, oh, God...

The sound of that very husky laughter again.

And another touch. On the bodice of her silver dress.

She heard another sound. A ripping.

Her dress coming apart.

She opened her mouth to scream.

A hand clamped down over it, nearly smothering her.

And once again that wretched whisper fanned her cheek. "Let's play chicken, Miss Carlyle. I want to hear you talk. While you talk, I'm distracted. I need to be distracted."

Slowly the hand moved from her mouth.

"Don't scream," he warned her.

She inhaled raggedly.

She felt a rounded fist fall lightly against her heart. "Where life beats! Right there, your heart, Miss Carlyle. To kill you quickly, I could slip a knife right through you, there. But then, I would never want to kill you quickly."

"Don't kill me. Please."

"Then tell me what I want to know."

The whisper again brushed her cheeks with deadly menace as the fingers fell upon the bare flesh now exposed at her navel. "Don't scream, Miss Carlyle. Just talk. Talk to me. I'm dying to listen. And surely, surely, my lovely Miss Carlyle, you must be dying to talk...."

Adam knew who was in each cottage; he had made a point of determining just who was staying where during the first hour he had spent on the island.

The door to Avery Smith's cottage was locked.

No matter. He didn't wait. He hefted a shoulder against the door.

"Damn you, you bastard!" he cried out.

The door gave, and he went flying into the darkened parlor area of the one-bedroom cottage, Jem, Matt and Yancy following behind him. "Astin, you bastard, get out here!" he shouted, striding toward the bedroom.

But before Adam could reach the hallway, James Jay Astin, alias Avery Smith, came walking out of the bedroom, tying the belt on his robe. He'd obviously been sleeping.

"Young man, just what the hell is your problem?" he demanded.

"I want Sam Carlyle."

"I've been under the impression that you already have Miss Carlyle."

Jem, apparently afraid that Adam would take a swing at the older man, stepped up behind him.

"Where is she?" Adam demanded.

"Mr. O'Connor, I'm well aware that your opinion of my means and methods is not high. And I admit, as well, that I came here to find out just what Miss Carlyle knows about the *Beldona* and the disappearances that have occurred in the search for her. I want that ship. I am the one who's best suited to solve the mysteries regarding her, to bring up her treasures, to show her in her very best light."

"Do you want that ship badly enough to threaten Sam?" Jem suddenly demanded from behind Adam. "Enough to kill?"

"No matter what the rumor might be, I've never killed anyone, nor caused anyone to be killed. And take a look. Do you see the young lady here?" Astin demanded. Hands on his hips, he stared at Adam. "You're looking in the wrong place, and you should damned well know it!" he snapped.

"What's he talking about, Adam?" Yancy asked.

Adam and Astin stared at one another. Adam realized that Astin must know the truth about Jerry North, just as he did himself. Justin Carlyle had been out with Astin several times before his disappearance. If Astin was as legitimate in this as he was claiming, the two men might even have been friends.

Justin Carlyle might even have shared some information with Astin regarding a possible reconciliation with his ex-wife, Jerry.

Justin wouldn't have told Sam about Jerry. He wouldn't have told her anything that might hurt her. And unless Jerry was definitely going to become a part of their lives again, there wouldn't have been much of a reason to tell Sam about her.

"She couldn't have come to hurt Sam," Adam said.

James Jay Astin threw up his hands. "There are different ways to hurt people, aren't there, Mr. O'Connor?"

"She wouldn't put Sam's life in danger."

"There are different ways to do that, as well. You can endanger someone's life without ever intending to."

"I'm going to see Jerry North," Adam said to Jem, Matt and Yancy. "You go over to the Walkers'."

"That won't be necessary."

Adam spun around to stare at Astin. "Why not?"

Astin exhaled, shaking his head. "As I said, I have been looking for the *Beldona*. I wanted Justin Carlyle's help looking for it, and I think that Justin would have taken on my company to do the actual salvage. Samantha Carlyle hates the ship—she wasn't willingly going to help anyone, so I had to try to find out what she did know, and where she'd go if she was diving herself. I'm too old myself for the kind of diving required to find the ship. I hired the Walkers to tail Samantha Carlyle, to get her diving around the Steps, to try to discover just what was down there.''

''Then—'' Adam began.

''I'm telling you, the Walkers are guilty of a certain deceit in their reasons for being here, but that is it. They are innocent of any wrongdoing. Judy Walker is extremely fond of Miss Carlyle, who has been very kind to her children. I can promise you, the Walkers would not harm Sam. You will not find Miss Carlyle with them.''

''God help you if you're lying to me, Astin!'' Adam said. Then he turned on his heel and exited the cottage.

It was time for a showdown with Jerry North.

He kept touching her.

Fingers moving over her flesh like maggots.

But she *did* want to live.

''The English captain of the *Beldona* was still in love with his Spanish mistress. She and her new fiancé were both aboard the *Beldona*. The rubies and other Spanish gems were aboard the ship, as well, and my father believed ..."

"Yes, what did your father believe?"

His fingers stroked her thighs.

"That ... that ..."

"Yes?"

Oh, God. She couldn't speak, couldn't breathe.

He was straddling her.

She could tell that he was lean, tightly muscled.

And he was nearly naked. Shirtless, barefoot, he wore bathing trunks and nothing else at all. He sat over her own barely covered hips. The hair on his legs grazed vulnerable flesh.

He leaned closer to her again. She could almost feel the full length of him. The texture of his flesh. The strength of his body.

All of it ... so threatening.

Evil. Eerie.

His lips nearly upon hers, his breath coming in and out, a whisper forming on his mouth, against her own.

"Now ..." he began.

Then another voice suddenly cut the air. A female voice.

Furious.

"My God! Just what in hell do you think you're doing?"

15

Oddly enough, Hinnerman was at the door of the cottage as Adam made his way toward it.

"What the hell is it, cop?" Hinnerman demanded nastily. He was wearing boxer shorts and an open robe, and he held a glass of liquor in his hand. A nightcap.

"I'd like to see Miss North, please."

"Why?" Hinnerman demanded belligerently.

"That's between Miss North and me."

"You want to talk to Jerry, big man, you gotta go through me."

But Adam didn't have to go through Hinnerman. Jerry was standing behind him.

Such a pretty woman. Looking so much younger than her years. Except for her eyes. Her eyes looked so much older.

"Adam, what's wrong?" Jerry asked.

"We're looking for Sam."

Jerry, in a white cotton robe and delicate white slippers, shook her head worriedly. "She isn't here."

"Of course she isn't here! What the hell would she be doing here at this hour of the night?" Hinnerman's eyes narrowed on Adam. "Maybe she's decided you aren't such a hotshot in bed after all, huh?"

Adam clenched his teeth, forcing a false smile to his lips as he faced Hinnerman. "Maybe she feels just that, Hinnerman. But you know what, butt head? At least I never had to beat a woman to get her to stay with me."

Jerry gasped. Hinnerman swore.

"You wiseass piece of shit!" Hinnerman bellowed, starting toward Adam. Jerry leaped between them. Hinnerman looked as if he was about to slug her, but Jem instinctively came forward, sweeping Jerry up, just as Adam stepped forward, flinging up an arm to ward off Hinnerman's blow while carefully aiming his own right.

Hinnerman went down.

Adam discovered that he was shaking. "Why the hell do you stay with him, Jerry? Why the hell do you need him when . . . when—"

He broke off, shaking his head.

Jerry eased from Jem's hold, looking down at Liam, who was just beginning to try to pick himself up. "You . . . know?" she whispered.

"Yes."

"Does Sam?"

"No, not yet. I thought it was something you might like to tell her yourself. But then again, I kept other information from her, and that's why she's missing now."

Hinnerman had made it to his feet. He was staring balefully at Adam.

"Sam Carlyle seems to like you just fine right now, doesn't she, Jerry?" he jeered. "Wait until she finds out you're the mama who deserted her and her daddy on this island. Wait until she finds out that you were snooping around her daddy right before he disappeared from the face of this earth!"

Jerry was white. She looked at Adam. "He's right. How can I tell her? She'll hate me."

Adam shook his head. "How can you not tell her? How can you keep away from her? You've got a beautiful daughter."

"Too beautiful, maybe, inside and out. She'll hate me."

"I don't think so." He glanced contemptuously at Hinnerman. "You need to get away from this abusive bastard. She'd help you."

"You mind your own business, you cop asshole."

"I'm not a cop anymore."

"Who the hell are you working for?"

"Myself. I'm my own damned employer. Jerry, we've got to find her. Want to help us?"

"Yes, yes, just let me change."

Adam nodded. "Jem, you stay here. If he lifts a finger against her, deck the bastard again."

"Gotcha, Adam," Jem agreed.

"Yancy, we'll try Jim Santino's next."

"Want me to go to Sukee's?"

"No, I don't want you alone anymore, either. Just stick with me. Behind me," he added after a moment. "Santino is the son of a gangster."

Yancy took him at his word. She hung just behind him, holding his elbow as they hurried across the beautifully manicured lawn to Santino's cottage.

Yet even as they neared it, they could hear the screaming. Adam glanced at Yancy quickly, then started to run.

"You bastard! I'll kill you!" cried the furious female voice.

Sam heard a whacking sound.

Then her attacker, speaking again, contrite, pleading now.

"Stop it. Calm down. You don't understand what I'm trying to do."

"It's obvious what you're trying to do."

"Bullshit! Her old man killed mine. What possible interest would I have in her?"

"Your libido seems to have no problems with her!"

He was off her, Sam realized, inhaling raggedly and fighting a different battle. She could hear the blows that were raining against him.

"Sue, stop it!"

"You slimy, two-timing, gigolo son of a bloody bastard. You said—"

"Oh, my God!" Sam gasped, realizing to whom the voices belonged. The Emersons. "Joey, you bastard. Get this blindfold off me and untie me. I don't know what you think—"

"Great!" Joey broke in. "This is just great, Sue. Now she knows who we are. We're going to have to kill her."

"Now wait—" Sam began.

"Don't be an ass, Joey. If you just explain—"

"Explain? Are you out of your mind?"

"Oh, no, don't explain!" Sue said sarcastically. "Your way is much better. Beat her. Rape her. That will make the both of us just adore you."

"I wasn't going to—"

"Then what the hell were you doing?"

"Trying to scare her. I was working—"

"What a chore that must have been!"

"Sue, I love you!"

"For the love of God, will you at least take this stupid blindfold off me?" Sam pleaded.

The Emersons were silent. A moment later Sam exhaled a sigh of relief as the blindfold was wrenched away from her eyes.

She was on a boat. A nice one. The bunk she was tied to was surrounded by mahogany cabinetry and shelves lined with books. She was staring at a complete entertainment system.

Joey and Sue were staring at her. They were both in bathing suits.

Not formally dressed, but in far better shape than she could claim herself at the moment. Her dress was in tatters. She felt both frighteningly vulnerable and ridiculous at the same time.

"Would you please consider untying me?" she demanded icily.

Sue glanced at Joey, who had the grace to look ashamed.

"Please, these ties are really painful. I can barely feel my arms anymore."

Sue stepped forward. Sam realized that she had been tied up with a pair of Sue's stockings.

"Sue, I didn't tell you that you could untie her."

"Shut up, Joey."

"All right, Sam. I'm actually sorry about this," Joey said, "but I want you to know that I've got a gun on you now. Don't try anything."

"Thanks," she told Sue, rubbing her wrists to bring some life back to them and ignoring Joey's threat.

Her feet had been secured by one of Joey's belts. She freed herself. Joey did indeed have a gun. It was very small, the size of his hand. But considering some of Joey's family ties, Sam was sure that the gun was both real and lethal.

Sue stood next to Joey but kept staring at Sam, shaking her head.

"You're slime, Joey. And to think that I married you, that I fell in love with you!"

"Dammit, Sue, I didn't really intend to do anything to her. I knew you were sleeping in the other cabin, just waiting for the drug to wear off her."

"This was idiotic to begin with," Sue insisted.

Joey sighed deeply. "It is not idiotic. I want to find that ship. My mother wants me to find that ship, and my brother wants me to find that ship. My dad was stabbed. And I'll bet you she knows it."

"I just found that out this afternoon," Sam said awkwardly. "Joey...Shapiro?"

"Yeah. Son of a dead man. Knifed through the gut. He was half consumed by fish when they found him."

"Your dad was a gangster. Joey, come on!" Sue pleaded suddenly. "You don't want that life."

"He was a diver."

"He was a criminal, playing rough games for high stakes." She glanced at Sam. "I told him not to do this! The day he came after you in your living room, he was nearly decked by that cop friend of yours. Idiot!'' she told Joey.

"How was I supposed to have known they had a past history and that Adam O'Connor would come rushing to her rescue? This should have been all over that night. She should have passed out nicely, wakened terrified and answered all my questions.''

"I don't have the answers you want!'' Sam insisted. She looked at Sue. "And he didn't attack me in my living room,'' Sam added, deciding it might serve her well to keep the argument going between the two of them. "He broke in through my window and attacked me in the bathtub.''

"The bathtub!'' Sue shrieked at Joey.

She'd never realized before just how young the Emersons were, Sam thought. Right now, they looked like a pair of squabbling children.

Except that they were children with a prisoner. Playing cowboys and Indians, cops and robbers.

And she still might get an arrow—or a bullet— through her heart.

Joey was attempting to be placating once again. "Sue, you knew I was going to get her to talk, no matter what it took.''

"No, you're wrong on that one, Joey. I knew you were getting obsessed with this thing, but not at the cost of everything else.''

"Sue...''

"Joey—" Sue broke off, staring at Sam. "He really attacked you in your bathroom?"

"I was right in the tub."

Sue swung around, slapping Joey as hard as she could. "You son of a bitch! She was naked."

"Well, it wasn't my fault! How the hell did I know what she was going to be doing when I went through the window?"

"Amazing! She's nearly naked right now! Oh, Joey, I just do not believe this!" Sue cried. She swung at Joey again.

And hit him.

Hit him so hard that she knocked him off-balance. Trying to regain his footing, Joey grabbed at his wife.

They went down together.

Sam stared at them for a split second, then decided that opportunity might not come again.

She sprang from the bunk, wincing in pain as the sudden movement stabbed straight through her arms and legs. Joey's gun had fallen. If she took the time to reach for it, Joey might well drag her down, as well.

She kicked the gun. It went flying under the bunk and clattered as it slipped between the boards of the cabinetry.

"Look what you've done!" Joey shrieked at Sue, gaining his feet.

Sam didn't wait for Sue's reply.

She flew out of the cabin, past the salon and galley, and bounded up the steps that led to the upper deck.

And there she stood dead still.

She was surrounded by darkness.

The darkness of the water.

The Stygian darkness of the sea at night.

The wind whipped around her. The boat was rocking wildly.

The storm was brewing wickedly.

And she was in the center of a wild black void.

She swung around. Thank God. Light. She could see light. Seafire Isle. If only she could judge the distance. They hadn't come so far.

But far enough.

They'd come somewhere between one and two miles from shore, perhaps.

What a difference! she mocked herself. What was a mile on a night like this?

The difference between life and death, perhaps. Say it was two miles. With a whipping wind, a churning dark sea. The undercurrents would be as volatile as the air around her.

"Damn it, Sue, I know you can reach the damned gun. Get it!" she heard Joey cry.

She saw a pair of flippers leaning against the port side decking. She grabbed them and slipped them on.

"Joey, I've got it!" Sue cried. "I've got the gun."

Sam plunged into the sea.

* * *

Adam shouted, banging on the cottage door. "If you've hurt her, I'll rip your heart out, you bastard!" He set his shoulder against the door, slamming at it with determined strength.

He burst into the cottage.

The living room was dark. Adam rushed through it. Into the bedroom.

He stopped short.

Jim Santino was in bed. Doing nothing evil to Sam. He wasn't even with Sam. He was with Sukee.

Sukee, naturally, had been doing the screaming.

But she hadn't been in any pain.

She was staring at him with the sheets drawn around her breasts.

Sukee smiled very slowly. "Hi. Did you come to join us?" She looked at Jim, taunting him. "Did you hear the way he threatened you? I really like tough guys!" She sighed, lashes fluttering as she looked at Adam. "But no, he didn't hurt me. Still, if you want to rip his heart out, we can make it into a wild night."

Yancy had come up behind Adam. He spun around.

"The Emersons?" she said.

He shook his head. "The Shapiros," he murmured.

"What?" Yancy demanded.

"A very long story," Adam said, turning to leave Jim Santino's bedroom.

"Hey, wait, what's going on?" Jim yelled after them.

"Sorry we interrupted!" Adam shouted.

With a sense of urgency building inside him, Adam started to run again.

He reached the Emersons' cottage and started to bang on the door.

It swung in at his touch.

He stepped into the living room. It was dark and empty. "Sam!" he cried, moving into the kitchenette, the bedroom, the bathroom.

The cottage was completely empty.

He turned around to leave and slammed into Yancy. "They've taken her," he said huskily.

"Where?" Yancy demanded.

"Where else do you go when you leave an island?" Adam demanded bitterly. "The water. They've taken her out to sea."

It was amazing how cold the water—the usually wonderful, temperate water—could be in the middle of the night when a storm was approaching.

Sam was a good swimmer. A strong swimmer. The water had been her life. She was almost as comfortable in it as she was on dry land.

Usually.

But then, usually she had the sense to stay out of the water when a storm was nearing the island. And she never swam in these depths in the middle of the night.

In the chill of the wind....

In such unbreakable darkness.

Life. How she wanted to hang on to it.

She wondered now what her father had felt, fighting for his life. Surely it had seemed as precious to him during his last few minutes as it now seemed to her. Had he thought of her? Had he fought against the possibility of going away forever until the very last minute? She was strong, and the flippers helped, but it didn't matter. For every few feet she managed to make toward the island, another swell came by and swept her back. The salt was stinging her eyes. Tears filled them. As afraid as she was for her own life, she suddenly felt her father's suffering.

And if she perished here...

Yancy had Hank and her baby to sustain her. Jem had his family. They would hurt, but they were strong. Then there was Adam. Adam, whom she had thrown away. Adam, who had played his own games of deceit. Adam, who had told her that he loved her.

She had to stop crying, she told herself furiously. She would definitely die.

She was going to die.

No. She could survive in the water for a very long time. She squinted, drawing her wrist above her head, grateful that she wore a diver's watch with a luminous dial.

Nearly five o'clock.

Nearly morning.

How long had she been in the water already? How close was the storm?

The storm that hadn't been due to come near them for at least another twenty-four hours.

The rain hadn't started yet, thank God. Just the wind.

The wind . . . and the vicious swirl of the water.

She'd shed the remnants of her dress and was swimming in her underwear, nothing restricting her movements. She reminded herself that when she got tired, she only had to float. The current should take her toward the island.

It was just that the current kept changing with the erratic whipping of the wind.

Sharks.

There *were* sharks in these waters. Lots of them. She'd faced them so many times.

Faced them. At their level.

Now her legs were dangling. Temptingly. And she was blind to what lay below her. She'd always had a healthy respect for sharks but never a fear of them. Until now.

Terror suddenly filled her. From below, she would look just like a smorgasbord.

She had to float, rest, relax.

She flipped onto her back, breathing deeply. The sea was rising, the water slapping over her face. She had to take care with every breath. No matter how experienced she was, her muscles were tiring.

Adam had tried to protect her. He had stuck to her like glue. She'd thought herself so much older and wiser than the last time. She'd lost her temper without seeking an explanation again. She'd been hurt. Last time she had forced him away.

This time she had run.

Now she was going to die, and it wasn't going to matter if he did love her or he didn't.

Still, she'd been so close. She'd wanted Adam from the time she had first seen him, and she'd wanted him more with each hour that passed. They'd shared the sea. A knowledge of it, a love for it. The secrets within it. A love for the life around it. Adam loved her island. He'd said that he loved her....

She closed her eyes briefly, trying hard to breathe easily and regain her strength, to keep herself afloat on her back so she wasn't constantly fighting the swell of water into her nose. She sneezed, coughed, choked. The salt water stung through her nostrils to her eyes. Thank God she was so accustomed to it. She would have been dead already if she wasn't. She had to keep going, keep fighting. Fighting until she was dead. Oh,

God, though, this was hard. A bullet in the heart would have been an easier way to go.

No, hope was best.

Except she had no more strength.

Adam would come for her, she realized suddenly. He was probably looking for her already, scouring the island. He had undoubtedly dragged everyone on the island out of bed. If he loved her . . .

He did.

The things people did for love. . . .

She was going to die, Sam thought, and she had just figured out what her father had known about the *Beldona*.

If given the opportunity, she could most probably find the ship.

Water lapped over her head again. She turned, trying to swim hard.

She heard the sound of a motor. She flipped over again, blinking against the wind and the rising sea. A boat was coming toward her. A flashlight was seeking her out in the waves.

Adam.

Adam had come at last. . . .

"There she is!"

It was a woman's cry. Sam blinked against the sea and salt. Oh, God. No.

Joey and Sue were standing portside, pointing at her. Joey's little gun was thrust into the waistband of his swim trunks as he leaned over the wooden railing.

"There! There!"

Sue seemed to be reaching toward her.

Had they come to rescue her? Or put that bullet through her heart?

"Get her, Joey!"

She could slip beneath the surface. Let the sea take her.

She was tired. So tired.

Something tugged on her leg. Pulled her down. Oh, God! She panicked, choked.

A shark. That was what survivors said. That there was no pain at first, just a jerk, a sensation of being pulled downward. They'd never known what hit them, just looked down to see a pool of blood spreading around them. . . .

There was no blood that she could see. Just the darkness of the water.

And another jerk. Hard.

Oh, God, so hard! She couldn't possibly fight it. It was like a vise. She was being bitten right in two, and now she could feel the pain as she was tugged, pulled. . . .

Pulled irrevocably downward into the cold, black, swirling void of the sea. . . .

16

Down...

A shark.

Not a shark.

Adam.

He was in front of her in complete diving gear, thrusting his regulator into her mouth, drawing her downward. His arms locked around her, and despite the darkness, his silver-gray eyes met hers through the glass of his diving mask. They both kicked the water with their swim fins, moving through the silent, salty darkness of the sea, sharing the air from Adam's tank with slow, practiced breathing. Sam didn't know where he was taking her, and she didn't care. It seemed that they were merely drifting in the chill blackness, but Adam seemed to have a strategy.

She was alive.

She had believed that he would come for her.

And he had.

He lifted a thumb, indicating the surface, then adjusted his buoyancy control vest, filling it with air.

They kicked upward from the fifteen to twenty feet to which they had descended. She was grateful to see that they had come up just twenty or thirty feet from the *Sloop Bee*. The dive boat was rocking strenuously in the turbulence of the ocean. Adam pulled off his mask and spat out his mouthpiece.

"Are you all right?"

She nodded, then threw her arms around him. "You found me. Oh, my God, you found me. I didn't think that anyone could find me in the wind, in the darkness.... I thought I was going to die. Oh, Adam, I didn't want to die, but I kept thinking about my father. It must have been so horrible for him—but you came for me." She clung to him with such energy that his vest couldn't quite maintain them above the surface. She didn't care. If they were to drown now, at least they would go together. She found his lips. They tasted of salt, but they were warm. He kissed her back, and his warmth filled her. She wasn't going to die. She was going to live.

And she was going to love him.

Adam suddenly kicked the water hard, and they broke the surface again.

"You found me," she whispered.

He smiled, inhaling deeply. "It wasn't difficult. I had Jem head for the Steps. I was sure that was where they'd be."

"Where did Joey and Sue get that boat?" Sam asked. The last word was a gurgle; she'd been hit by a wave.

"Hank stole it."

"Hank stole it?" she repeated incredulously.

"He had to—to escape. He'd been kept in the garage of a marine company for a year. When he got out, he didn't know who to trust, so he escaped to the water—and Seafire Isle. He left the boat in the harbor. Joey and Sue must have discovered it, and decided that it would make do for their own use."

"I still don't understand. Were they keeping Hank prisoner?"

Water slapped her in the face again. She was shivering; her teeth were chattering.

"Let's get out," Adam advised.

When they made it to the *Sloop Bee,* Yancy and Jerry North were at the ladder to help her out. She was instantly wrapped in a blanket, hugged, handed from person to person. And there were a lot of people—Adam, Yancy, Jerry, Liam Hinnerman, Jim Santino and Sukee. Behind them all, she saw that even Avery Smith was aboard.

Not Avery Smith. James Jay Astin. She had to remember that.

"Where's Hank?" she whispered to Yancy.

Yancy explained softly that Hank was with the baby.

Sam looked around, not seeing Jem and Matt.

Adam read her mind. "They're bringing the Emersons around," he told her.

A cup of coffee was pressed into her hands. She accepted it gladly, sitting on the starboard side of the boat.

"I'm so grateful to be here, to be alive. To all of you for coming out, but I'm still so confused."

Adam sat down at her side. "You certainly have every reason to be confused. Because just about everybody is guilty of something."

Sam arched a brow. James Jay Astin cleared his throat and came around and sat on her other side. "Well, you know who I am," he said. He looked forward, then at Adam, and then at Sam again. "Lew and Judy Walker have recently resigned from my employ."

"What?" Sam gasped.

"They were working for Mr. Astin," Adam explained evenly.

"But they're actually good people, Sam. All they were trying to do was find the *Beldona* for me. They didn't do a thing illegal. And neither one of them would ever harm you in any way."

"What a relief," Sam murmured. "So—neither of them knocked me out or killed my father?"

"No, of course not!" Astin told her. "And neither did I," Astin said grimly. "I was your father's friend,

Miss Carlyle. That's the absolute truth. I am sorry for the deceit we practiced. I beg that you forgive me.''

Sam nodded slowly. "You're forgiven. All of you," Sam said.

Jim Santino cleared his throat. "Sorry, Sam. I guess it's pretty obvious. I've been trying to use you, too, to find the *Beldona*." He hesitated. "I've been working for my dad, but honestly, I would never have hurt you, either."

Sam nodded at Jim, then looked at Adam. "Who have *you* been working for?" she demanded.

He smiled. "Myself. Actually, I was using the *Beldona* to find you again. And my brother, naturally."

She nodded, lowering her eyes, smiling. Then she was jolted, her coffee stingingly warm and yet reassuring as a drop bounced onto her hand. The boat with the Emersons on board was suddenly brought alongside the *Sloop Bee*. Jem and Matt stood grimly behind the Emersons, ready to force them aboard the *Sloop Bee*.

Jem had Joey Emerson's little gun in his hands. He dumped the remaining ammunition from the weapon and slid it into the waistband of his pants before he lifted Sue, setting her flatly on board the *Sloop Bee*.

"I don't know what the hell you all think you're doing," Joey protested.

"I imagine Miss Carlyle intends to press charges against you for assault and battery, kidnapping, and maybe even attempted murder," Adam advised him dryly.

"Oh, don't be silly. I was just trying to scare her," Joey protested. "And you're not a cop anymore."

"Think of this as a citizen's arrest," Adam said. "We can probably also charge you with another case of kidnapping, wrongful imprisonment—and murder."

"Murder!" Joey said, furious, standing his ground against Adam. "I didn't murder anybody. I just wanted the truth. Nothing but the damned truth. My mother has been sick all these years, wanting to know what's going on."

"Your mother?" Jem queried skeptically.

"Yes, my mother. I've been working for my mother, trying to find out exactly what happened to my father! Damn! Everyone keeps saying that Sam's father was so wonderful. Well, all right, mine wasn't a saint, but he was murdered. By Sam's father. And I deserve some answers just like everyone else here."

"Sam's father didn't kill Marcus Shapiro," Jerry North said suddenly, her voice soft, yet somehow filling the silence that had risen after Joey's words.

"The hell he didn't!" Joey said. "He followed Justin because he had heard that Justin was about to make a deal with James Jay Astin, which meant Justin was pretty sure he had discovered where the ship lay. He knew your father, too, Sam, because SeaLink had been tentatively negotiating with Robert Santino about splitting both the expenses and rewards in bringing up the treasures of the ship.''

"Yes, Justin knew where the ship was, but he didn't kill your father, Joey," Jerry said.

"How can you know that?" Joey demanded.

Jerry stared at Adam. Sam frowned, watching the strange cry for help that seemed to be in Jerry's gaze.

"How can you know that?" Joey repeated furiously.

"Because she killed him, kid. Jerry killed your old man," Liam offered suddenly, chuckling.

"That's enough," Adam said quietly. "We'll get back to the explanations in a minute, Joey. Sam, Jerry, come down to the end of the boat for a minute's privacy, will you?"

"Oh, that will help!" Liam exclaimed dryly.

"You shut up," Jem warned Liam.

"Or else . . . ?"

Adam had Sam's arm, and Jerry's. Sam had never been more confused. Adam was insisting she needed a private moment with Jerry in the midst of Liam casting murder accusations Jerry's way.

"Wait—" Sam protested.

"This can't wait," Adam said.

He led them both to the aft of the *Sloop Bee.*

"Adam, what's going on?" Sam demanded. "Jerry, did something happen to you?"

"I—" Jerry began.

"Jerry, everything is coming out now. Matters are going to get worse before they get better. This isn't exactly the right way to do this, either, but the best I can do under the circumstances is buy you both a few seconds here."

"Please, what is going on?" Sam persisted.

Adam walked two steps away, his back to the women. He stood like a bulldog, guarding them from the others.

"I'm—" Jerry began.

"Yes?"

"I'm—your mother, Sam."

"Mother? My mother's been gone. I don't even remember her. I think she's dead. I—"

"No, Sam. I'm not dead."

"This can't be."

"It's the truth."

"Oh, God!" Sam felt as if she'd been hit.

"I'm so sorry, you deserved so much better. I mean, you deserve to be told in a better way. And you deserved more noble relations. Like your father."

Sam felt as if she was going to fall. The information was numbing. Jerry, her mother? It explained Jerry's interest in her. Jerry's quiet longing to be with her. It explained the pain in the woman's eyes, and her discomfort now.

Seconds that seemed like hours passed before Sam could feel, think or speak. Then she saw the slow trickle of tears falling silently down Jerry's cheeks. A strange surge of emotion welled within her. Love? She hadn't even known she had a living mother. Love could take time. And understanding. But she realized that Jerry had been hurt. Whatever her actions, she had known pain as well. And Sam realized that she wanted to protect the woman.

"Oh, Sam, I am so sorry—"

"Don't you be sorry!" Sam said fiercely, catching Jerry's hand, squeezing it.

"But—"

"Don't be sorry. Don't you be down on yourself. I don't understand anything anymore—"

"This friggin' family reunion has got to stop!" Liam bellowed.

"Go to hell!" Jerry cried, pulling from Sam and brushing past Adam to come and stand in front of Liam. "You go to hell!" she cried furiously again.

"Tell the Emerson kid—the Shapiro kid!—and your daughter the truth. Tell them that you murdered Shapiro's old man."

"I don't believe it!" Joey snapped.

"Tell him, Jerry," Liam insisted.

"Liam, you leave her the hell alone and let her talk in her own time," Adam warned, stepping forward again.

"Please!" Sam insisted, following him.

Jerry swung back to look sadly at Sam, speaking softly, her words for the two of them alone. "What I've told you is the truth. God forgive me. I left your father right after you were born. I was young and stupid and didn't think that I could bear life on his island. But he was a good man, the best man in the world. He still wrote to me on occasion. When he could find me. He sent me pictures. Years later I had become involved with—with Mr. Santino's father. Oddly enough, I discovered that he was in the process of some business that had to do with Justin. I saw Justin again. We began to talk. I thought that maybe after all that time... But I was just being used against him." She turned from Sam then and stared at Joey, her voice rising on a strong note. "Your sainted father tricked me. We followed Justin—to the ship. To 'celebrate' with Justin, so your father told me, Joey. I was there when he slit Justin Carlyle's throat." She raised her hands, staring at them. "When I saw what he had done to Justin, I stabbed him."

She looked at Sam. "I'm sorry. I'm so, so sorry."

Sam stared at her, stunned. She felt numb again. Cold. Colder than she had felt in the sea, fearing death.

"I'm sorry about your father," Jerry whispered painfully. "He was the only truly good person I ever knew. And I'm so sorry that now you know you're related to me.'' The last was barely a whisper.

Her father was dead. Definitely dead. She had known it. Of course, Justin wouldn't have left her. The finality hurt. But the pain had been with her for so many years now that this finality was a bearable anguish.

Her numbness began to fade as the warmth of pity filled her.

This was her mother. This beautiful butterfly who didn't look much older than she was herself. This woman who had apparently made such a pathetic disaster of her life, but now spoke with a strange, sad dignity. Jerry had hurt her, abandoned her. But there were so many things she could see in Jerry now. In her beautiful blue eyes. Remorse. Anguish. And a fear that had apparently lived with her for a long, long time. The fear that she could never, in a thousand years, change things.

"Jerry..." Sam began, but Jerry was staring at Joey Emerson née Shapiro again.

"*I* killed Marcus," Jerry said. "I killed him when I saw what he had done to Justin. I didn't think about it, I simply reacted. He had meant to kill Justin all along. Your father planned to murder Justin. He slit Justin's throat. I can still remember the blood surging into the water... I—oh, God, Sam, it was quick. I swear it. Justin died quickly. He couldn't have been in any pain, it was so fast. I can't say it enough. I'm sorry. So sorry.''

Sam stood there, heedless of the others around her. "You killed Marcus Shapiro because he murdered my father," she said evenly. "But why did Marcus kill my father?"

Jerry's head fell, tears silently streaming down her face. "Robert Santino had hired a lot of divers on his treasure searches. When all this happened, he was still negotiating with SeaLink and, through SeaLink, with Justin Carlyle. Other than Justin, most of the divers Santino hired weren't the most reputable men in the world. Santino wanted the rubies. He didn't give a damn about the historical value of the *Beldona*. He just wanted the Eyes of Fire rubies. Well, one of his men, a nasty little drug-smuggling murderer named Chico Garcia—"

"Chico Garcia!" Adam interrupted. "He disappeared a long time ago. You mean, Garcia disappeared because of the *Beldona*, as well?"

"It's quite a story," Liam Hinnerman said coolly. "Chico wanted a lot more money from Robert Santino than he was getting. He was also fooling around with Santino's previous girlfriend—the woman he had been dating just before Jerry. He went out diving with one of Santino's men, unaware that the guy was ready to break out on his own. Anyway, the best Chico was willing to do was to bring up gems one at a time and see what Santino was willing to pay him for each one. But the guy he was out with intended to keep everything for himself. Chico was actually the first man to find the ship—though he never had a chance to share what he knew about it. After he came up with the rubies, he realized that his buddy intended to shoot him. He must have been mortally wounded, but he went back down to the *Beldona,* stuffed the rubies into the eye sockets of an old skeleton, and died himself. The buddy never managed to follow him, never managed to discover the exact location of the ship."

"I still don't understand why my father was killed," Sam said.

"Or mine," Joey said.

"Your father was a murdering bastard who deserved to die!" Jerry informed Joey passionately.

"Shut up!" Liam Hinnerman suddenly snapped. Taking a step toward Jerry, he swung his palm at her face with a blow that sent her sprawling to the floor.

"Don't you dare do that! Don't you dare!" Sam cried out. Leaping to her feet, she attacked Hinnerman.

"Sam!" Adam started after her, but Hinnerman pulled a gun and pointed it straight at Adam's nose. Jerry struggled to her feet and caught hold of Sam, dragging her down before Liam could strike her, as well.

"Leave him alone, Sam, please."

"He has no right! He can't do that to you!" Sam insisted angrily. "I won't let him! He can just damned well shoot me—"

"Sam, Sam, please stop. He *will* shoot you." Jerry stared at her, her blue eyes damp. "Sam, I knew the story. I—I went into shock after your father was killed. I don't know how I survived...except that I was saved by one of Santino's divers."

"Hinnerman," Adam guessed.

"Yes, sir!" Liam said quietly, smiling, the gun still pointed at Adam's face.

"Sam, I swear to you, I didn't realize it myself until we were on the island. Liam is—"

"Liam is the bastard who pretended to be working for Robert Santino while he was striking out on his own," Adam said coolly. "He rescued Jerry and kept in close contact with her while she had to lie low. Justin had been killed, and she had killed a man herself. Liam probably convinced her that she'd get the chair for murder if she whispered a word to anyone. Of course, Liam wanted her to find the ship, but she was terrified of diving, and shock had given her complete amnesia about what she knew about the ship. How am I doing, Hinnerman? Is that about right?"

"In a nutshell," Liam said. "I've killed before, and I wouldn't mind killing again at all. Of course, I need Sam alive for a while. Sam can find the *Beldona*. And

Sam is going to find the *Beldona*. Because if she doesn't, every single one of you is going to die."

Adam crossed his arms over his chest. "Okay, Hinnerman, you've got a gun. But you're facing six men, not to mention some very inventive ladies. You can't shoot us all at once. And there's a storm coming."

"I don't need to shoot you all at once. I'll shoot you one by one—you in the knees, first. That should make Sam very amenable to following my orders."

"And he's not alone, honey," a sexy voice said wryly from behind Adam.

They all spun around. Sukee had drawn a little pearl-handled revolver from the windbreaker she'd been wearing.

"Sukee?" Jim said incredulously. "But you were working for my father!"

"'Fraid not, honey," she said sweetly.

Sam stood again, protectively placing herself in front of Jerry. "I just don't believe this," she said flatly.

"Sorry," Sukee said with a shrug.

"Why?" Jim demanded, still astounded.

"Well, now, lover, it seems that no one on this island goes by his or her right name. I made up all that Pontre crap. You're all too trusting."

"I doubt that I will be in the future," Sam commented.

"If you have a future," Liam warned.

"Just what *is* your real name?" Adam demanded of Sukee.

She smiled. "Garcia. Chico was my father."

"This is sick!" Yancy offered. "You're in league with Hinnerman—who killed your father?"

Sukee tossed her short, sassy hair. "Unlike Joey over there, I can see the truth. My father wasn't just a criminal, he was a complete asshole. I don't need anyone to tell me that he deserved to die. But he was the first to find the stinking ship, and I deserve my cut of those rubies. So we're going to get to them. Right now."

"It's night, and there's a storm brewing," Adam said.

"It's nearly dawn, and I suggest Sam finds the damn ship before the storm actually gets here," Sukee said.

"She doesn't know where the ship is," Adam insisted angrily.

Hinnerman suddenly pressed the nose of his gun against Adam's temple. "Where's your brother?"

"None of your business."

"He came straight here. To you. To his kid."

"Well, he isn't here, is he?" Adam backed away from the nose of the gun, staring at Sukee. "Who was keeping him prisoner? A relative of yours?"

Sukee smiled. "I have a brother, too. He met up with Liam soon after poor old Dad met his fate. We spent a very long time planning this. Hank happened to dig his way out of his imprisonment just a little bit too late to be of enough help to do you any good now, huh? A few days earlier, and he could have kept you from the predicament you're now in. But the little bastard is on the island, I'll bet," Sukee said.

Hinnerman said, "It *is* an island. He's not going anywhere."

"So you're planning on killing all of us here, then going to Seafire Isle and killing everyone there?" Adam asked.

Hinnerman smiled in reply.

"Sam doesn't know where the ship is," Adam insisted.

"Sam hasn't wanted to know where the ship is because Sam has known she'd find her old man's body on it," Liam said flatly. "Now she can find the ship or I can start killing people."

"You can't just kill everyone," Adam began.

Hinnerman turned his gun on Joey Emerson. He fired. Sue screamed. Joey fell, clutching his shoulder.

"Want me to keep shooting?" Hinnerman asked Adam politely.

"Jem, get the first-aid kit," Sam said quickly.

"Sam, if you don't want to see anyone else bleeding and in pain, you'd better start suiting up."

"Am I supposed to dive alone?" she demanded.

"I'll go with her," Adam offered.

"Oh, no, not you, he-man!" Sukee said sweetly. "You're just a little bit too dangerous. I'll be going with Sam while Liam and his Magnum keep you all company up here."

"It's all right, Adam," Sam said, looking at him. But oddly enough, Adam wasn't looking at her. He was looking beyond her.

Day was just beginning to dawn. Blackness had receded. A crimson sky allowed them to see the foam-tipped waves rising all around them.

What the hell was he looking at? Sam wondered.

And what in God's name was she going to do? She was fairly certain that she actually did know where to find the ship.

Oh, God...

"Miss Carlyle, Jerry has been a real pain in the ass lately. If you don't move quickly, I think I'll shoot her next. Right in the kneecap. Not a lethal shot, but one that will cause her excruciating pain.

"I'll get my suit," Sam said flatly. She turned to get her equipment.

"Better get suited up yourself," Hinnerman told Sukee.

"Yeah, all right." Sukee followed Sam, smiling as she carefully slipped her gun into a pocket of her jacket. She kept her distance from Sam while she shed the jacket. "Don't get any ideas, Sammy. I can see it in your eyes, you'd love to make a grab for my jacket—and my gun. Liam will shoot Jerry if you make one false move. Take my word on that." She smiled and started toward Liam. He took the jacket, then Sukee walked to Sam to put on a dive suit. "You going to be okay up here?" she called to Liam.

"Yep," Liam assured her. "I won't mind killing anyone who moves."

"You'll just have to be fast to do it," Adam said matter-of-factly.

"What?" Hinnerman demanded.

"Look, look out there! On the water!" Adam said.

Hinnerman spun around, firing blindly and automatically.

And as he did, Adam took his chance.

He leaped on Hinnerman and sent them both catapulting over the port railing and into the water.

Sam didn't dare risk the time to glance overboard.

Sukee's jacket had gone overboard with Liam, she was certain. And without her gun, Sukee was just an obnoxious little half-pint bitch.

Who'd been willing to kill them all.

Sam grabbed her by the shoulder. She'd never really taken a good solid punch at anyone's face in all her life.

The ability to do so now came with amazing ease.

Her right knuckles connected with Sukee's jaw. Sukee screeched, trying to sock Sam in return. She made an ineffectual lunge for Sam's stomach, but Sam didn't feel the blow at all. She clenched her fist again, and this time caught Sukee beneath her jaw. Sukee swore, ranted and tried to strike Sam again. She missed completely. Sam struck her once again.

Sukee screamed wildly, clutching her face, falling to the floor. "You've broken my nose, you bitch. You've broken my nose!"

Sam swung around. Half of the *Sloop Bee*'s passengers were staring at her.

The other half were staring over the port side of the boat. "Can you see them?" Sam demanded, ignoring Sukee, who was moaning on the deck.

"No!" Yancy cried to her.

"I'm going after them," Jem said, diving into the water.

They heard shots coming from the water. Someone still had a gun.

It didn't matter. Jem was already over the side.

Sam swore, zipping up the suit she was already half into. James Jay Astin was reading her mind, standing next to her, ready to help her into her vest and cylinder. Jerry was behind him with her mask and fins. She accepted both, looking at Jerry.

Her mother.

What a night.

Psychologically, of course, she would never get over it.

But she *would* get past it.

And she would help Jerry get past it with her. It was just that right now . . .

Right now she had to find Adam. She started to move. Sukee grabbed her ankle, trying to trip her.

"Could someone please take care of Sukee?" she asked politely.

"They just shot Joey," Sue said. "You bet I'll take care of her."

Perhaps that wasn't such a good idea, but Sam couldn't waste any more time on Sukee. Besides, she realized, as she went over the side, Sue wasn't a vicious killer. Sue wasn't a killer at all. She was just in love with a man who came from a family with a shady past.

Joey's father had killed hers.

Her mother had killed his father.

Sweet Jesus . . .

No more killing. No more deaths.

She went over the side.

Her dive gear gave her the same advantage Adam had used to sweep her away from the Emersons. She sank down a good fifteen feet, grateful that dawn was breaking, that she was also being given the advantage of the light that was just beginning to break through the water. She could see the kicking legs of all three men.

Jem was perhaps twenty feet from the other two.

Liam Hinnerman was still in possession of his gun and still shooting. But he was finding it almost impossible to get a good shot at Adam in the midst of the waves that were buffeting him.

Adam . . .

Adam was perhaps fifty feet from her. Diving, rising, diving, rising.

Trying to beat the waves and avoid Hinnerman's shots at the same time.

She swam toward Adam.

Tugged on his feet. Jerked his ankles.

He came shooting downward in front of her. To her amazement, he was smiling. Her weights balanced them against the buoyancy of the water. They went pitching downward together for a long moment. She started to offer him her regulator so he could breathe, but he pulled her mouthpiece away for a moment instead, gripped her head and kissed her hard as they plummeted.

Interesting way to drown. . . .

But they didn't drown. Adam released her, sharing her air. He motioned, indicating Jem, and she knew he was telling her that they had to do something to help Jem.

When she realized what he wanted to do, she shook her head fervently.

He nodded.

She couldn't stop him.

He was going to bait Hinnerman. Force the man to keep taking potshots at him.

Sam was to drag Hinnerman down until Adam could turn and struggle with the man.

"No!" she mouthed.

Adam was already gone.

Even in a shirt and jeans, he was still amazingly smooth and supple in the water, like a dolphin. He went streaking by Hinnerman, who fired.

Again...

How many bullets were in that damned gun? How many had he used?

Sam didn't know, but she heard the peculiar sound of another bullet streaking through the water. She couldn't bear it anymore.

Time to move.

She filled her vest with air and shot upward with a prayer, directly beneath Hinnerman. He was kicking madly against the waves, looking out at the water surrounding him. Looking for Adam to surface.

She caught his feet and dragged him downward with all her strength.

He catapulted down, startled by her attack. Then he tried to recover, doubling over, reaching for her.

He was stronger than she was, and in damned good shape. He worked out. He was powerful.

He reached for her regulator, ripping the mouth-piece from her. She lost her mask as his fingers wound around her throat.

He raised his left hand. Aiming the gun directly into her face.

He smiled as he prepared to fire.

His arm was suddenly jerked upward, and he fired. A bullet ripped toward the surface of the water, missing Sam by mere inches.

It had been intended for her face....

But Hinnerman couldn't fire again. Adam's fingers were around his throat, and the man was turning blue. His eyes were beginning to bulge, his tongue to protrude. He tried to gasp in air.

And received nothing but water.

Sam watched in horror, mechanically dragging her mask and regulator back into place. She gasped in air.

As Hinnerman tried to break free he slammed against a coral shelf that rose just above the Seafire Isle Steps.

Blood from a cut he opened on the coral spewed into the water, and the man went limp.

Sam caught Adam's arm, and his eyes met hers. He was still furious, in a deadly rage. But he read in her eyes what she had realized earlier. It was time for the killing to stop.

She hadn't spoken, but he nodded. He took a long draft of her air, then indicated that she should take her mouthpiece back and surface. She did, with him behind her, dragging Hinnerman's wounded form.

Sam broke the surface first. Jem was holding on to the ladder on the back of the dive boat.

"Sam?" he demanded.

"Adam's coming. Hinnerman's hurt," she said.

Jem nodded, dragging himself up the ladder to help Sam emerge first, then turning back for Adam. Sam sat at the back of the boat, doffing her flippers first, thanking James Jay Astin as he helped her out of her vest.

Adam reached the ladder. Liam Hinnerman must have really gashed himself, she thought, and the sky, crimson itself with the rising of the sun, was adding to the deep red tone of the water that surrounded Hinnerman.

"Come on, Hinnerman, we're going to take you to a hospital so you can be nice and healthy when you stand trial for murder," Adam muttered, setting Hinnerman's arms on the ladder. "Hold on!" he said, grasping the ladder to drag himself up so he could turn with Jem to heft the man out of the water.

But even as Adam emerged, Jerry suddenly started to scream. Sam jerked her head up. Adam swung around.

Hinnerman let out a startled cry as he was jerked off the ladder.

"What the hell—" Adam began.

"Shark!" Jerry whispered, standing there, shaking.

Hinnerman disappeared beneath the surface as Adam positioned himself to dive in.

James Jay Astin made a dive for Adam instead.

"It's the blood, O'Connor. You can't help him now."

They were all frozen, stunned.

Hinnerman's head appeared above the surface one more time as he gurgled something unintelligible.

Then he disappeared under the waves that were growing fiercer with each passing second.

They heard a strange wailing. Sukee, starting to cry. Sam didn't think she was crying for Hinnerman, just for the loss of what she thought should have been hers.

Adam moistened dry lips, slipped an arm around Sam and spoke to Jem. "We've got to get back before the storm hits, Jem."

Jem nodded. "Yeah."

Adam led Sam to a wooden seat, his arm around her. They passed Jerry, who was sitting with her wind-whipped blond head bowed.

Sam paused and knelt beside her.

"I'm not sorry to have a mother," she said softly.

Jerry started to cry. Sam winced, but James Jay Astin smiled wryly at her and Adam, taking a fatherly position beside Jerry.

Sue had tied Sukee to the ice chest with her belt. Joey was lying on the floor, with Yancy packing towels against his wound.

"Yancy?" Adam said.

"He's going to make it. If we all survive the storm, that is."

Sam looked at Adam, who smiled, touched her chin and kissed her gently.

"We'll survive the storm," he assured her. "We will."

They took a seat side by side, Sam leaning against his shoulder.

"There's probably still a lot to explain," Adam said softly to her. "But I meant what I said, Sam. I love you."

She smiled. "I love you, too."

"Want to marry me before you get mad and walk off again?"

She looked at him. Nodded slowly. "Yeah. Yeah, marriage sounds kind of good right now."

"I'm glad. I don't think I could leave you now for a while."

"I don't think you'll need to leave me," she whispered.

He kissed her again. Her lips. Softly. Tenderly.

They made a good team, she thought. "You're definitely one good dive buddy," she told him.

He laughed.

The sound was carried away on the wind.

And Jem brought them speeding to the dock at Seafire Isle just before the heavens burst open.

———————— Epilogue

Dead men tell no tales.

But those on the *Beldona* had done so, each man crying out his own story in poignant silence.

It was the second day Adam had dived to the wreck. Though Sam had led him there the first time, she had stayed outside the crusted hull of the ship.

While the storm raged around them the other night, she had told him what she was certain her father had known. Their group—plus Hank and minus Liam Hinnerman—had huddled in the main house while the storm winds whipped around them. Sukee had ranted and threatened, promising that she was going to bring Sam up on charges of assault and battery. Joey Emerson née Shapiro had told Sam that she should tell the authorities everything she saw fit, but Sue had cried and pleaded, promising that she would get her husband psychiatric help. Sam was still a soft touch. Joey Emerson was probably not going to pay for the way he had behaved. However, even Adam had to admit that he was extremely contrite.

It also seemed as if his wife meant to make him pay dearly anyway.

So, except for Sukee, their group seemed to be a comfortable enough one while they listened to the winds rage beyond the walls of the house. And while the winds tore around them and the lights went out and they sat huddled together in darkness, Sam told them what she thought her father must have discovered.

"A ghost story, I think—it's absolutely all I can figure out. I was thinking about Adam and nearly drowning when it occurred to me."

"Me and drowning—in the same light?"

She smiled. "Well, I especially wanted to live—because of you. And I was thinking about the things that people did for love—and for money. My dad had hinted about his theory, but I guess I really never listened. I think that Theresa-Maria Rodriguez was still very much in love with Captain Reynolds when he seized the *Yolanda* and took her and Don Carlos aboard the *Beldona*. Don Carlos had stolen the Eyes of Fire rubies for her, and she knew it. She wanted the rubies, *and* she wanted to be with Captain Reynolds. I think the two of them planned to sabotage the ship, murder everyone aboard and blow it up, then disappear together with the gems. There were dozens of places they could have gone in the New World and lived like a king and queen on the price they could have gotten for the rubies."

"I don't understand," Judy Walker said. "What difference would it make who or what destroyed the ship? It would still be sunken, right?"

"Sunken, but in pieces," Sam said. "Hunks of debris covered by the coral cliff where the steps are, just before the drop-off. Beneath the steps, I imagine that coral and barnacles and all sorts of sea life have grown over what remains of the hull and decking, making it almost impossible to see."

"I had gone out, figuring she was in pieces," Hank said. "I thought she had to be under the steps, as well. That drop-off would have been a perfect place for a ship to sink and disappear."

"Sam is right," Jerry offered painfully. She looked at Sam. "You're right—I'm certain."

"But the rubies are supposedly still on the ship," Jim Santino said. "Jerry, you saw them, right?"

She nodded. "In the eye sockets of a skeleton."

"The rubies are still on the ship because Don Carlos Esperanza, and maybe even Captain Reynolds' own shipmates, discovered what he was up to. They probably mutinied with their Spanish prisoners, but too late to save themselves from the explosives Reynolds had set to destroy the ship," Sam said.

"So..." Judy Walker encouraged.

"So when he knew he was about to die, I imagine Don Carlos Esperanza took out his sword and pinned Captain Reynolds right through the heart with it. He probably stuffed the rubies right into the man's eyes then and there—and Sukee's dad must have put them back when he knew he was dying himself.''

Sam paused, looking at Adam.

''I think maybe Hank and I should go down alone first. You and Jerry could dive with us to find the ship, but I don't think you should go in at first.'' He hesitated a little painfully. ''I don't think either of you should find Justin Carlyle.''

Sam had agreed.

So when the storm had cleared and the police had come from the mainland, they had gone out for the first time. Adam and Hank had found their way through the holes in the coral shelf until they were under the overhang. But even once they were there, it was still almost impossible to find the wreckage of the ship. They had almost used up their air when they found what had been the captain's cabin.

Adam and Hank had very carefully removed the remains of Justin Carlyle, then Chico Garcia. They decided not to move anything else at all until Sam had a chance to see the ship.

And now Sam was with him.

Seeing the ghosts of the past she had re-created in those strange moments when she had been afraid she was going to die herself.

Dead men . . .

Their skeletal remains lay about eerily, some held together by remnants of rusted armor, one with its head uncannily perched on a bookcase while the disjointed body sat on the desk beneath it.

Don Carlos Esperanza.

The sword that had brought about his death lay at his side. The sword that had once pierced him, through flesh and sinew and organ, a sword that had once been bathed in blood.

The sword with which he had slain Reynolds, then himself, with the sure knowledge of his impending death from the explosion he could not stop.

Now the sword lay on the handsomely carved desk where the pieces of the dead man remained, side by side with the small bones of what had been his hand.

It looked as if Don Carlos might, at any minute, pick up the sword and avenge himself upon his enemies.

Dead men did tell tales. . . .

This one shouted silently of his own murder.

A tiny yellow tang darted in and out of the cavernous eye sockets of the long dead man.

Sea fans wafted over oak. Anemones rose against the rotted core of an inkwell.

Another skeleton lay by the side of the desk, shadowed in darkness. Though time and pressure had blown out the master's cabin window of the *Beldona*, the ship was down deep enough that the sun's rays offered little light inside.

This skeleton looked at them.

Stared at them like a demon, a devil, dead hand drifting, fingers seeming to point....

Stared at them with blazing red eyes that seemed to dazzle and blind.

Captain Reynolds.

Seeing now through the Eyes of Fire....

Captain Reynolds! A man who had received his just punishment for the murder of so many innocents. A finger lifted now, drifting in the remnant of a glove, seeming to point, just as he seemed to stare and scream....

Sam didn't touch the jewels. Adam hadn't thought she would. Sam had found the ship because of them, and Jerry probably could have done the same, yet neither woman wanted anything to do with the treasure.

Adam was glad, however, that Sam seemed intrigued by the wreck itself. They explored it, then slowly and carefully surfaced together, their information intact to hand over to James Jay Astin, who would arrange salvage with the state of Florida.

According to the salvage laws, Sam had earned her share of the treasure. She wanted it donated to a children's hospital. Some good, she had told Adam, should come from the loss of her father.

Back on the *Sloop Bee,* Adam held her, ruffled her damp hair and told her, "It's a rare woman who wouldn't even touch those rubies!"

Sam shuddered. "They're cursed."

"Sam! You're not superstitious."

She said nothing, and he shrugged, holding her close.

"I have a jewel I'm hoping you *will* like. It's nowhere near as grand as those rubies, but then, I've been working for myself lately, and I don't pay well at all." He drew a ring from the little pocket of his bathing trunks. "It's an engagement ring, even though I'm hoping we can just fly away and get married."

She offered him her finger. He slipped the ring on it. "Well?" he asked a little nervously.

"Now, this," she said, "is the most beautiful jewel I've seen in all my life."

He kissed her lips, then her forehead, her eyelids. She gazed at him, content. "Now those," he said, staring intently at her and pointing, "are the wildest Eyes of Fire I've ever seen. When you're mad, Sam..."

She tapped him on the chin. "You've got a temper yourself, you know." She smiled. "But I love you. And I think as soon as we can take a trip to the mainland, we should get married. Quite frankly, I'm afraid to wait too long."

He grinned, then sobered. "Sam, quite seriously, the ship cost you your father. But it gave us back to one another, and, well, there's Jerry...."

"My mother." She smiled. "How strange. I was stunned. I thought I might hate her, but I don't. She never had the kind of love I had, and she didn't know how to accept it from my father. She almost had it back again—then lost everything. You don't think she'll go to jail, do you?"

Adam shook his head. "To all intents and purposes, she killed in self-defense. She'll be fine. Mr. James Jay Astin is determined to get her the very best lawyers there are. She's been allowed to stay on the island. Things will work out."

Sam nodded. "We can actually thank the *Beldona* for more."

"What?"

"Well, Hank coming here. Creating Brian along with Yancy. Yancy is determined to marry him right away, too, you know. She says she was an idiot, that she lived in hell when she thought he was dead, and she wasn't letting any fool prejudice—including her own fear—keep them apart anymore."

"I'm glad. My brother really adores her."

"We've also got Mr. James Jay Astin."

"How so?"

"I think he's in love with—with my mother."

"Really?"

Sam nodded.

"And you're happy?"

"Very happy."

He rose, pulling her up beside him. Jem was bringing the *Sloop Bee* to the dock.

Sam pointed. "Our island," she murmured. "I mean, you are . . ."

"Working for a private concern now," he assured her. "And you, my love, are definitely my greatest private concern."

Sam laughed and landed happily in his arms. He kissed her deeply.

They were home.

And if the Eyes of Fire had offered up a curse, it was over now.

For the Eyes had closed.

And love had set them free.

Award-winning author!

This October uncover the passion that results
when two worlds collide in

PROMISE ME FOREVER

Tragic circumstances brought them together, but their
differences threatened to tear them apart. Although
they were from two different worlds, they shared one
glorious passion. He was convinced that together they
could overcome anything...she wasn't so sure that love
conquers all.

Opposites attract...but can they last forever?

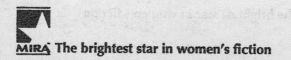

MIRA **The brightest star in women's fiction**

MDM2